A FOOL'S KABBALAH

T0348928

ALSO BY STEVE STERN

FICTION

The Village Idiot, a novel

The Pinch, a novel

The Book of Mischief, stories

The Frozen Rabbi, a novel

The North of God, novella

The Angel of Forgetfulness, a novel

The Wedding Jester, stories

A Plague of Dreamers, 3 novellas

Harry Kaplan's Adventures Underground, a novel

Lazar Malkin Enters Heaven, stories

The Moon & Ruben Shein, a novel

Isaac and the Undertaker's Daughter, stories

FOR CHILDREN

Hershel and the Beast

Mickey & the Golem

STEVE STERN ◇ A FOOL'S KABBALAH

◇ A NOVEL ◇

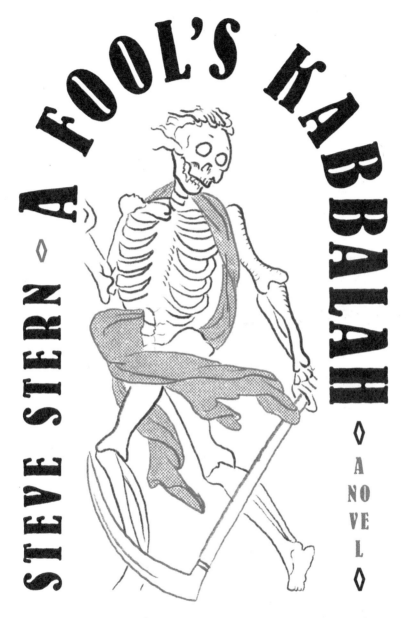

🛆 MELVILLE HOUSE
BROOKLYN • LONDON

A FOOL'S KABBALAH

First published in 2025 by Melville House
Copyright © 2023 by Steve Stern
All rights reserved
First Melville House Printing: December 2024

Melville House Publishing
46 John Street
Brooklyn, NY 11201
and
Melville House UK
Suite 2000
16/18 Woodford Road
London E7 0HA

mhpbooks.com
@melvillehouse

ISBN: 978-1-68589-165-7
ISBN: 978-1-68589-166-4 (eBook)

Library of Congress Control Number: 2024946531

Designed by Beste M. Doğan

Printed in the United States of America
1 3 5 7 9 10 8 6 4 2

A catalog record for this book is available from the Library of Congress

For Kathryn Davis, friend and inspiration,
and Sabrina, without whom, bupkes

The soul demands
your folly, not your wisdom.
—CARL JUNG

A FOOL'S KABBALAH ◊ A FOOL'S KABBALAH ◊ A FOOL'S KABBALAH

He'd started out in Paris, then on to Zurich and Prague, cities still vital and unblemished in their appearance; then Frankfurt, Munich, his native Berlin, Vienna, and points east, which were ashes. He had begun as the renowned scholar Dr. Gershom Scholem, dispatched by the Hebrew University in Jerusalem as emissary of the Otzrot HaGolah, the Treasures of Diaspora Archive, and returned to the nervous calm of Prague a broken man.

On the train from Frankfurt he'd neither looked out the window nor read a book. He had no book with him, nor did it even occur to him that, perhaps for the first time in his life, he'd brought along no classic theological or philosophical text to peruse. From all the dogmas and mythologies, canons and wisdom literatures, that had been his food and drink, he was fasting. Wasn't every day now its own Yom Kippur, the Day of Atonement? But like Kafka's hunger artist his fast was not to be admired; the "banquet" of existence had no special appeal for him. He felt no flicker of sensation upon his arrival in the city that he and Walter had declared as consecrated to its native son Franz. Gershom checked into the Hotel Europa on Wenceslas Square where he had previously stayed, signed the guest book with an illegible scrawl, and accepted the key. But as he followed the bellhop carrying his suitcase through the plush lobby toward the gilded glass cage of the lift, he broke down. Perhaps it was the rich warmth of the Empire furnishings, the sienna sconces fastened to the polished mahogany woodwork—an atmosphere that seemed impervious to adversity—that thawed the ice around Gershom's heart enough to admit an ache; then the pain, really a body blow, halted his forward movement, whereupon he folded himself into an armchair beside a stained glass Tiffany lamp and began to weep like a child.

The young bellhop, red pillbox cocked at a jaunty angle atop his Pomatumed head, waited patiently for the guest to get over whatever afflicted him. At length Gershom dried his eyes with a sleeve and rose to plod behind the bellhop, who, without a missed step of decorum, proceeded him to the elevator. The room, with its half tester bed and faux balcony outside the high windows, had a soft-hued elegance, which should have been inviting after the barracks-like accommodations at Offenbach. But Gershom was indifferent to its vintage décor; he was slow in realizing that the bellhop's departure was contingent upon his receiving a tip. Left alone, he struggled to recall his confident state of mind when he'd stopped at the hotel all those long months ago—the mistaken sense of security he'd felt before waking up to the realization that Europe was a charnel house. But the memory, like so much else lost in the maelstrom, was irrecoverable.

HE HAD BEEN TASKED WITH salvaging what was left of a world. It turned out there was quite a bit of it: the still intact Torah scrolls, the books both sacred and secular, menorahs, spice boxes, kiddush cups, seder plates, documents—but no people. To be sure, there were ghosts, a multitude of them and some still living, but *their* rescue was a haphazard proposition. The books, however, were as palpable as flesh and blood.

Those that had survived the flames had been hidden in impromptu *genizahs*: airless cellars, attics festooned in cobwebs; antiquities of inestimable value were immured in dank catacombs, buried in forests. Much had been squirreled away by the victims but much more had been confiscated and held hostage by the rapacious predators. It seemed that the enemy had as great a mania for collecting as for destroying; those books that they refrained from incinerating would remain a resource for studying the perverse customs and convictions of an odious race. Academies would be established for that purpose. As it happened, many of the commandeered volumes were stumbled upon by the liberators, who, with the best of intentions, stored them in warehouses for redistributing to their original communities. The problem was, those communities no longer existed. So the books, ritual objects, incunabula, all remained in storage, quarreled over by opposing committees charged with finding them homes.

The temporary home for most of these effects was the Offenbach Archival Depot in the city of Offenbach a few kilometers downstream from Frankfurt on the River Main. The depot was a requisitioned factory building of the I. G. Farben Corporation, which had manufactured the cyanide-based pesticide used to exterminate lice and the inmates of concentration camps. The building itself was a characterless five-story concrete cube with two tall smokestacks, an unlikely site for a depository of treasures.

Gershom's first sight of the depot left his brain reeling as from a concussion. It was a formidable brain, Dr. Scholem's; it was, by his own measure, nimble, incisive, and cunning. It was the brain of the man who held the Chair of Jewish Mysticism at the recently established Hebrew University on top of storied

Mount Scopus in Jerusalem. There had never before been such a position, and this one was created expressly for Gershom, who had swum against powerful currents of history to attain it. The Jewish historians, in their eagerness to present to the Gentiles an eminently reasonable and unthreatening version of their religion, had consigned an immemorial tradition—namely Kabbalah—to oblivion. Gershom had single-handedly (as he liked to think) resurrected that tradition, with all its dangerous, heterodox, and anarchic reverberations. The impact among scholars and laymen alike had been, in the words of his bosom friend Walter Benjamin, like "a mighty paw" lifted against the Philistines. For Gershom, personally, it was as if he'd raised a lost continent from beneath the sea.

To accomplish the endeavor, he had spent years ferreting out ancient texts from every antiquarian bookshop in Berlin, Munich, and later Palestine. In Jerusalem he'd stalked the booksellers—some wearing fezzes, some with sidelocks and patriarchal beards—to their dusty, back-alley lairs. In them he'd discovered priceless volumes the sellers in their ignorance believed to be worthless curiosities, though they nevertheless touted the books' "pricelessness" and bargained fiercely with the prospective buyer. He conned their brittle pages, some still bearing the smudged fingerprints of generations of aspiring sages and sorcerers. (Books written in the hoary biblical tongues that Gershom had taught himself as a teenager, much to the consternation of his comfortably assimilated family.) He'd distilled their fantastical wisdom into weighty volumes of his own, which revealed, in precise dialectical language, recipes for conjuring creatures from other worlds and formulas for entering the mind of God.

So who could have been better equipped for undertaking the

job at hand than he, a universally recognized professional in the field of recovering dispossessed literatures? With a messianic zeal, he would redeem the invaluable books scattered by the planet's premier cataclysm and spirit them back to the Promised Land where they belonged. Such was his arrogance when the pillars of the university packed him off to Europe to assess the situation and collect the stray Judaica for the university's precious reserve. But once he'd entered the stagnant air of the Offenbach Depot, escorted by a beleaguered Captain Isaac Bencowitz of the U.S. Army's Monuments, Fine Arts, and Archives Unit, all of his high-minded designs were confounded.

Four of the five loft-like stories were stacked floor to ceiling with books, scrolls, and manuscripts, many of them bound in bales of scalloped pages. Many volumes were piled willy-nilly like slag from a volcanic eruption, the sacred alongside the profane, holy scripture in Hebrew and Aramaic bundled cheek by jowl with Yiddish storybooks. All were damaged, worm-eaten, mildewed, some with pages scorched by fire or gnawed by rats. Others, retrieved from damp bolt-holes and subterranean vaults, were draped over ropes stretched beneath the ceiling like clothes on a line. Here, in the moted shafts of amber light that filtered through the wire-glass windows, was the mountainous residue of an extinguished culture disposed of like rubbish. Relentless bibliophile that he was, Gershom had come to respect in essence the gospel of the kabbalists: that words—Hebrew words in particular—had souls. The language of the mystical texts assumed a life exclusive of the mortals who had written it, its authors mere conduits for transmitting visions, symbols, and myths; they were expendable, those entranced archaic authors, once their task was accomplished. But here, seeing the books in such heaps minus the righteous folk that had honored them, they appeared as so much detritus, lifeless as bodies from which the souls have been expunged.

Standing before them, Gershom was struck dumb, his legs weak as water, his eyes clamped shut against the sight. There was a compartment in his brain, hermetically sealed but expanded over the years, wherein the hidebound scholar preserved a perception of himself as a wild-eyed seeker of revelation. This was an alternative Gershom—"the shadow Scholem" as his dead friend Walter had it—conceived to complement the deviant history he'd chronicled as a foil for the conventional. That Gershom, with his elfin ears and rudder-like nose (which he often exaggerated in his own mind to grotesque proportions), enticed him on occasion into places where the scholar feared to tread. The Gershom that resided in that seldom-visited, timeless compartment of his brain sank to his knees, called for a skullcap and prayer shawl, and began to recite, in his classical Hebrew, *Kaddish*, the prayer for the dead—while the professor and dignitary in his funereal suit only sniffled and wiped his nose with a monogrammed handkerchief, furtively dabbing an eye in the process. The good captain pretended not to notice.

"We've catalogued nearly a million items so far," he announced in his official capacity, though his slack, deep-furrowed face looked anything but official; his khaki uniform, with its soup-stained lapel, appeared as if slept in, his rimless spectacles befogged. "But, as you know, so many libraries and Jewish holdings still remain in unsympathetic hands." He assured Gershom, who'd composed himself enough to reclaim his capable face, that he would have his work cut out for him when dealing with those ill-disposed national entities. "The question is of course what to do with all this stuff once we've gathered it."

Gershom's English was discerning enough that he winced at the word "stuff," but the man's rueful expression was at variance with his cavalier language; it was clear that his reverence for the labor weighed heavily upon him. Then he removed his glasses and began to wipe them with the hem of his military tunic, peering at his visitor through tired, red-rimmed eyes.

"Sometimes," he sighed, "I get the urge to strike a match and make a bonfire, then jump into the flames along with the books." He replaced the glasses and attempted a smile that his eyes could not support.

Gershom shuddered, unprepared for such a confession. "The distribution, as you might imagine," he reassured the man with a purposeful emphasis, "is our gravest concern."

The captain appraised the scholar as if to determine whom exactly he was speaking for. Had he asked, Gershom, so previously secure in his role, would have been hard-pressed to answer with confidence. So unmoored did he feel. He was grateful when, once they'd adjourned to his small office, also deluged in books, the captain opened a cabinet and offered Gershom a tin coffee mug into which he poured several fingers of dry gin. He did the same for himself.

"*La chayim,*" each said in his turn.

HE'D COME FIRST TO A Paris still resonant with memories of his dead friend Walter. Not the Walter of their last encounter, with whom Gershom had quarreled over his friend's tortured attempts to reconcile his Marxism with his devotional nature. ("A losing battle," Gershom had insisted.) It was on that occasion when Walter, forswearing their shared convictions, had advocated the elimination of magic from *his* own theory of language. *That* Walter, short-winded and paunchy, his signature pompadour prematurely graying, was so torn between one fixed idea and another that he was incapable of taking steps to save himself from the coming storm. What Gershom remembered most was the time before that. Then, virtually penniless as usual, vacillating as always between competing enthusiasms, Walter Benjamin was the most magnetic personality on earth.

The neon of Montparnasse burned as brightly in 1946 as it had in 1927. The boulevards were awash in its ruby glow; the lights coruscated off the windscreens of motorcars whose Klaxons vied with the blare of jazz trumpets in the clubs and cabarets. Lovers were still entwined like caducei in the cathedral niches and along the embankment of the Seine. But no one was deceived by the music and the incandescence. The liberated city had had its moment of shrill celebration, leaving the population to salvage what dignity it could from a sediment of shame and regret. It had been different nearly twenty years before, when they'd met in the midst of what came to be known as *Les Années Folles*, the Crazy Years. Then, even the decorous Gershom had not been proof against the city's antic energies. He was further buoyed by his hopes that, after a decade of persuasion, his friend would soon come to Palestine.

"There's a position waiting for you at the university," Gershom had assured him over herbal liqueurs. "The chancellor Magnes has agreed to vouch for you. You can write your lectures on the lilac-scented verandah of a Jaffa café while looking wistfully at the Mediterranean sunset."

"Gerhard," replied Walter—he'd never been comfortable with Gershom's adopted Hebrew name—"Gerhard, you needn't twist my arm." The prospect was genuinely attractive. Under the auspices of an aspiring new nation, the critic could pursue his uniquely metaphysical approach to the great Jewish texts. This was his latest hobbyhorse, which he might soon swap, as was his custom, for another in midstream. But at that time, Eretz Israel was, as it would remain for the rest of his days, an alluring possibility.

Of course, his Aliyah, his ascent to the Land, would have to wait until Walter had first attended to his current literary commitments. "There's the commissioned piece I'm doing for an anthology of the writings of Wilhelm Von Humboldt, a positively revolutionary essay on the philosophy of language for *Die Literarische Welt*, and another on Hölderlin for *Die Neue Rundschau*, not to mention my half-completed monographs on Baudelaire, Proust, and Franz Kafka . . ." (Kafka being the writer with whom he and Gershom had lately come to share an obsession.) There was also—and this Walter needlessly confided to his friend in whispers—the apocalyptic idea he'd recently conceived for what he called "an enchanted encyclopedia." The yet uncopyrighted idea was inspired by his fascination with the lavish shopping arcades of Paris, around which he would construct "a unified field theory of practically everything." That these projects were never-ending and would dog him in his hand-to-mouth peregrinations back and forth across Europe until the bitter end, was not yet apparent. All that was clear then was that Paris was a carnival, and Walter was as intoxicated with it as he was with his own mercurial brilliance.

They were seated on the awninged terrasse of Le Dôme Café on the busy Carrefour Vavin, whose sundry patrons included various luminaries of the moment. Walter, who fancied himself one of them, nodded in the direction of a sylphlike figure affectedly sniffing the lily in his lapel. "Jean Cocteau," he murmured in Gershom's ear. Cocteau, a man who (according to Walter) seemed to appear everywhere at once, sat in the company of some mutually admiring representatives of the surrealist circle that Walter had become so enthralled with. There were also a few artists from the so-called School of Paris: the jocular Jules Pascin, flanked by his wife and mistress whose rivalry would soon drive him to suicide; Moïse Kisling with his pudding-bowl haircut, an arm flung casually about the bare shoulders of the notorious Kiki, self-proclaimed Queen of Montparnasse; there was Marc Chagall, with his striped blazer and chestnut curls, disdainfully tossing a coin into the outstretched palm of his flea-ridden compatriot Chaim Soutine. These were mostly East European immigrants who—as Walter alleged—had traded their jerkwater *shtetls*, where the making of images was forbidden, for a city where everything was allowed, if not encouraged.

"Praise God, who permits the forbidden," Gershom uttered sardonically under his breath. This was the blasphemous prayer attributed to the false prophet Sabbatai Zvi, Gershom's current focus of study, and the impious words made him feel bolder even as they gave him a chill. They made him feel in any case less humbled by these Babylonian surroundings, as did his preoccupation with challenging Walter's vaulting ideas.

They had been sparring since their omnivorously bookish youth in Berlin, each a bit thrilled by the range of his own sweeping references. To support an argument, they could call upon authorities—even during their adolescence—from every historical epoch, with a fluency that defied national and chronological boundaries. Nietzsche rubbed shoulders with Paracelsus, Pindar with Franz Rosenzweig; Walter mourned technology's diminishment of the "aura" (his favorite word) of all art; Gershom lamented what he viewed as God's failed ambitions for man and speculated on the birth pangs of Messiah. Often they spoke at cross-purposes; sometimes their theories dovetailed. Occasionally they soared to such rhetorical heights that they entered a rarefied zone approaching pure nonsense.

Said Walter: "A dictatorship of poverty is essential for invoking the Messiah."

Then Gershom: "Religion's supreme function is to destroy the dream-harmony of man."

When they touched down again from the ether of their exchanges, they were surprised, and not a little gratified, to find their table hovered over by kibitzers no doubt rapt by the hairsplitting sagacity of their dialogue—or was it that their cosmopolitan auditors were simply amused by such pedantic bombast?

"Bouvard and Pécuchet," judged one yawning flaneur, in reference to the eponymous dogmatists of Flaubert's novel.

When not involved in ideological skirmishing, they swapped misgivings and pet gripes. Gershom aired his ongoing ambivalence with respect to the Zionist project—he feared that political incumbencies would ultimately betray its spiritual roots—while Walter expressed his own ambivalence toward almost everything in his experience. He catalogued his physical ailments (sciatica, neuralgic spasms, arrhythmia), the women he'd lately fallen in love with (the fanatical Bolshevik muse Asja Lacis being foremost), and the bodeful headlines by which he was consumed. As it occurred, their meeting in Paris coincided with the execution in America of the anarchists Sacco and Vanzetti, and Walter insisted they attend a rally in the Place de la Concorde to protest their "murder" at the hands of the plutocrats. Gershom, who defined himself, often to the amusement of his colleagues, as a "theological anarchist," was cautiously game.

But he was taken aback when Walter showed up for the demonstration, organized by the French Communist and Socialist parties, in a kind of apache-like proletarian uniform. This included a black leather-paneled donkey coat and a red kerchief knotted around his throat. On his head he wore a cloth student's cap tilted at a rakish angle. The contrast with his ordinarily mandarin aspect—owlish eyeglasses, bristly mustache, tall sooty-black coiffure—was somewhat startling. Thousands of rowdy demonstrators filled the broad plaza on that windy afternoon, waving placards calling for justice and boycotts of American products. When the crowd around the giant Luxor obelisk became unruly, breaking ranks to smash shop windows and loot merchandise, the police waded in on horseback, wielding truncheons to disperse them. To escape their onslaught, people clambered up lampposts, climbed walls onto hotel balconies, and jumped into the ornate fountains. Gershom and Walter, having only narrowly missed being trampled in the stampede, ducked down a side street and beat it several blocks before taking refuge in a café. Once they had seated themselves, conspicuous in their effort to be unassuming, Gershom, having finally caught his breath, was a little awed by his companion's radiant flush.

"Walter," he observed, "revolution becomes you!"

Walter grinned in an attempt to appear dauntless, while the hand at his breast tried to still his galloping heart.

The next day, still light-headed, Walter urged his friend to tour with him a sampling of *passages couverts*. These were the arcades, roofed over in scrolled wrought iron and glass, that tunneled like interior boulevards through the architecture of entire city blocks. There had been scores of them in the nineteenth century, most of which were demolished by Baron Haussmann's wholesale reconstruction campaign. Those that remained still preserved a faded splendor, their embellished neoclassical and art nouveau corridors framed by marble panels and lined with elegant boutiques and galleries. There were wax museums, shops showcasing mechanized toys and brilliant assortments of exotic stamps, swank restaurants catering to the wealthy.

"Walter," complained Gershom, as he was dragged from passage to passage: one called the Dauphine, another the Choiseul, the Grand Cerf, the Vivienne, all of them located in the chic 9th and 10th arrondissements. "Walter, what is it you see in all these glittering bourgeois tschatskes?" (They both liked to pepper their speech with quaint Yiddishisms, which functioned in their conversations like sandbags to hot-air balloons.) As Walter moved ahead of him in a kind of trance, Gershom repeated the question. He knew his friend was an ardently acquisitive type; his purchases of rare books and paintings, far beyond his means, had often caused Gershom to cringe from the extravagance. But why such an interest in these exclusive commercial arteries with their mother lode of overpriced bibelots?

"Ah, Gerhard," replied Walter, taking his friend's arm and assuming a spooky tone, "think of us as intrepid spelunkers." Though the parties of deep-pocketed collectors and browsers that passed in their vicinity looked anything but "intrepid." "Don't you see how these caverns call to mind the secret entrances to the labyrinths of the ancient Greeks, luring us into an underworld as into dreams."

"Tschatskes!" repeated Gershom.

"But that's just the point." Walter's voice shifted into its forensic mode. "The dreams of the capitalist era are embodied in commodities. Even works of art, having forfeited their magic through reproduction ad nauseam, are now mere commodities. It must be our program, dear Gerhard, to awaken the masses from their besotted enchantment with things."

But Gershom could see how Walter was himself infatuated with these retail grottoes wherein he extracted mysteries from gimcracks and elaborate Louis Quinze furniture. Still, was his friend's new passion so different from Gershom's own zeal for those convoluted systems the mystics constructed, the arteries through which the enlightened might travel in due course to paradise? He and Walter were at heart co-conspirators in their grand ambitions, each intending to rouse the consciousness of the planet's sleepers with their own respective noise.

They went on two consecutive nights to the moving pictures. Walter preferred any film starring Adolphe Menjou, who was featured in a turgid allegory called *The Sorrows of Satan* at the Grand Rex Theater on the boulevard Poissonnière. Its only redeeming scene, thought Gershom, was the one in which the voluptuous Lya De Putti bared her alabaster breasts, though he didn't say so. He couldn't understand how Walter could glorify an actor whose only distinguishing gesture was his incessant raising of a single eyebrow. The next night it was Gershom's turn to choose. In a spirit of gaiety—he was forever trying to demonstrate a lightheartedness he lacked—Gershom selected, "as an antidote to Menjou," a three-reeler called *Saint Farceur*. In it a loose-limbed funnyman of some indiscernible ethnicity steals his scythe from the Grim Reaper himself, who pursues him up ladders, across rooftops, and through a bathroom in which a plump matron is luxuriating in her tub. In the end the dreaded

Reaper recovers the scythe with which he manages to snag only a tail feather of the giant bird that the comic has hopped astride to make his escape. (Its flapping wings were apparently attached by invisible cords to a moving cloud overhead).

Having no athletic ability whatsoever, Gershom appreciated the acrobatic comic actor's literally death-defying leaps and pratfalls, while Walter simply surrendered to helpless laughter at the knockabout romp. Afterward, over drinks on the pandora-bowered terrace of Les Deux Magots, Gershom felt called upon to discourse on the character of humor. Jewish humor in particular.

"Honesty directed against ourselves" was how he defined its essence. "I give you an example," adopting a pathetic voice, "'Oy, am I thirsty; oy, am I thirsty!' Now give me some water." Walter slid the bottle of Perrier tentatively across the table and Gershom drank. "'Oy, was I thirsty!'" he moaned.

Walter looked puzzled, then said, "Oh yes, ha."

Gershom went on to explain how no punitive action could follow the self-accusation inherent in Jewish comedy. "An age-old Jewish legal principle maintains that someone who accuses himself cannot be condemned. Laughter, you see, is the acoustical resonance of adjournment. There's an adage: *Aggadah*, which as you know is the narrative dimension of Talmud; Aggadah has a laughing face. Another example . . ."

"Please, Gerhard," Walter held up a hand, "no more examples."

Gershom was a little offended, but then, who was he to school Walter Benjamin on the nature of laughter? He was anyway soon appeased when Walter began to actively mull over his friend's proposition: that a subject's indictment is often its best defense. "One might perhaps amend Machiavelli's contention in *The Art of War* that 'the hand that strikes also blocks' to 'the hand that strikes *itself* . . .'," he opined, removing his spectacles to pinch the bridge of his nose as a spur to thought. "Then," replacing the glasses, "you have Nietzsche's announcement of the death of God, which is ultimately a left-handed argument in favor of God's necessity." But the paradox, he asserted, was best illustrated in the writings of Franz Kafka, whose work the friends had been following since its first appearance in obscure literary journals. Now they had the novels, which Kafka's friend and betrayer Max Brod had seen published after the author's death—this despite Kafka's wish that they be destroyed.

Here Gershom could not help inserting his somewhat ecstatic judgment of the Czech writer's virtuoso *oeuvre*: "As a secular expression of the kabbalistic world-feeling, it comes to us wrapped in an almost canonical halo."

Walter nodded; they were on the same page. "Did I tell you how I just missed seeing Kafka read from his work in Munich?" he asked.

"Every time we meet," Gershom replied.

Undeterred, Walter brought the conversation full circle. "More and more the essential feature in Kafka seems to me to be humor." Gershom cocked his head skeptically; it was like Walter to take up a theme of his friend's and run with it toward some far horizon. "They say his circle was in stitches when he read to them from *The Metamorphosis*: Gregor waking to find himself changed into a monstrous bug . . . Kafka was finally a holy schlemiel, Gerhard—a Svejk, a Sancho Panza, a clown! I think the true key to his work is likely to fall into the hands of the person who is best able to extract the comic aspects from Jewish theology."

Gershom flinched. "I'm not sure I follow you." It was often

difficult to follow the erratic, frequently non sequitur leaps of Walter's mind. Sometimes Gershom elected not to follow at all. Ignoring Gershom's scruple, Walter persisted in his rumination. "Has there ever been such a shrewd and percipient person?" Then leveling his gaze point-blank at his friend, he asked, "Might you be man enough to be that man?"

"Walter, you're drunk," said Gershom, squirming under the intensity of his friend's gimlet stare. He was accustomed to playing straight man to Walter's more spirited imagination, but tonight he felt that his bluff was somehow being called. Hadn't Gershom declared himself more than once "a metaphysical clown"? There was the Nadar photo of a baggy-smocked Pierrot he'd hung on the wall of his house in the Abarbanel Road, which he invoked when making fun of his own pointy ears and the "child-bearing hips" that made clownish his otherwise gaunt anatomy. Wasn't the clown, the jester, the *shkotz*—wasn't he the ideal archetype to mediate between religion and nihilism, which Gershom regarded as the opposing poles of the mysticism that was his principal concern?

"One must be a fool if he is to help," pronounced Walter imperiously. "In fact, only a fool's help is a real help."

Gershom wagged his head in agreement, then asked, "Help for what?"

But Walter only raised a shaggy brow Adolphe Menjou–style and left the question hanging. In lieu of an answer, he sharpened his mind-reading stare and sadly assessed, "Of course, Gerhard, you're not a very funny guy."

They parted soon after. Gershom returned to his fitfully patient wife, Fanya, and his omnibus library in the eucalyptus-shaded stone cottage in Jerusalem. There, in relative security (if anything could be deemed secure in that volatile land), he proceeded with the work of unearthing a lost tradition and, as an unintended consequence, setting loose its resident angels and demons on a modern world. Meanwhile Walter continued his restless progress as a wandering Jew, gadding about the European continent while promising throughout those ill-starred years that his emigration to Palestine was imminent. He wrote his uncategorizable Promethean essays, many of which he rehearsed in his voluminous correspondence with Gershom, and kept his head just above water on a mingy stipend from the Frankfurt Institute for Social Research. He maintained his hot-and-cold embrace of Marxism, even in the face of Stalin's show trials, and fled the Nazi invasion of France as far as the Pyrenees. There, denied entry into Spain, he took his own life with an overdose of morphine in the charming seaside village of Portbou.

"**O**y, am I thirsty!" groaned Menke Klepfisch upon encountering Blume, Rabbi Vaynipl's beautiful daughter, as she crossed the market square with a jug of water fetched from the well. She held the large clay jug on her shoulder, its shifting weight somehow accentuating the sway of her hips beneath her woolen skirt as she walked. "Oy, am I thirsty," groaned the gangly young man. Blume paused, leaning toward him with a wry expression to pour a trickle of water into his wide-open mouth. He swallowed with a bobbing of his pronounced Adam's apple and groaned again just as pathetically, "Oy, was I thirsty!"

Blume rolled her black-currant eyes. "Menke Monkey," she scoffed, using the English homonym; she was an educated girl. Then she laughed with a sound like—to Menke's ears—a bird skittering over piano keys. He never knew whether she was laughing at his jokes or at him; not that it mattered, just so she laughed.

He was the shtetl scapegrace, Menke Klepfisch, whom the virtuous enjoyed disdaining for his antics. This was their general attitude even before he had run off with—such was the rumor whose source was himself—a traveling circus. If that was truly the case, he gave no evidence of having learned any special skills during his time away from Zyldzce; though he'd come back with a store of *vitzn*, of well-worn jokes for all occasions, with which he constantly assailed his defenseless victims. He also laid claim to an ability to ropewalk. He had even gone so far, shortly after returning to town, as to string a rope between trees on either side of the narrow River Bug. Then he collected kopecks they could ill afford to spend from a handful of gullible spectators. From his perch in the crotch of a leafy water oak, he called down, "*Mayn froyen un mentschen*, I confess I'm a fraud. Should I attempt to do what I promised, I will surely fall into the river, and since I cannot swim," though the river was no more than knee-deep in that season, "I will drown. So, if you think it's right that a son who is the sole support of his ailing mother should drown on account of your few measly kopecks, then I'm ready to commence my performance . . ."

Had he not been out of reach, the gathered might have hanged him from the very tree he had climbed.

It was true, however, that he was caring for his aged mother; he may even have come back to Zyldzce for that purpose. But even with the sick woman, Menke couldn't help taking occasional advantage of the opportunities her maundering mind provided to tease her. If, for instance, she mistook him in her dementia for Menke's worthless dead father, he might say, stroking her thinning hair, "I'll bring your tea just as soon as I get my furlough from the world to come." If she asked him in a moment of rare clarity to please close the window, it's cold outside, he might answer, "If I close the window, will it be warm outside?" Which is not to say he didn't spoon-feed her from the pot of mashed groats Froy Dubitski, the sexton's wife, regularly brought over. He emptied her slop jar, read to her from the vernacular women's Bible, and now that she seemed to have relapsed back into her childhood, told her tales she'd once told him when he was a boy. The tightrope sham notwithstanding, some said Menke was different after returning from his travels. He'd been seen, shortly following his homecoming, to fall into uncharacteristic bouts of self-absorption and was heard to utter vague warnings about approaching calamity. But since his reputation as an irredeemable wag had long preceded his departure, nobody paid much attention to his admonitions, and in the end Menke himself reverted to his unrepentantly feckless behavior.

Out of charity, he was given the occasional odd job. For a time he assisted Reb Tubal Boynbaum in his bakery, where his capricious attendance to the fire-breathing brick oven led to no end of burnt challah loaves. When not frightening customers with the ghostly features he cultivated from the dusting of flour that covered his face, he made jokes at his boss's expense: He confided to Froy Pruchnik that the swag-bellied Reb Boynbaum made the divots in his bialys with his extruded navel, and to her further horror he whispered, "You should see how he makes the holes in his bagels." Sacked from the baker's, he was taken on for a trial period as a waiter at Shmulke Goiter's fleabag "hotel." There, unable as always to curb his tongue, he might approach the random patron with the breezy question, "So, you want dinner?" And when the patron, in the absence of a menu, inquired, "What are my choices?" Menke responded, "Yes or no." If the customer complained that he'd served the brisket while holding it pinned to the plate with his thumb, he replied, "Did you want it should fall on the floor again?" Served his own meager portion as was included along with his meager wages, Menke remarked, "For this they had to kill the whole ox?"

Turned out of Shmulke's tavern, he tried his hand at peddling. With the pittance he'd earned waiting tables, he bought fruit past its prime from the local peasants and hawked it from a barrow in the clamorous market *platz*. When the wives turned up their noses at his produce, he grew impatient; in his idleness he hollowed out a mealy apple with a paring knife, dropped in a live blister beetle, and replaced the cap of its stem. To a spectator astonished by the apple's rocking to and fro, Menke explained, "It's possessed by a *dybbuk* who will offer riches to the one who buys the apple and sets it free." He informed the potential customer that the resident spirit naturally increased the price of the apple accordingly. More skilled at discouraging than enticing clientele, Menke incurred the outright ire of some, such as the *frumeh* pupil of Rabbi Vaynipl before whom he dangled a pair of shriveled figs.

"Behold the Sacred Relic of the Holy Testicles of the Baal Shem Tov," he solemnly announced.

With the intention (never realized) of painting a sign to attract more business, he'd left a primed sheet of veneer leaning against his barrow. When asked by a curious passerby what it was for, Menke feigned surprise. "It's a picture of Moses crossing the Red Sea of course." And when the onlooker remained confused, he gave him to understand that "the Jews are gone, the Egyptians haven't yet arrived, and *dumkopf*, the sea has parted!" Adding, "For you, only five groschen."

Nuisance that he was, the Zyldzcers regarded Menke as largely harmless. Even as they disapproved of his irreverent tongue, they might spare him a kopek or two in recognition of his incorrigibility. Having no official *shtot meshugener*, no village idiot to endow, the townspeople seemed to have tacitly acknowledged that Menke's chicanery had its place. The only element of his conduct that might raise the brows of the Jews, however, was his perceived courtship of Blume, the rabbi's much sought-after daughter. Of course, the term "courtship" was a stretch when applied to the succession of gambols and wisecracks with which he was forever trying to divert the girl. Still, the townspeople questioned whether such frivolous company as Menke's was appropriate for the only daughter of a holy man.

They needn't have worried; Menke was as deft at frustrating intimacy as he was at encouraging it. Close to Blume since infancy, he had always been leery of making the girl aware of his desire to be more than friends. Walking together along Fish Mouse Street, flanked by the wooden houses buckling under the weight of their moss-grown roofs, Blume might begin to divulge some confidence to her companion: She felt guilty, for instance, for reading non-religious books behind her father's back . . . But Menke, afraid of the very familiarity he'd invited, would interrupt her to perhaps call attention to a stout woman hurrying home from the market.

"How I love to watch Froy Mukdoyni's russet hair blowing in the wind," he might observe and, as Blume looked to see if he might possibly be sincere, add, "What a shame she's too proud to chase it."

Blume would typically roll her soulful eyes, suppressing a snicker that, on a good day, would burst into full-throated laughter.

If, on a brief ramble on the towpath that ran alongside the river, the girl ventured to ask him about the sights he'd seen during his travels, Menke would recall a floating island solely inhabited by giant rabbits or a country whose population's only nourishment was the scent of apricots.

"Menke," she repeatedly scolded him, tendrils of midnight hair escaping her headscarf, "are you never serious?"

"Only when I'm talking to you," he confessed, which was a rather transparent dodge, since he was seriously in love with the girl.

As were a fair portion of the young men of Zyldzce. There was no shortage of candidates for her affection and—through appeals from the good offices of Breine-Freydl, the cross-eyed matchmaker—her hand. She'd been trailed about since childhood by boys fascinated by the spectral lights in her hair, the blush of her buttermilk cheek, the careless rhythm of her slender limbs (so at odds with her otherwise modest demeanor) beneath her aproned skirt. They were an impressive lot too, Blume's suitors. Among them was Yoysef Blokzilber, Reb Reuven the lumber merchant's son: He wore in *shul* a bespoke Prince Albert suit imported from Lemberg, and was often seen to take from its breast pocket a hunting watch in a gold-filled case. There was the pudgy prodigy Moyshele Kaganowicz, foremost among the study house benchwarmers, a memory artist and Rabbi Vaynipl's star scholar. Stick a pin in a word on a page of scripture and the young phenom could tell you the exact word pierced on the other side. There was the lamblike Yitzkhok Sumac of the golden sidelocks and delft-blue eyes, which earned him the nickname of Seraph-and-a-Half among his fellows. It was said as well that his family was related on his mother's side to the saintly Gaon of Vilna. To name but some of the chief contenders for Blume's fond regard.

It would not have occurred to Menke in his ill-fitting sack coat with its empty pockets, with his potato shnoz and his heron-like stalk of a body, crowned by an outsized head rank with rag-mop curls—it wouldn't have occurred to him that he could ever compete with those favored lads; just as they would never have considered him a serious rival. He was content, or so he told himself, to remain Blume's clown. But while she received the earnest petitions of her suitors with an equitable grace, and exasperated her father with her indecision, none of them made her laugh.

On a chance encounter with the girl in Lantern Fly Alley (Menke was skillful at orchestrating "chance" encounters), he reported, "I heard old Reb Shepske Szcuczynski was sent to a specialist in Wroclaw."

"I'm sure I'm very concerned about Reb Shepske's health," replied Blume flatly.

"'Doctor,' he complained," continued Menke, "'I can't pish.' 'How old are you?' asks the doctor—he's very professional, with degrees from Poznan and the Jagiellonian on his wall. 'Ninety-three years, thanks God,' Reb Shepske proudly announces. 'Hmm,' says the good doctor, stroking his beard, 'you already pished enough.'"

From Blume, a long-suffering sigh, a furtive snicker, then outright laughter. What could you do with such a boy?

Once, having bumped into her on a cloudless afternoon near Shavuot, Menke, in a gesture of reckless prodigality, offered to buy Blume a strawberry kvass. Berl the vendor, in his perpetual stoop beneath the large copper urn strapped to his back, was beckoning. When she graciously declined, telling him he should save his money, he informed her of a recent windfall.

"What are you saying?" she asked, suspicious. The sunlit down on her cheek was like pollen on a petal: How he would've liked just to graze it with the blunt tip of his nose.

"Well," replied Menke a bit diffidently, "I got an advance from the burial society on my mama's funeral expenses."

Blume tilted her head as if she hadn't heard him correctly. "The burial society doesn't give advances."

"So I told them my mama was already dead."

The girl's jaw fell open: Even by Menke's standards, this was beyond shameful! Though it was difficult to tell whether she covered her mouth in outrage or the better to stifle her mirth.

Then Menke's mother Taybl-Beyla really was dead. (Dr. Slutzki, with his syrupy bedside solicitude, had promised her death would be easy—her soul would leave her body as smoothly as a hair plucked from sour cream. But it seemed more to Menke as if her soul had been ripped from her diaphragm without benefit of anesthesia, the wisp of her body whiplashed by pain.) The townspeople gave her a proper burial among the lichen-encrusted stones in the beech-shaded cemetery on the far side of the river. They paid their condolences during the *shivah* to her orphan, who assured them it was a blessing that she'd had the good sense to expire before the uninvited guests arrived and the unthinkable began.

"Death," he said, more perplexing than usual, "is as good a place as any to hide in."

In Kabbalah God makes the world out of words. Now, brooded Gershom, lulled by the tattooing of the passenger train wheels en route to Stuttgart, the world has had its day. So didn't it follow that, after the catastrophe, words were what the world should retreat back into? Then it fell to Gershom to retrieve those words—the ones inscribed in the moldy volumes of Mishnah removed from the embrace of corpses, the disinterred scrolls and obsolete Yiddish Baedekers, their pages nibbled to lace by worms—and see them returned to the place where they were finally meant to be. But where exactly was that? Where else but Zion, as Gershom had determined, the uncontestable treasure house of all things Jewish. The task, however, not unlike the rigorous spiritual ascents described by the sages in Gershom's driven studies, was easier said than done.

He was moved in part by the ruling theory posited by the sixteenth-century mystic Isaac Luria. He held that the real exile of the Jews predated the destruction of the Temple and the ensuing expulsion from Jerusalem. Exile, according to Rabbi Luria, was a cosmic tragedy dating back to the beginning of time, when God sent forth from the void gleaming vessels filled with primordial light. But the effulgence of that light was more powerful than the vessels could contain, and they burst, scattering their divine sparks throughout the universe. Had the vessels arrived at their earthly destination intact, the world would have remained in its sublime prelapsarian state; we would never have fallen from grace and been banished from the Garden. As it was, the separation of the light from its source echoed not only the historical Jewish Diaspora but a kind of personal diaspora of the soul.

To gather those sparks from their fallen condition among the shards of broken vessels and return them to their original source, thereby heralding a messianic age, was the task that Rabbi Luria, known as the Ari, the Lion, had assigned—by order of his visionary authority—to every Jew. By this act, called *tikkun*, the Jews themselves would assume responsibility for healing and perfecting the world. The recipe the Ari had provided for recovering the sparks was simple; it was accomplished through *mitzvot*, that is, through study, prayer, and good works. Of study Gershom had done more than his fair share, though he'd been notably delinquent in the prayer and good works departments. This expedition would help compensate (and maybe atone?) for what he'd thus far omitted from the Ari's program; it would also help salve the terrible pain inflicted by the abominations of the past several years. Or so Gershom had believed, until his travels led him into landscapes where the Ari's myth of universal redemption seemed to disintegrate into so much claptrap.

From Paris he took an overnight train to Zurich, which was mostly undamaged despite having been "accidentally" bombed by who knew which side. The trams rattled along the bustling Bahnhofstrasse; the churches and guild houses duplicated themselves in the shimmering mirror of the lake, their steep gables reprised by the snowy peaks of the Alps in the distance. Prague too was remarkably untouched, its ancient synagogues spared by the enemy as the repositories for Hitler's projected Museum of an Extinct Race. True, the city's Baroque spires and dusky serpentine streets remained agitated from the bloody uprising at the end of the war, but Gershom could sit with a cognac in the tall windows of Kafka's preferred Café Louvre and still feel somehow sheltered from harm. What harm was left that had not already been perpetrated in that quarter? Heidelberg, behind a curtain of wavery mist like northern lights, was also unharmed but for its pulverized bridges, but Vienna, Frankfurt, Munich, and Gershom's home city of Berlin were in ruins.

He'd been prepared to view the devastation, or so he assumed; had even perversely looked forward to it. Total annihilation was the least of what the Germans and their allies deserved—"May the sins of the fathers be visited on the children unto the third and fourth generation." There would be a certain splendor in such providential justice. Hadn't *das Volk* believed the *Gotterdammerung* a necessary prelude to the regeneration of their Nordic race? But so great was the magnitude of the destruction Gershom beheld that it was impossible to imagine that civilization could ever recover from such an incalculable laying to waste. It was a destruction so complete that it seemed to exceed what the imagination could apprehend, and Gershom was sickened by his inability to make sense of what he saw. Hadn't making sense of the inconceivable always been his strong suit?

The blasted houses and public buildings, when not reduced to dust, showed either crumbling facades without interiors or interiors without facades. Sometimes a structure's exposed cross section revealed inhabitants on its various floors: a stick of a man in a hammock furiously biting a hangnail, the silhouette of a family by candlelight behind a burlap drapery. The avenues were bordered by dunes of rubble between which the people passed as if through some petrified version of a parted sea. They passed— the tattered population, much of it homeless and displaced— through one zone of oblivion on their way to another, wandering as if in search of some piece of the planet that might still support life. Along their route they picked through the debris for scraps of coal, a table leg for kindling, an eyeless bisque doll for a child, some morsel of humanity lost beyond retrieval. They carved slabs of greenish meat from the flank of a fallen truck horse and stood in mile-long queues for a ration of watery gruel. A widow pushed a pram piled high with memories usurping the place of her murdered innocent. An old man with no apparent shadow planted turnips in a grassless lot; a sallow girl sold herself in exchange for a wedge of streusel; a gang of half-feral orphans paused in their scavenging to watch a puppet show in the window of a bombed-out factory. Demobbed soldiers, once the pride of an invincible Master Race, the telltale collars torn from their shabby field tunics, scrimmaged over a slice of leberwurst.

Among the surviving structures of these blighted cities was the occasional library, a few of which contained collections of Judaica and Hebraica—*sheerit hapletah* as they were called, the scattered remnants of Jewish culture. Some of these collections had been substantially increased thanks to the work of the Reichsleiter Rosenberg's taskforce. With a horn-mad avarice they had plundered the great estates of the Rothschilds, the Rathenaus, and the Wildensteins, and sacked the libraries of the Hochschule für die Wissenschaft des Judentums in Berlin, the Etz Chaim in Amsterdam, the Staatsbibliothek in Krakau, the majestic Strashun in Vilna, and countless other treasured repositories.

What the Nazis didn't incinerate in the public squares or save for heating fuel or sell to the paper mills, they selected for use in their ideological warfare. Ultimately the chosen books and archival materials were to be consolidated in various institutes devoted to the research of the Jewish Question, a subject the Germans had been hard at work on throughout the war—even as the question was being definitively answered. Many of these collections were consumed in the fires following aerial bombardments, but Gershom, in his office as repossessor of plunder, set out to visit those that had survived.

He knew some of them from his youth: the Bavarian State Library in Munich where, in his student days, he'd pored over medieval manuscripts, their pages crisp and delicate as filo pastry; the library on the Bockenheimer Landstrasse in Frankfurt, with its parqueted floors, frescoed ceilings, and tall stained glass windows; the palatial Berlin Congregational Library on the Oranienburger Strasse, denuded now of its overarching elms. Sequestered by galleried bookshelves, bent beneath emerald-shaded lamps at polished oak tables, Gershom had fed, once the bacillus had taken hold in his teenage years, his passion for Jewish learning. In those days he didn't read so much as devour the pages of Mishnah and the Babylonian Talmud for their sometimes bitter but frequently ambrosial contents. "Turn it and turn it again, for everything is in it," went the old saying with respect to the bounty of Torah and its commentaries, and the young scholar had taken the watchword to heart. He coveted not only the rough wisdom of their texts but also the physical volumes themselves, their smooth vellum and pebbled calf bindings, the buff yellow parchment, the blind tooling, the gilt spines, the whorls of its marbled boards—and the words: the blazing black characters with their savor of holiness.

He delighted in handling those books, sometimes experiencing an erotic frisson similar to what he'd felt when, still a virgin, he'd dared to caress the curve of his first wife Escha's hip through the light fabric of her summer frock. In his soberer moments he was embarrassed by such rapture, which prompted his penchant for inspecting the volumes in private, preferably amid his personal library in the stone cottage on the Abarbanel Road. Now he was possessed by a different though equally intemperate desire, to gather up every remaining Jewish book in Europe and ship them all for safekeeping to Palestine.

Not everyone was uncooperative. Most librarians had compliantly sported their party insignia throughout the war years and knew enough to keep their heads down; if they viewed their fatherland's native barbarism with disfavor, they knew better than to censure it. Some were now prepared to acknowledge that a degree of injustice had been committed and were amenable to the authority of the officials from Jewish agencies seeking to reclaim the assets of their tribe. But the majority, who had willingly embraced the Reich's assertions of universal sovereignty and applauded the suppression and literary autos-da-fé—these, still at their posts despite the ongoing denazification, retained a proprietary attitude toward holdings they deemed eminently worthy of preserving. Usually they were courteous if rigidly formal, often speaking with a saccharin intonation that only thinly disguised their contempt. But when it came time to actually negotiate over what they regarded as their own lawful reserves, their lips tightened and their eyes became chillingly opaque. They hedged, waffled, and referred Gershom to superiors who were never available. They sent him into unnerving bureaucratic warrens that rivaled anything in the pages of his sainted Kafka.

Such was the case with the lady librarian in Berlin, in whose office Gershom was kept waiting for an unconscionable period, cooling his heels as he looked out a window onto an ugly bomb crater in the street below. When she finally appeared, pencil-skirted, lynx-eyed, and severely coiffed, she was profoundly apologetic: So much had been undone since the armistice, she complained ambiguously, that needed doing all over again. Gershom spread the corners of his lips to approximate sympathy. Bidding her guest to take a seat, the woman installed herself behind a barge-sized executive desk and wasted no time in coming to the point.

"You must understand, Herr Scholem," she began, clearly well-informed as to the nature of his visit, "that our library has acquired and maintained its extensive Judaica archive since the time of Napoleon's emancipation edicts."

Gershom exhaled; he'd been here before. "And you must admit, Frau Reuter," he replied just as evenly, "that circumstances have changed since then."

"Fraulein," she corrected in an undertone, smiling thinly, her eyes narrowing like gunports; her heavy makeup gave her face the look of painted crockery. "I can assure you," she said, "the collection here is well cared for and accessible to all who are interested."

Gershom felt his throat constrict until he had to clear it. Struggling to control the tremor in his voice, he stated, "Everybody here who was 'interested'," making aggressive air quotes with his fingers, "is dead. There is no one left in Berlin who can even read these Hebrew codices."

Fraulein Reuter heaved a sigh; the man was being difficult. "Herr Scholem, can you not appreciate that it was the German people under the patronage of their government that have kept these books safe from destruction?"

Gershom's brain hurt from the heat it was generating. "Frau . . . lein Reuter, I'm sure we are all very grateful for the Reich's tender care of our property." He paused to pluck a speck of lint from the knife-edge crease of his trousers, then lifted his head again. "But now it's time to give it back."

"Give back to whom?"

"To the Jewish people and the Israeli polity which is its most significant representative."

"You speak as if they were one and the same."

"They are."

Her expression was cold: Galatea turned back into marble, thought Gershom; he imagined a smooth enamel nub where her sex should have been. "I know of no such collective legal entity," she put forward matter-of-factly.

Gershom bit down: The worst of it was that she was right. Since the beginning of the slaughter, he'd campaigned from his outpost in Jerusalem for international recognition of the authority of the Jewish people: They constituted, in effect, an organized corporation laying claim to the treasures of which they had been despoiled. But even now, despite the stupendousness of the crimes committed against them, there was no common consent among nations willing to grant them that license; the Jews were dependent on the largesse of their enemies. He took a breath: He was Dr. Gershom Scholem, far-famed scholar and emissary of the esteemed Otzrot HaGolah; his dignity was sound, inviolable. So how was it that he found himself shouting, "We have a right to our cultural heritage, you Nazi hag!"

Fraulein Reuter had retreated into complete petrifaction. "Herr Scholem," the statue spoke, "I suggest you refer your request to the proper municipal ministry."

She must have known that, amid the postwar chaos, no such ministry existed.

The officials in Bratislava were even more intransigent, perhaps further stiffened by the starched military uniforms they'd lately been issued by the Soviets. Even the lowest of weak-chinned, soft-bellied functionaries demonstrated a sort of practiced impatience with Gershom's requests. Frustrated by their mulishness, he sometimes abandoned all pretense to diplomacy. "What do you even want with these books?" he wondered aloud. For those in question were not the irreplaceable volumes, the ones with embossed spines, silver clasps, and illuminations commandeered from the libraries of Jewish Junkers along with artworks of inestimable value; the books in the Soviets' possession were only the soiled, age-mottled *sifrei kodeshim* impounded from the sagging shelves of tumbledown village study houses. Books gone limp from centuries of sedulous handling then reverently kissed by their users in apology for the abuse.

"How can they profit you?" Gershom pled.

To his question some officials went so far as to shrug; they were simply following orders dispensed from above. But when the scholar attempted to trace those orders to their source, the hierarchy dissipated into vapor.

Though it was only a stone's throw from Vienna, Bratislava, on the Danube near the border of what had been the old Pale of Settlement—the territories to which the Eastern European Jews had been historically confined—was a world away. It was the farthest east Gershom had traveled on his mother continent. But he didn't stop there: From Bratislava he pressed on to Cracow, then Lublin, Warsaw, and Vilna. Reduced now mostly to moonscape, these cities had once been the vibrant seats of

Yiddishkeit, where the indigent Ashkenazim had dwelled for a millennium in their thronging, lice-ridden rookeries. Between the cities lay the beggarly little towns in which the Zhids had cohabited uneasily with their gentile neighbors, who might turn on them at any excuse and savage them for sport. This was the somber country of the Ostjuden, a species of Jew that had always been an embarrassment to their acculturated Western European coreligionists, among whom Gershom was reared. The German-Jewish Bürghers of Berlin and their fashionable wives were appalled by the unwashed squalor of these primitive types in their untidy beards, corkscrewing earlocks, and rope-girdled caftans. But they were also the Jews for whom the chain of tradition had remained virtually unbroken since Sinai. In his *Jung Juda* days, inspired by Martin Buber's sepia-toned Hasidic legends, Gershom had believed every Jew from Russia, Poland, or Galicia to be a reincarnation of the miracle-working Baal Shem Tov. They had kept the faith, these threadbare *luftmenschen*, and maintained their ability to abide beyond history; they could rise to heights of spiritual bliss in their worship that the dour intelligentsia of Gershom's generation could never touch. Not even if they should become familiar with the secret symbolism of the Kabbalah.

But history had had the last laugh, the unwashed and urbane alike having shared the same obscene fate. The few that had managed to climb out of the crucible, more or less alive, would most likely never know elation again, and even a garden-variety melancholy might be too galling an emotion to endure. In his travels Gershom had made reluctant stops, admittedly more out of a moral obligation than compassion, to meet with the displaced persons in their camps. Some occupied the same stinking barracks in which they'd awaited the death that had somehow overlooked them. Many, frail to the point of near transparency, resented having been overlooked.

One such skeletal survivor, a former professor of natural philosophy at the University of Leipzig with broken teeth and a jarring cough, blithely explained to Gershom, of whose work he was aware, "We here are refuse from the death factories which they haven't yet decided where to dispose." He accepted the skullcap and prayer shawl from the American Joint Distribution Committee that Gershom was helping to dispense, but assured him he donned them for warmth rather than devotion. "The phylacteries I will use for sock garters or maybe a belt." He followed Gershom's gaze toward a child with pipe-stem legs who had succeeded in flying a kite a few feet above the muddy yard. "You see perhaps a metaphor?" the professor asked Gershom. "You should know that the kite was made by an adjutant for the camp commandant's son from the flayed hide of a former inmate." To complete the metaphor, the kite became entangled in the barbed wire surrounding the camp's perimeter.

The detainees had received, along with toothpaste and soap, an assortment of recaptured books of Psalms and Torah scrolls—though some of the scrolls were so damaged that they were given a ceremonious burial and properly mourned. Internment, however, was not incarceration; the people were free to range from camp to camp, which they did in stateless legions scattered across Europe, driven forward by the sheer novelty of motion. Palestine as an ultimate destination had been instilled in the minds of many, and Gershom encouraged those he spoke to in this. He often felt, when they were roused by the idea, as if he'd planted in them a questionable posthypnotic suggestion. For even as he proselytized the enlistment of new citizens for the Yishuv, he worried about how they would alter the swelling ranks of the original settlers. The pioneers had largely been motivated by the hope of a glorious Jewish renewal realized through the quixotic Zionist experiment, whereas these wintry leftovers, so harrowed and oblivious, were mobilized only by an instinct for self-preservation. They would do what they must to create a secure new nation, and in so doing trample the ideals that had drawn the dreamers to the Land in the first place.

"I must not entertain such thoughts," Gershom told himself.

Though he harbored even pettier thoughts. The restituted books dispersed among the survivors—what would become of them? Gershom pictured himself taking them back, wresting them from the hands of the refugees as forcibly as they'd previously been confiscated by the barbarians in order to insure their deliverance to Israel. *The sparks must be returned to their source.* But could he really be so base as to believe that the preservation of the books should take precedence over the survivors' need for them? It was a reflex triggered by his inveterate bibliomania, and it shamed him that it endured even now beyond the catastrophe—the "Holocaust" they'd begun to call it, though the word for some reason rankled, its melodrama seeming to catapult the horror beyond the human sphere. Gershom was aware of his own hypocrisy, though he'd become "political" with only half a heart. But how could one retain fidelity to a progressive Zionism and remain an apostle of the starry-eyed philosophies of Buber and Ahad Ha'am, who had championed the idea of Palestine as a "spiritual center"—how continue to argue for utopia in the face of the Arab uprising of '29 and its deadly aftermath? And now, how could you discourage the absolute necessity of creating a nation-state?

Yet even when confronted with the enormity of the moment,

Gershom remained, God help him, a creature of his study, the mortal embodiment of the content of his books. "At his appendix surgery," the cheeky Fanya had quipped, "they made an incision and out seeped words instead of blood." Truly, he was more at home among his fusty volumes than he had ever been in the world beyond them, and this posthumous Europe was all the more reason to remain ensconced between the pages of hermetic texts. In a carrel in the fortresslike university library on Mount Scopus, Gershom had devised a unique system for cataloguing its increasing holdings, and for his erudition had been awarded the Chair of Jewish Mysticism. It was a title so improbable that it seemed almost to mock its possessor. How was it that he, an avowed rationalist and skeptic from his precocious boyhood, had become the century's preeminent interpreter of mumbo jumbo? In the beginning his esoteric studies had been mere affectation, a rebellion against the bloodless bourgeois milieu of his family and the aridity of their moralistic religion. He'd taken an arrogant pride in his independent learning and his self-taught ability to translate the ancient texts with their abstruse nomenclatures. These were the texts the old guard of Jewish historiographers— Heinrich Graetz, Simon Dubnow, the mossbacked Leopold Zunz—had dismissed as an inconvenient aberration in their effort to formulate a "science" of Judaism. Highlighting mysticism, they determined, would only antagonize the *goyim*. By bringing this aberrant mystical strain like some ramping primeval behemoth out of the shadows into the broad light of the present day, the young Gershom had thumbed his nose at the accepted wisdom. So what if he'd yet to comprehend the immensity of what he'd set loose.

The books had been impenetrable at first, and then, gradually, they weren't. Something of their elusive essence began to infect him. The strange, phantasmal language of the titanic *Zohar*, the Book of Splendor, and its precursor, the compact *Bahir*, the earliest known Jewish mystical tract—the savor of that language seemed to have entered his bloodstream, and there incubated until it began to make a kind of visceral sense. The numinous logic of the books simmered in the alembic of his organs and bowels, releasing the odd coherent message through potent spirits that reached his brain.

"What I feel," Gershom had reported in his exaltation to Walter, who had his own weakness for states of grace, "is an intuitive affirmation of those mystical theses that lie at the narrow boundary between religion and nihilism." This was the sort of language that Gershom could present to the professors and use to explain the experience to himself. But the truth was, the passions that had overtaken him in his studies had no name he could apply to any of the philosophical or philological categories he knew— and he knew them all. If they had any name, these passions, it was one that could only be found among the inscriptions in the hidden annals of the heart and genitals.

But that was then. There was the Talmudic proverb that claimed that on the day the Temple in Jerusalem was destroyed the Messiah was born. So tell it to these walking demi-cadavers in the resettlement camps, thought Gershom, that from destruction springs redemption, and prepare to have your head heaped upon with well-deserved scorn. He was ashamed to recall, when among the survivors, his own grandiose youthful delusions, how he'd aspired as a green adolescent to the role of a universal redeemer. Once he and Walter had joined forces, there seemed no project so outsized that it could not be realized by sheer force of intellect.

Together they would rouse the nations from their soulless capitalist stupor and alert the people to the venality of their religion. What did it matter if they proved in the end to be imposters, since even false messiahs—as for instance, the infamous seventeenth-century charlatan whose sociopathic exploits Gershom was lately captivated by—could play their part in a great awakening. That was his mission before he'd viewed firsthand the consequences of what a false messiah had wrought.

At word of the invaders' approach Rabbi Eliakim Vaynipl gathered his "disciples" in their dilapidated study house to enact a solemn ritual. His scholars were not actually disciples and Rabbi Vaynipl not actually a rebbe nor a scion of any Hasidic dynasty; he was merely a lone, self-professed follower of Yeshayahu Funzundel (called the Odd Fellow of Medzybizh) of blessed memory. Rabbi Vaynipl led no congregation and was, in point of fact, no more than a poor *melamed*, a teacher of Talmud Torah, but his circle of young scholars were so devoted to the ingenuous old man that they regarded themselves as his acolytes and hung on his every word. He had gathered them on this night with the assurance that each had fasted since the night before and prayed throughout the daylight hours; they had cleansed themselves in the ritual bath and purged themselves, in the case of the more zealous, with the use of a clyster syringe. The ceremony they were about to perform was not without danger and so required the utmost purity of body and mind.

"I have summoned you here tonight," said the rabbi, his hooded eyes plaintive beneath papery lids, "to perform a holy rite for the purpose of hastening the coming of Messiah."

A bumblebee murmuring was heard among the assembled.

They would execute this rite, the rabbi informed them, according to the formula imparted in the ancient *Book of Raziel.* "This is the book," affirmed Rabbi Vaynipl, holding up a dog-eared and beschmutzed little volume, "that was given to Father Adam by the Angel Raziel and later transcribed by the exemplary Eliezer of Worms from the original text, which was engraved in sapphire."

Of course, the prescribed liturgy for invoking celestial beings was known to be a hit-or-miss operation: You might call up, God forbid, a devil instead of, say, a dead saint or the prophet Elijah, who commuted between heaven and earth in order to interfere in the affairs of men. But desperate times demanded the undertaking of great risks.

Only recently had the rabbi and his steadfast circle begun to recognize the urgency of their circumstance. Who wanted to believe that the threat was really so dire? Naturally, even they, in their sleepy provincial outpost, had heard of the laws being passed in Germany that forbade Jews to engage in almost anything beyond breathing—and it was rumored there was a growing number of places where they were denied even that. But Zyldzce, located in its remote backcountry corner of Poland or Byelorussia or Lithuania—the borders were always shifting—Zyldzce was not Germany. So what if the Reich had come to think differently on that score? Another nation's bellicose ambitions were of little concern to the simple shtetl folk. Besides, hadn't they learned to live with your bog standard oppression and the menace of indiscriminate bloodshed for a dozen centuries? Jew hatred was a fact of life, like bedbugs and hives.

So they'd discounted the warnings, which had come in any event from dubious sources, such as the scamp Menke Klepfisch, whose unreliable reports were dismissed out of hand. Then there

was the old Galitzianer *schnorrer*, a prune-faced, tussocky-bearded
vagabond who'd traveled through their district from somewhere
near the Czech border. Obviously addled, he told tales of
nightmarish atrocities in a voice so bereft of expression that who
could believe him. Nor had such farfetched stories yet found their
way into the regional journals or even the national radio. But then
came a trickle of refugees from Czchuków and Pszczyna, whose
similar accounts of what they'd witnessed were harder to ignore.

Though their town had thus far been spared any injurious
symptoms of disruption, the people sensed that an unkind world
was encroaching, and was perhaps set to hedge them about.
Germany and Russia had jointly squeezed Poland and its border
states with poison pincers, and after the mutually approved
partitioning, the Soviets had occupied Zyldzce for a spell. While
far from benign, the commissars had tended to target their
abuses more toward the restive gentile population than the Jews,
a number of whom—at least among the young—styled themselves
Communists and freethinkers. Some of the Jewish youth had even
been given positions of authority, which they used to lord it over
the sons of Ham—behavior for which they would pay dearly later
on. But when the German tyrant betrayed the Russian despot
in '41, the Soviets abandoned the field before the arrival of their
insuperable new foe. There followed a brief interlude of uneasy
peace. But now all of Poland and its neighboring states were
under the "protectorship" of the Reich, and while its lowering
shadow was felt far and wide, its minions had yet to enter Zyldzce.
Villages and shtetlach in its vicinity, however, were already seeing
an infestation of the enemy, and news of its enormities had finally
penetrated the Zyldzcers' complacency.

Rabbi Vaynipl, as he faced his devotees, could not in all

honesty vouch for the provenance of this particular edition of *The Book of Raziel*. Zalman Tafshunski, apothecary and bibliomane, had declared it a worthless imitation, but the peddler that the rabbi had purchased it from insisted it was an incunabulum dating from the fifteenth century.

"It's what your sages call a 'grimoire'," the humpbacked little man had explained, his whiskery jaw in constant motion as if chewing a cud, "which is a book of magical spells and incantations."

He claimed the legacy versions of the selfsame book had been instrumental in countering various scourges and plagues of the Middle Ages; it was responsible as well for minimizing the rampaging incursions of Chmelnitzki's Cossack revolt generations ago. The rabbi was keenly aware of what a disastrous toll the depredations of those times had taken on the Jewish populace, which did not lend weight to the peddler's truthfulness or speak well for the efficacy of the book. Nevertheless, the slender volume was numbered among the canonical texts of the hallowed mystical tradition that Rabbi Vaynipl was a devout adherent of. So perhaps the book had been used incorrectly during the ravages of those olden days; maybe its users had lacked sufficient faith. The rabbi had been scrupulous in his study of the book's coded contents, its necromantic icons and symbols, and he was confident of the spiritual fortitude of his followers, unfledged youth that they were. They simply could not afford to fail.

Granted, the old timber *beit hamidrash* was an inauspicious venue for staging the advent of . . . if not King Messiah Himself, then at least one of His emissaries. The wind whistled between the logs of its termite-riddled walls, and the windows were papered over where the broken glass had yet to be replaced. The relic of a large masonry stove belched and sighed but provided little heat, and there was a noxious stench from the unplucked game that the sexton had hung to smoke in the choked chimney flu. But the room itself seemed capacious now that the *shtenders* and desks had been shoved against the walls, and the presence of an *aron koydesh*, the freestanding ark of the Law, lent the place a somewhat sanctified air. Some questioned why an ark had been installed in the lowly study house in the first place. The answer was simple: When the "new" synagogue (since called the Old New Synagogue) was built in the previous century, an elaborate new ark was also constructed. That one, hand carved and velvet curtained, replaced the plain cedar cabinet salvaged from the medieval wooden shul that was torched during the Chmelnitzki massacres. So the town's handful of resident Hasids, among whom Rabbi Vaynipl figured conspicuously, had offered their study house as a home for the orphaned ark.

The rabbi and his circle, always relatively conservative in their ritual observance, had not previously involved themselves in practical Kabbalah. Never before had the students been called upon by their teacher to resort to incantations, white magic, and such in the interest of summoning supernatural entities to intervene in earthly affairs. Heretofore they'd been limited in their efforts to theoretical pursuits and the use of prayer and meditation as a means of hopefully attaining *dveykuss*, a cleaving to God. The rabbi was well acquainted with the Talmud's injunction against divination, not to mention his own mystical discipline's caveats against trafficking in the occult: One should first have a minimum of forty years, a wife (the rabbi was several years a widower), and a substantial paunch. (The latter was meant to provide ballast against too rapid a spiritual ascent.) By such standards, neither the wizened old Rabbi Vaynipl nor his youthful followers qualified for their enterprise. Moreover, the rabbi knew the cautionary tales about those who'd attempted before him to force the hand of the Lord; such as the Seer of Lublin, who was defenestrated from a tower for his wizardry, and Rabbi Joseph della Reyna, who was drowned by angry demons for having tried to cage Satan himself. But *they* had miscalculated by prematurely anticipating Apocalypse. Rabbi Vaynipl would not make that mistake: He had no doubt that in this moment extreme measures were called for, as the End of Days was likely upon them.

"Let us begin," he pronounced, dropping his chin into the nest of a dove gray beard as wavy as the grain of weathered wood.

The young scholars, already instructed in what to do next, pulled their prayer shawls over their heads and formed a circle. Moyshele the Prodigy, an exalted expression on his ordinarily smug face, came forward to place a spirit lamp on the floor in the center of the ring. At the same time Fayvl Kochlefer, padding behind them, stretched the simian length of his arm to extinguish with a pewter snuffer the kerosene lanterns hanging from the rafters. Then the flame from the single lamp illumined the beardless faces of the yeshivah scholars and allowed them to see one another for a moment as a worshipful quorum of holy theurgists from Talmudic times; though they knew in their hearts they were amateurs and the task before them unimaginable. Still, they believed in their righteous rebbe if only because he believed in the undreamed-of endeavor himself. Several perspired despite their gooseflesh from the chill in the room; Shimon Ishkowicz passed gas with a sound like the quack of a duck.

"All that is formed and all that is spoken is one Name," intoned Rabbi Vaynipl, rocking as if in prayer, his reedy voice like a scraped fiddle string. "And that Name is . . ."

The scholars uttered in unison the letters of Tetragrammaton, the hidden name of God: "*Yud . . . Heh . . . Vov . . . Heh,*" then shuddered in a body with the sense that from this point there might be no turning back.

They were enjoined by the rabbi to chant the letters in various preordained configurations "until we achieve the *chochmah* consciousness between being and nonbeing." This they did, vocally rearranging the letters for an inordinate period in compliance with the method specified by the initiates of old. An asthmatic Yekhiel Blakarowitz, wheezing like a melodeon, looked to his fellows to see whether they'd yet been endowed with the crown of light that the said "consciousness" was supposed to confer. He waved a stealthy hand over his own head in the hope of feeling that saffron crown's peculiar warmth.

"Now let us chant," said the rabbi, consulting the grimoire and speaking with an increasingly ragged breath, "let us chant the mother letters which are the secret root of Tetragrammaton: *Shin, Mem, and Aleph . . .*"

The quorum repeated after the rabbi, again for what seemed like an endless stretch of time, the exhaustive permutations of the three letters: "*Mem Shin Aleph; Shin Aleph Mem,*" and so on. The eerie tension in the atmosphere created by their collective drone overruled any restlessness that might otherwise have infected the scholars.

Rabbi Vaynipl, grown hoarse, squeezed the hump of his yam-like nose and alerted his flock that they should prepare themselves to receive the miraculous vision of Ezekiel's chariot, "whose wheels will shimmer like the sunlight reflected on a wall through a bowl of water. But," he suddenly shouted, having momentarily found his voice again, "we must not allow the shimmering to persist!

For," raising a crooked forefinger, "the least vibration can cause the chariot to break apart with unspeakable consequences for us here on earth."

The injunction was enough to freeze the scholars in place. The runty Shimon Ishkowicz tried hard to control his flatulence for fear that he might destroy the necessary tranquility and by extension the world. While most clenched shut their eyes rather than be struck blind by the awesome spectacle of the chariot, some peeked, if only to glimpse their ethereal rabbi gazing as far as the coast of paradise.

"Together we have passed out of *tohu*, the Universe of Chaos," Rabbi Vaynipl assured them, no longer referring to the book, "and entered tikkun, the Universe of Rectification. Here we may begin to repair the vessels that were shattered by the divine light of the Almighty at the Creation."

Each vessel, he explained, had been blasted apart into 613 fragments, which corresponded to the 613 parts of the body, which in turn were equivalent to the 613 commandments of Torah. The mending of a single vessel, reassembled with the incorruptible glue of prayer, represented the reconstitution of the entire *Sefirot*, the Tree of Life, which would itself be translated into humanoid form.

But all the chuckle-headed Mordecai Wisznik could conjure in his mind's eye was a copper pot with chicken legs. Standing next to him, Peshke Ezjyszki, barely out of knee pants, was so overcome by the unsettling creepiness of the whole affair that he began silently to sob, his tears mingling with a trickle of urine that pooled at his feet. By now the majority of the *minyan*—with the exception of Moyshele the Prodigy, who may have been faking it— had lost the thread of the arcane ritual, and having given up on the idea of revelation, contented themselves with observing their rabbi in his transports. They worried he might burst into spontaneous flame from an overabundance of holiness.

Having allowed the book to fall from his arthritic hands, the old man began to babble assorted combinations of letters in a hemorrhage of nonsense syllables. It was a phenomenon Moyshele identified in a whisper to the doltish Mordecai (who nodded sagely) as "the circumcision of the tongue." The rabbi's moist eyes, shot with broken capillaries, were rolled back into his head, which was tilted toward the ceiling, and he seemed to be in the throes of either deep ecstasy or excruciating pain.

"The Thirty-Two Paths of Wisdom," he warbled plangently, rocking to and fro like an accelerating metronome, "are attained by the addition of the ten Sefirot to the twenty-two letters of the Hebrew alphabet, which must then call forth the dreadful forces that will vanquish evil forever. Shaddai!" he blared, beating his meager chest with one hand, lifting the other toward the exposed ceiling rafters, "*Adonai! Yod Chavah! Ehyah Asher Ehyah!* Hallelujah! Hallelujah! Hallelujah!"

Silence. Then nothing, nothing happened at all. The rabbi's head eventually righted itself, though his arm remained uplifted and he still seemed to be gazing at distances beyond reason. But a feeling of acute embarrassment, even shame, had pervaded the gathering; no one spoke or ventured to look now at Rabbi Vaynipl, though neither did any dare to break the circle. At length a sound was heard like a squeaking of mice but was ultimately determined to be a creaking of hinges, which had its source in the rehabilitated ark. All heads turned toward it as its twin doors began slowly to open. The spines of the scholars went uniformly rigid and Peshke Ezjyszki sank to the floor planks in a dead faint. No one made a move to come to his aid. The rabbi opened his arms toward the homely oaken cabinet in a gesture of welcome. At that, the doors of the ark abruptly swung wide and a slight, crouched figure in a peasant shirt, a tallis tied round his throat like an opera cape, dislodged himself from among the Torah scrolls and sprang into their midst. It took the assembled a moment to recognize the intruder as the scoundrel Menke Klepfisch.

"Pogroms, we got," he submitted earnestly, stepping into the circle of scholars and edging aside the spirit lamp with his foot. "Cholera we got, and gout, blood libel, idolaters, Nazis, *apikorsim* ... Oy, maybe it's better we were never born. But who is so lucky, I ask you?" He swiveled his tousled head left and right as if expecting an answer. "Not one in fifty thousand," he said.

Nobody laughed.

When the intruder shrugged and made his slouching exit, Rabbi Vaynipl returned by degrees to his doleful self. He rubbed his tired eyes with his swollen knuckles and looked about as if to ascertain precisely what had happened. He picked up the fallen book, kissed it, then sighed and offered this cold comfort to his stunned followers: "Even when the gates of prayer are closed, the gates of tears are open."

It was a given that everywhere he went he arrived too late. The old legend-drenched Baluty district of Lodz was shards and broken bricks; Warsaw, shards again (and the exposed network of tunnels out of which the remnant of the ghetto fighters had crawled after their ill-fated rebellion). In Vilna, once called the Jerusalem of the North, home to the august Gaon of Vilna, the sacrosanct YIVO Institute was rubble (though much of its Yiddish archive had been saved, smuggled out at the risk of their lives and shipped to New York by an intrepid few who called themselves "the paper brigade"). But the once teeming Jewish quarters of these cities were ashes, as were their populations: *Judenrein*, as the vanquishers had designated them. Gone were the folk that Gershom and his Zionist brethren had endowed with such mystery in his student days—the impoverished rabbis and patch tailors, the arm-twisting shopkeepers, vinegary market wives, sausage makers, rope spinners, and *shamuses* with beards to their *pupik*, speaker ladies with their remedies for neutralizing the evil eye. The centuries of Czarist ukases and Cossack bloodbaths had finally culminated in this moment, and all before Gershom had had a chance to view these living persons in their natural surroundings.

"What am I, an anthropologist?" he admonished himself; though if he were honest, he would have had to admit that he'd been satisfied with knowing such folk primarily through their naïve incarnations in Buber's fairy tales. With those ill-clad, herring-scented yokels and their childish beliefs, he had frankly nothing in common. What could he have learned from their woolly-headed rebbes? Unworldly cranks, they'd closeted themselves in their dingy chambers employing the very books that were the bedrock of Gershom's *gestalt* to try and meddle with the order of the cosmos. He'd had scarcely any desire to meet them—until now.

Still, he could commend himself, could he not? After the news of Walter's suicide and the gut punch of his own brother Werner's murder at Buchenwald (where he'd been sent by the Nazis for being that worst of all degenerates, a Jewish Communist), after his mother's recent death and notwithstanding his witness to a devastation beyond historical measure, he had carried on. He remained "active," to use his colleague Hannah Arendt's catchword, though she wielded it like a bludgeon. What a nudge the woman was! Despite it all Gershom could still lay claim to successes. He had negotiated tirelessly, often with grudging officials; had listened patiently to their invented stories of having "rescued" rare Hebraic manuscripts for display in their special divisions, then patiently explained to them that they were liars. After a time he'd learned to control his temper—he had not known he had such a temper—and remain his tactful self. In this way Gershom had secured many of their prior possessions from the libraries he approached, as well as items from the Jewish communities, rabbinical seminaries, and yeshivot that had been sacked to augment those libraries. But he'd been defeated as often as he'd succeeded, and so many masterworks remained in the hands of the kleptocrats. The coveted Frankfurt collection in the Deutsche Nationalbibliothek, for instance, had eluded his grasp, as had the Codex Hebraicus of 1343 in Riga, the only extant near-complete manuscript of the Babylonian Talmud from the medieval era. All his impassioned appeals had failed to move the directors of the institutions (allegedly purged of Nazis) that housed them, and his efforts had cost him the better part of his strength and peace of mind—though he chastised himself for succumbing to such faintheartedness.

He knew he should have done more and the knowledge desolated him. In Kaunas, his previous driver's commission having expired, Gershom hired another to take him back to Germany. Disappointment and enervation aside, it was time he returned to the Offenbach Depot, where he hoped to be allowed to oversee a shipment of repossessed goods sent to Palestine. In deference to conscience, he requested that his driver stop at some of the DP camps that lay outside the cities; he'd had enough of ravaged cities. Soon he'd had enough of the camps. Their route through the June countryside was meandering, and with his duties temporarily suspended, Gershom thought he might settle back and enjoy the ride. Immediately he was nauseated by the thought. The idea of enjoying anything in this fallen world was repugnant to him and seemed a betrayal of all he'd seen. Besides, the biscuit-brown East European landscape had so little in common with the *gemütlich* quilt of poppy-flecked chartreuse meadows and upland pastures that still peacefully abided between the arenas of wreckage in his native Germany. The barren hills resembled the rust-cankered backs of pachyderms, and even the pine forests had an ominous, marauding look. Antique ruins were indistinguishable from the more recent, which contributed to a disjointed sense of having strayed outside of the ordered sequence of time. Then there were the towns and villages.

Most were nothing but rural slums, places so desolate that the war had not wasted them more than had their ordinary attrition. These were places situated sometimes in Poland, sometimes Russia, Belarus, Lithuania, Ukraine, depending on the winds of realpolitik. Gershom wondered if the people themselves knew where they lived and to what nation they owed their allegiance—or if, in the case of the Jews, they had even cared. Due to their depleted male populations, the villages were largely given over to forlorn widows, urchins, and the elderly marooned in their neglect. You saw them digging puny potatoes in unplowed fields or leading a spindle-shanked goat by a tether—the women of indeterminate years, their faces, in the oval sling of their headscarves, a fretwork of leathery wrinkles. They refrained from looking up at approaching vehicles, as if by ignoring them they might be taken as mere features of the landscape, rather than mistaken for human beings. It could still be dangerous to be regarded as a human being.

Gershom had asked his driver to stay away whenever possible from main-traveled roads, advice the man had taken perhaps too much to heart. So be it, the roundabout route they followed avoided military checkpoints and also gave Gershom more time to collect his thoughts—a task as subject to trial and error as collecting a lost heritage. He wished he could keep his overwrought brain from thinking at all. Closing his eyes to the passing backcountry, rocked by the rhythmic knocking of the old odorous Škoda sedan, he made no effort to communicate with his driver. But the driver, to his irritation, sought to initiate a conversation with him.

"Yitz," he began, jolting Gershom out of his solipsism. Was this some panicked ejaculation?

"What's that?"

"Yitzhak, my name. Yitz. Yitz Kabatcznik."

"How do you do," replied Gershom with his usual reserve. "I am Dr. Scholem."

"I know, the book collector."

Gershom nodded to the man's phlegmatic eyes in the rearview mirror. "One of many," he conceded. He appreciated, though, that given the alphabet soup of organizations with competing aims involved in the business of cultural restitution, the man should distill his role into so quaint a calling. *Book collector.* As a line of work, it sounded like a venerable complement to *book peddler,* which was the humble trade the grandfather of Yiddish literature had chosen to assign to his pseudonym: Mendele Mocher Seforim, Mendel the Book Peddler. Untold editions of his caustic satirical tales had turned up in the pillaged libraries.

The driver spoke again in his offhand way. "Books are drek."

Gershom wasn't sure he'd heard him correctly. "Sorry?"

"You heard me."

This was a hostile reply, was it not? Though there was no hint of malice in the man's voice, Gershom was shaken. From the backseat he again surveyed the face in the mirror—the bushy brow in the shadow of his flat cap, his broken-nosed, Tartar face, the impassive eyes. The fellow had claimed to have some connection to one or another of the organizations sponsoring the continental scavenger hunt for Jewish souvenirs, but Gershom had neither asked for nor been shown any credentials. He chose not to dignify the man's assertion with a reply.

Nevertheless, Yitz persisted. "What are they good for?"

A barbarian, thought Gershom. How could a Jew ask such a question? And the man was a Jew, as the numerical blue brand on his forearm below his rolled sleeve attested. Gershom always felt a sense of humility in the presence of survivors, but this one, so seemingly self-possessed and disagreeable, invited no special sympathy. Let alone that his question flew in the face of all that Gershom held sacred. Called upon to answer, however, he could offer in his weariness only a rote response: "Books form the soul of the Jewish people."

"Like I said, drek. I prefer a nice glass schnapps."

Gershom could feel his ears beginning to burn. Had the man no moral compass?—though it was said that conscience was among the first "illusions" one lost in the camps. Nevertheless forcing himself to meet the occasion, Gershom declared what had become his principal postulate: "Saving the books amounts to saving the People of the Book!"

An inaudible grumble was heard from the driver's seat.

"What did you say?"

"I said," replied Yitz, "about that, I wouldn't know." He stuck a cigarette between his meaty lips and flicked a match into flame with a thumbnail. "You be a person of the book," he said patronizingly, taking a deep draw from the cigarette, exhaling. "Myself, I'm a person of the *oyseh mukem*. You know oyseh mukem?" Gershom's Yiddish—if this was indeed Yiddish— was patchy. "*Hoomentush?*" tendered Yitz by way of further enlightenment. Then, in case he still hadn't made himself clear: "Pussy," he said in his crude German. "I like the ladies. Schnapps and ladies."

Shocked now out of his fatigue, Gershom gnashed his teeth, but Yitz was not done.

"I like to squeeze a soft tsitske, and also a fistful fat tooshie."
Taking his bony fingers off the steering wheel to knead the air,
Gershom didn't know whether to clap his hands over his ears or
his eyes. "I like shmitsn mit a zaftig maidel that throws over my
belly her big leg . . ."

Gershom was no prude, but this was blatantly disrespectful.
"Enough!" he barked, then thought he perceived the driver's
slight smile in the rearview mirror. Was this his idea of *épater les
bourgeois?* The plebeian out to get the goat of the staid professor?

"Nu," said Yitz, "you don't want to talk pussy?" He was clearly
pleased with himself. "So we'll talk scripture."

Gershom gasped as, driving uphill, the man did literally shift
gears as he changed the subject..

"It tells us in Deuteronomy," he submitted, affecting a
pedagogical tone, "is prohibited from plowing a field, a farmer with
a ox and a donkey yoked together. But in Talmud, the tractate
Bava Kama, Rav Ashi asks, 'What is the law if the farmer drives
his wagon with a goat and a fish?'"

Gershom had begun to massage his temples with his fingertips.

"Rav Pappa asks in Tractate Nedarim," he went on, "'What is
the law if you find sitting on a person's head a bird's nest? Must you
send away the mama bird before you take the chicks?'"

Gershom groaned. How could it be that he, who'd discussed
the future of Zionism with redoubtable intellects such as Agnon
and Chaim Bialik, and explored the mathematical theory of truth
with Walter Benjamin, was now reduced to being persecuted by
this boor?

"Ben Zakkai says yes," said Yitz. "You must, before taking the
nest from the top of a person's head, chase away the mother bird."

At that point Gershom, stiffening his spine, resolved to be

the passive victim no longer; when necessary, he could fight fire with fire.

"In Tractate Hagigah," continued Yitz, "it says a high priest is permitted to marry only a virgin. But, asks Rabbi ben Lakish, can the priest marry a virgin if she's pregnant . . . ?" At which juncture his passenger suddenly interrupted.

"The Bava Batra maintains," pronounced Gershom, "that a baby pigeon found within fifty cubits of the coop belongs to the owner, whereas a pigeon outside of fifty cubits belongs to the finder. Rabbi ben Bag Bag asked, 'But if one of the bird's feet is within the fifty cubits and the other outside, to whom does it belong . . . ?'"

Said Yitz, a shade triumphantly, "For asking this question they expelled ben Bag Bag from the academy."

Gershom was about to cry foul, when a loud report like the sound of a gunshot made him jump in his seat. The car swerved briefly out of control before it was brought to a precipitous halt within inches of the trunk of a chestnut tree.

"Flat tire," Yitz coolly announced. Then suddenly all business, he got out of the car to remove the jack and the spare from the boot.

Reeling from the fright of their near accident—to say nothing of the unsettling dialogue that had preceded it—Gershom dislodged himself from the backseat with the object of stretching his unsteady legs. Their vehicle had fetched up beneath a tree overlooking the market square of one of those habitations too large to be called a *dorf*, or village, and too small for a proper *shtot*, a town. Had the flat not occurred, Gershom might not even have noticed the clustered provincial eyesore they were traveling through. The houses were the usual haphazard arrangement of out-of-plumb wood and mortar structures, some displaying hand-painted shop signs, all with crippled chimneys and swayback roofs of shingle or tin. From their midst reared the verdigris onion dome of a Russian Orthodox church. Like so many similar backwaters, this one had an untenanted feel, though here and there, slinking round a corner or ducking into a courtyard, you might spot some dreary citizen.

"What is this place?" asked Gershom more or less perfunctorily.

Yitz paused in his vigorous pumping of the jack handle, looked left and right, and shrugged. Then he rose from kneeling on one knee and squinted, as if the scene might have struck some familiar chord. He walked round to the front of the car, stuck his head in the driver's side window to consult a map taped to the dashboard, and returned to the jack. Kneeling again to resume working the handle, he uttered a single syllable with a breathy full stop.

"Zyldzce."

"Menke, how could you?" demanded Blume; she was apparently not amused.

Menke assumed a shamefaced expression. "You didn't think it was funny?"

They had come upon each other (as usual by Menke's design) in the narrow lane behind the public bathhouse, in whose musty vestibule Menke had lately set up shop as a letter scribe. It was a cloudy day in early April, the air keen with the metallic edge that augured an impending storm. Blume was on her way to retrieve the Sabbath cholent from Boynbaum's bakery. In this activity she was among the mob of women who routinely took their covered dishes on Shabbos eve to heat overnight in the baker's oven— that way they needn't violate the sanctity of the Day of Rest by cooking. The girl was in a hurry; she was often run off her feet with managing her father's household, which included cleaning the beit hamidrash and providing Shabbos meals (with mostly imaginary funds) to the poor scholars and mendicant drifters the rabbi ceaselessly welcomed into their home. Tasks that kept her from her omnivorous reading.

"Funny," said the girl in response to his question, giving no emphasis to the word. "You nearly gave my papa a stroke."

Still feigning mortification, Menke muttered, "I guess you had to be there."

Rather than lend dignity to his answer, Blume brushed past him and began to walk away. Menke savored for a moment the fragrance of fresh dill that trailed in her wake, then chased after her.

"Blume, I couldn't help it," he protested, "they're such a bunch of *shmegegges*." She continued to ignore him; the defamation after all included her father. "Besides," he pressed on, "didn't I give them instead of disappointment something to talk about?" It was a fact that Menke's latest act of deviltry was the talk of the town.

The girl had proceeded into the broad street dubbed somewhat tongue in cheek "the Boulevard" to spite the prevalence of butchers' stalls and knackers' yards. Without stopping, she gave him a look. "What gives you," raising her voice over the clatter of a passing milk wagon, "what gives you the right to judge who's a shmegegge?"

Menke had to trot to keep pace with her irate stride, admiring the way indignation kindled a rosy glow in the hollow of her porcelain cheek. "I'm sorry?" he said, offering a clearly insincere apology.

At that Blume suddenly halted, kicking at a scrap of offal flung from a shambles. (A trio of slavering dogs instantly pounced and began to fight over it.) She studied the gawky boy in his high-water pants, with his sheep's eyes and borscht-stained lips, as if trying to come to some settled conclusion. Menke felt ticklish under her scrutiny, and a little dizzied by the unfathomable depth of her beauty. Thinking she might be on the verge of forgiving him, however, he ventured an anecdote to further divert her from vexation. He lived to divert her.

"I found a fly yesterday in my raisin bread, so I complained to the baker Boynbaum. '*Tahke*,' says Boynbaum, he's such a card; 'so give me back the fly,' he says, 'and I'll give you a raisin.'"

Blume's softened features stiffened again. "Menke," she said, "don't you think it's time you grew up?" then walked on.

Menke stood there taking some pride in having made her mad. This meant that she cared, did it not? Always in the past she was finally cheered by his antics, disapproving at first but moved in the end to reluctant laughter. But anger, that was something else, a sign of genuine concern. Or did it simply mean that she'd had enough of his monkeyshines?

He continued to contemplate the question even as he pursued his letter-writing activities in the well-trafficked entrance to the bathhouse. He sat on a low stool in the corner, which he rented for a few groschen from the inert, sour-faced attendant Netta Hilke, and scribbled missives on the tea chest he used for a desk. Scribing was a new vocation for Menke, taken up in response to the hysteria for correspondence among the Jews that those unfavorable days had bred. Zyldzce, it seemed, was at last convinced of the coming unpleasantness, and everyone was frantic to contact relations in those parts of the globe still safe from its reach. Reb Asher Golub, the longtime village scribe, had more clients at his booth in the market than he could handle, which gave Menke the idea of taking advantage of the overflow. Naturally there was little trust in his disreputable character among the townsfolk, and his claim to literacy was not much in advance of those he offered to serve. But on the other hand, the queue for old Reb Asher's services was long and his chicken-scratch penmanship shaky and slow. Moreover, it couldn't be said that Menke wasn't a clever lad, and if the glibness of his mouth was any indication, he might also turn out to have an epistolary flair.

The unschooled who brought him their requests for written communications, however, often got more than they'd bargained for. They pressed him to appeal to the consciences of far-flung uncles and cousins in the hope that they might send remittances to help defray the cost of their flight from imminent harm; they urged him to express, respectfully, their unrefined *cris de coeur*—and Menke complied, assuring them his transcriptions would have "the stink of righteousness." To give him his due, Menke did remain faithful at least to the spirit if not the letter of their messages. Things were bad enough that there was no need to amplify the extremity of his clients' circumstances, but the scribe couldn't resist taking liberties with the prosaic facts. A poor widow might impart to a sister in Pittsburgh, America, her fear of what might become of her and her children in the looming *churban* (the disaster); and Menke, impersonating the woman's woeful voice, would describe how her hair had turned white overnight and her children become toothless and incontinent. An illiterate glazier complained to a brother-in-law in Haifa that his business had fallen off, and Menke told how no sooner did he install a new window than it was smashed by anti-Semites: "Every night a Night of Broken Glass." Chronic diseases became terminal in his epistles. A woodcutter confided to Menke the curse of a swollen hernia, which the scribe graduated to an elephantiasis of the scrotum that compelled the man to transport his *beytsim* in a wheelbarrow.

As a consequence of his liberal edits to their dictation, the replies from relations often had small relevance to actual circumstances. Their bewildered responses in turn dismayed Menke's clients and ultimately discouraged them from seeking his further assistance. Later on, his dispatches would prove not so much distortions as prophecies. But by then scribing had become an obsolete profession, since uncensored letters were prohibited by the invaders, and the content of sanctioned letters was censored to the point of incoherence.

They had arrived without warning on an afternoon in spring, when the orange marigolds in the window boxes—the only ornaments the mole-gray town made a show of—had just begun to blossom. Then all of a sudden Zyldzce, for which the outside world had been essentially more rumor than real, entered history.

Menke might have said I told you so but for once held his tongue. Though hadn't he, in his travels, sometimes literally seen the writing on the wall? He'd worn many hats during that protracted *Wanderjahre*, one of which was teamster for a ragtag "circus" of gypsy jugglers. He'd driven the nag Ethelinda that pulled their painted caravan until her bones began to splinter, then liberated her in the night and led her on foot into Lublin, where hunger forced him to sell her to a factory for hoof glue. In Minsk he'd taken a job as a walking advertisement for a new kind of urine-diverting toilet, which he was made to wear strapped to his back as he marched through the congested streets. (Even Menke tired of being such a laughingstock and quit after a week.) In Cracow he opened crypts at a cemetery and removed the decomposed bodies from graves whose leases had expired, and in Przemysl he operated a hydraulic press at a plant that pulped and baled books deemed, arbitrarily, decadent and subversive. A yeshiva dropout, Menke was interested to find that many of the incendiary books were written in Yiddish, and was fired for browsing them on the job.

In Warsaw, needing no costume, he was hired for a walk-on appearance as a street Arab in a production of the film *Motke Ganef* (Motke the Thief). Sometimes, when he was unemployed—and he was unemployed for weeks on end—he would hang around the famed Café Ziemianska, where he eavesdropped on the bantering conversations of poets and journalists. Often he overheard grim prophesies of a rising blood tide, which, as one smug bard assured the kibbitzer personally, was "as plain as the honking schnozzle on your face." He heard the rabid speeches of the German Führer on the radios that the goyim played full volume in their windows with the intention of scaring the Jews. At night, avoiding his berth in a Chlodna Street doss-house, Menke haunted the cabarets such as Fat Josek's and the New Azazel in their louche cellar venues. There he absorbed the cornball jokes and slapstick didoes of baggy-pantsed, Yiddish-speaking comics, all of them schooled in variations of self-mocking schlemielerie. He paid for his attendance with the price of a watered-down slivovitz, which he purchased with the coins he collected after repeating those same cornball jokes at the tables of the Café Ziemianska—where more than one patron told him the donation was in payment for his promise to go away.

Often famished and destitute, Menke reminded himself that he was, at any rate, footloose and far from Zyldzce. He was at-large in the great wide world of possibilities. So why did he curtail his wayfaring to return to the shtetl? Well, for one thing he'd had word from Big Hadassah the corset maker, in a letter forwarded through many hands, of his mama's failing health. Hadassah and her neighbor, Froy Dubitski, would most certainly look after the old woman, who'd never been any great shakes at looking after herself, never mind her errant son. But still, Menke had a conscience, didn't he? Blume the rabbi's daughter might say no, but Blume—his childhood playmate, little knock-kneed Blume, who'd grown into the sable-haired, coral-lipped vixen whose utter unattainability had been instrumental in driving Menke from the town in the first place—Blume would have only been teasing. How he'd longed for her to tease him again.

He did make what he thought was a good faith effort on his return to warn them; he'd even pictured himself blowing a shofar as he led the people in a body across Europe to board a ship in Hamburg for the New World. But naturally, given its author's reputation, Menke's obviously exaggerated alarm went unheeded. Besides, everyone was still enjoying a collective sigh of relief at the hurried departure of their Soviet "guests," and by the time the Zyldzcers realized their peril, the borders were closed, visas were no longer available, and Menke had resumed his role as village reprobate.

For a while life continued in its ordinarily shopworn fashion—a life into which time and change had made few inroads during the past thousand years. True, some of the more prosperous Zyldzcers had radios, Bakelite console affairs with amber tubes, which those that knew a little English regularly tuned in to the BBC. They dutifully reported the thunderclap of Hitler's invasion of Poland, which rocked the planet and very nearly woke Zyldzce out of its willful slumber. But still the sun came up, the sun went down; the water carriers shuttled back and forth from the well in the marketplace, and the *shulklappers* called the faithful to morning prayers. Great Britain waved its saber, and France and Germany took potshots at each other across the Siegfried and Maginot Lines, all of which was of small concern to the shtetl folk. Subsequent broadcasts proclaimed that Germany had taken Holland and Belgium, that France had become a vassal state of the Reich, but still the townsfolk refused to appreciate the awful extent of their own jeopardy.

By then Operation Barbarossa was well underway: The Germans were in pursuit of the Russians who'd fled willy-nilly back east, with a number of the young shtetl Communists in tow. But the deceptive calm endured in the streets of Zyldzce; perhaps the Reich had lost interest in the whole campaign. Then one fine day, unheralded, a long procession of death-dealing machinery entered the town. First came the tanks of the armored panzer divisions accompanied by field artillery and siege guns, then the personnel carriers escorted by the hornet drone of motorcycles with sidecars, and the numberless battalions of Wehrmacht jackboots that rattled the town's flimsy architecture like the walls of Jericho. It seemed that the entire German infantry was marching over the trembling truss bridge that spanned the River Bug and proceeding down Hrubieszow Street in the direction of Moscow; the Polish residents (Zyldzce was technically in Poland now) cheered while the Jews peeked fearfully through drawn shutters. They waited, the Jews, for the endless columns of field-gray uniforms to pass out of town and leave the shtetl in its relative peace, but several units were ordered to break ranks and remain.

The orders, passed down like all orders through torturous channels from some empyrean high command, placed the town under the stewardship of the Obersturmführer Ulrich von Graf und Trach, who arrived in a gleaming black Mercedes cabriolet. A fair-haired, high-spirited, prepossessing gentleman with insouciant lips and a dimpled chin, he wasted no time in establishing an absolute jurisdiction enforced by his stolid troops. An immediate piece of business was to see the ground sown with leaflets declaring the Jews responsible for all of the earth's ills. A curfew was set and chilling directives posted on the walls of public buildings—one notably to the effect that any woman found guilty of infecting a

German soldier with venereal disease would be punished with death. (Death being the standard punishment for the least infraction of a dizzying array of ordinances.) The homes of merchants, as well as Shmulke Goiter's tavern and hotel, were requisitioned for garrisons, and the toadying Ignatz Wisniewski, a renowned pogromchik, was appointed to the puppet office of mayor. All manner of goods were commandeered from the Jewish shops and it was further authorized that a Judenrat council be formed to oversee the collection of "taxes" and the selection of work details. When no one was initially moved to volunteer for a place on the council, the commandant airily demanded that twelve men step forward, or else the rabbi—this was Rabbi Berel Moszczenik, the stately head of the Old New Synagogue—would be shot.

Then it seemed as if, in a matter of hours, the time-honored ethics of Zyldzce were turned *mit kop arop*, topsy-turvy. Cruelty was now a virtue, kindness a sin, and the very air seemed to have acquired a density that chafed the lungs. In fact, it was the lungs and heart, and *kishkes*, that registered the climatic change, because no one's brain seemed equipped to comprehend such a lightning transformation. It was in their gut where the Zyldzcers began to feel that even the surrounding landscape had become portentous: The grove of Swiss pines and lindens on the far side of the river was now a bloc of forbidding sentinels; the petals of the periwinkles that dotted the riverbank dripped poison. Deadly as well were the unsmiling eyes of the occupiers, which a Jew, whose own eyes were deemed an obscenity, must not meet on pain of grievous consequence.

Still marvelously inattentive in body and mind to the charged atmosphere, however, Menke Klepfisch turned a corner from the Boulevard into the market square. He was aimlessly knocking about—a risky occupation in itself—still brooding over the precise nature of Blume Vaynipl's anger, and how it might be defused. It was Thursday, market day, which the invaders yet tolerated, though the commodities for sale were much diminished since the Germans had already appropriated the better part for themselves. Horses whinnied, sheep bleated, cattle lowed; Jews and peasants spat in their hands and slapped palms to seal bargains. (Especially hard bargains, since the Jews despaired of ever replenishing their merchandise.) But the whole scene had about it the quality of a charade of authentic commerce—as if the buyers and sellers were dissembling normality for the sake of placating the occupiers, if not themselves. Even the striking commandant, overseeing the exhibition in his bottle-green field tunic—braided insignia adorning its collar, shoulder, and sleeve—had the look of a music hall brigadier. The people stepped aside for him as he strolled with his retinue through the throng, hands linked behind his back; everyone made way for him—all, that is, but a single woolgathering Jew, who, watching only his feet, walked straight into the ramrod-stiff officer.

The commandant took a step backward, allowing the affectation of his monocle to drop out of a piercing blue eye and dangle from the ribbon at his decorated breast. With withering irony, he touched two fingers to the patent leather bill of his cap and introduced himself: "Obersturmführer von Graf und Trach."

Replied Menke in a thoughtless reflex: "Menke Klepfisch," and clicked his heels.

The Herr Oberst's adjutant and lieutenants started forward, presumably to join forces in breaking the bones of the insolent Jew; but with a gesture their commanding officer held them back, and instead of administering the furious slap with his own gloved hand, delivered himself of a hardy guffaw.

ershom wondered if Zyldzce was the name of the place they were halted in or another of his driver's cryptic profanities. In any event, while Yitz went about the business of replacing the flat tire with the spare, Gershom decided to take a "stroll"—that was the word that first came to mind. English had become for him a default lingua franca ever since he'd composed the lectures that made up his magisterial *Major Trends in Jewish Mysticism* in that language. ("Magisterial" was the characterization that prevailed among the critics—some of whom admitted they had not previously known there was such a thing as Jewish mysticism—in their zealous praise of the book, and Gershom saw no reason to dispute them.) It had been a purely practical strategy, as the lectures were originally delivered by invitation in the United States. But since the book's publication Gershom had become as comfortable in English, his fruity accent notwithstanding, as he was in his native German and adopted Hebrew. It also served him well in his dealings with the Americans at the Offenbach Depot.

So, with the aid of a sturdy branch he'd picked up along the way, Gershom strolled, acutely aware of the word's infelicity in this context. You strolled at your leisure, secure in places where you belonged. Walter's cherished flâneurs strolled through the streets of Paris, idly absorbing its sights and sounds. But the sights through which Gershom had been passing all these fraught months were perhaps best observed with a cold eye.

This sorry little town, like a multitude of others, had forfeited its right to the label of shtetl. For a town to be called a shtetl it must have Jews, preferably in the majority. But all that was left of them here were the fragments of Hebrew characters scrawled on doorposts or peeking from beneath the peeling paint on Polish shop signs. So much, thought Gershom, for sheerit hapletah. De-Judaized, the skeleton population seemed to aspire to invisibility. They avoided the eyes of strangers, as if by not looking at them they were themselves unseen. Gershom wondered if, when the strangers left, the people reasserted themselves—like a tableau relaxing into animation—and exulted in the windfall inheritance of the properties that had once belonged to their vanished neighbors.

The low-lying, whitewashed shops around the square appeared to be sinking into their foundations, as if they too sought to evade scrutiny. That's how Gershom perceived them, wondering if his European odyssey had untethered his ordinarily empirical vision beyond recall. Several of the stores were open for business, though the jumbled assortment of goods they offered—beet shovels, pitchforks, ox yokes, horse tack—often belied the signs that still cited them as a greengrocer's or shoe repair shop. In the cobbled square itself, an old woman, cowled despite the heat, sat behind a small pyramid of bruised apples; another, her face warty as a gourd, hunkered under a torn umbrella peddling jars of honey and melting caramels. A legless wretch in a dog cart, honked at by toddling geese, stretched an arm to soften a piece of stale bread at a water pump. Gershom supposed that someone with a less jaundiced perspective might think that life here proceeded apace, as if there'd never been any Jews—though the negative space they'd once inhabited threatened to swallow him up.

Nevertheless, if only to extend his respite from the annoying driver with his Falstaffian pretensions, he walked on, entering a random passage too pinched for vehicles to pass through. The stuccoed walls of houses leaned toward one another, almost—*pace* Walter—like an arcade. Gershom noted that some of the uneven flags over which he trod bore Hebrew inscriptions, designating them as stones removed from a Jewish cemetery. Some were engraved with the priestly hands that identified the interred as descendants of Moses' elder brother Aaron. At the end of the passage was a house where grain was stored, across whose lintel the blistered denotation YESHIVAH KETANA could still be read; and beyond that the roofless shell of a building missing a wall, its interior revealing the cracked tiles of a ritual bath. There was a patch of scorched earth surrounded by soot-stained masonry outbuildings, which Gershom suspected of having once been a *shulhoyf*, the compound enclosing a synagogue courtyard.

It was time he should turn around; by now the spare tire must surely have been mounted. But goaded by some maverick impulse—had he not always been the prey of such impulses?— Gershom continued to pick his way through the sinuous streets. He emerged from an imbroglio of houses to find himself at the brow of an embankment sloping down to the sulfur-yellow river. On the riverbank was a decaying millhouse with its stalled waterwheel, and beside it a narrow wooden footbridge. The spot had a certain timeless charm that enticed Gershom to take a closer look. Waving away a swarm of gnats with his stick, he descended the bluff and gingerly crossed over the spongy planks of the bridge to the other side. There he discovered an overgrown cemetery containing a sparse plot of lichen-encrusted headstones. They were Jewish headstones, the remaining few that had yet to be appropriated for paving streets or reinforcing the walls of peasant houses. They tilted drunkenly amidst lamb's-quarter and a host of China-blue lupins wreathed in butterflies.

Overcome by a sudden drowsiness, Gershom resisted an unwonted urge to lie down among the weeds and thistles. What sort of dreams would this place beget? he wondered, picturing Jacob and his ladder: "Only mine," he mused sadly, "might be missing several rungs." His imagination had of late a way of outrunning his thoughts; just as now, before he snapped out of his reverie, he imagined that he saw, in the near distance, someone (or something) peering at him from behind a tree. Then he and the— what was it, ghost or homunculus?—locked eyes on each other, and instead of dematerializing or scurrying away, the creature stepped into the open and began to scoot toward him from beyond the forsaken burial ground.

Gershom backed anxiously away, gripping his stick more tightly as the man—it appeared to be a man—came closer. He paused a pace or two in front of Gershom, his whisk broom-bearded jaw in constant motion, chewing either a plug of tobacco or his toothless gums. "Vos macht a yid?" he croaked.

Discomposed as he was, Gershom stood his ground, scolding himself for his skittishness. Since when did Dr. Scholem begin to perceive these people as fabulous types out of his occult mythologies? Alone and having no doubt miraculously survived— as every survival was miraculous—the man was deserving of his attention. Though this one—rheumy eyes, crumpled skullcap atop a carbuncular head, ratty greatcoat belted with string—had a countenance, enhanced by the graveyard setting, that smacked more than most of an unearthly pedigree. Still somewhat on his guard Gershom answered his question—how *fares a Jew?*—with another as was the custom.

"Vos zol a Yid makhn?" he asked in his pidgin-Yiddish: How should I be? Which, despite its discourteous intimation, he'd always understood as a standard response.

The man made a slight bow, though perhaps not so much out of respect as from the weight of the hump on his back. Of course there would be a hump, thought Gershom, put suddenly in mind of the image that had troubled Walter's imagination from the nursery: *When I come into my room, my small bed to make, a little hunchback is there, with laughter does he shake.* This one, however, was not laughing. But neither did his grizzled features droop in that lackluster vacuity that was a hallmark of most survivors. Instead, the man kept nodding in concert with his perpetually working jaw, a movement suggestive of some manner of calculation. He stepped closer—too close, his gamey odor stinging the nostrils—and held out a talon-like hand for Gershom to shake.

"My name, Nachum ben Henich Aishishkin, merchant of fine and rare books."

Gershom eyed the hand before tentatively grasping its dry fingertips and letting go. "This was," he ventured, stating the obvious with regard to the man's profession, "before the war . . . ?"

"Is over, the war?" asked the old man, lifting his eyes from his bent posture, a turtle raising its head from beneath its shell. Then, in the face of the stranger's incredulity, he dissolved into a cackling laughter. The implication being that, whether or not the war was over, it was all the same to him.

Gershom recoiled, on the verge of turning away. These people, he groaned inwardly; if their ordeals hadn't left them virtual revenants and walking corpses, they were totally unhinged. They were hopeless cynics like his driver, or like this one—who was saying, "All kind books I got for the gentleman"—clearly mad.

"So come in mayn gesheft, my business," the old man invited, motioning with his bristly jaw toward the woods as he gave Gershom's sleeve a tug. Then, apparently assuming that Gershom would follow (or indifferent as to whether he did or didn't), he turned and began to scuttle back into the stand of pines beyond the graveyard.

Watching him walk away, Gershom saw, commingled in his mind, characters out of his childhood reading: Alice's White Rabbit upon *Treasure Island*'s Ben Gunn. You followed such figures at your peril. Then he thought: Nonsense, the fellow's nothing but a harmless, misshapen, old fossil whose trauma has left him believing that he is still what he had been. There was naturally no point in following him; following him was in fact unimaginable, but so, if you considered it, was so much else of Gershom's experience since he'd left his library in Jerusalem. And then there was the albeit remote prospect of redeeming more books . . .

It was cooler in the woods, shaded as they were by a fan vaulting of leafy black boughs, and the path was fairly well-trodden. But soon after they'd entered the thick of the forest, they passed out of it into a glade, where the grass was scant and the ground looked to have been disturbed. The earth was cushiony underfoot, as if its surface might actually give way. Ahead of Gershom the old man, apparently aware of his follower, looked over his shoulder to blurt a warning: "Softly here, you are walking on Jews." Gershom froze at so casual a reference to the ghastly fact. At once his curiosity, such as it was, dissolved into an acid stomach, and his heart sank; but somehow feeling he'd gone beyond the point where turning back was an option, he hastened to gain the other side of the clearing. After some minutes the beaten path became less distinct, though the hunchback continued to forge ahead through brambles and tall ferns. Finally, when the trail seemed almost to have covered its own tracks with foliage, the old man halted at the foot of a limestone outcrop. It was an imposing rock formation topped with trees and shaped something like the yawning head of a fish. A kind of ramshackle door, made of branches lashed together with flowering creepers, leaned against the boulder like a prop to keep the fish from snapping shut its jaws. On the forest floor at the base of the outcrop was a covered dish and a glass jar of gasoline-colored liquid. Herr Rumpelstiltskin, thought Gershom, though he remembered the man's name well enough—*Nachum*; Herr Nachum shoved the dish with the toe of his soleless shoe beneath the edge of the door and stooped to lift the jar to his lips. He took a long pull from the jar, spilling a quantity into his beard, then offered the liquid to his visitor.

"Black bread kvass," he said. "Keeps you regular."

Gershom shook his head in perplexity; the stuff looked flammable.

"The goyim," offered the old man by way of explanation, "they think maybe I am some bogey that they got to appease me." He cocked his hoary head in thought. "Or maybe they feel guilty?" Then he opened the flimsy door and bent over even further in order to enter a rough aperture in the rock. Gershom watched with some revulsion as the hump under his greatcoat was crushed like a collapsed soufflé by the limestone lip. Again Gershom asked himself, What am I doing here? as the old man extended an arm from inside his burrow to crook a finger. His throaty voice had acquired a slight reverberation.

"Treasures I got, come gib a keek."

So preposterous was his circumstance that Gershom felt the need to rehearse his own credentials in his head: Dr. Gershom Scholem, chair of etcetera and renegade scholar of forbidden texts, texts that led (some might say) to thresholds even stranger than this . . . though none of it seemed to matter anymore. Tossing aside his stick, Gershom ducked into the cave.

He emerged into an ill-defined space dimly illumined by a kerosene lamp poised atop a pickle barrel. Herr Nachum welcomed him by attempting to dust the clinging twigs from his suit coat, until Gershom irritably brushed away his hand. "Touchy," chided the gibbous old party. The murky globe of the lamp shed light on only the objects in its immediate vicinity, so that it was impossible to determine the contours of the grotto. If the forest was cool, the air in the cavern, though rancid, was practically nippy, almost justifying the hunchback's heavy coat. The floor crunched underfoot, either from the remains of food or the excrement of bats, or—Gershom's thoughts leapt helplessly ahead to the bones in a dragon's lair. There were a few items that passed for furniture—a manger-like bedding of rushes covered in gunnysacks, more rag-stuffed sacks appointed like club chairs in a lounge. (Was he expecting guests?) There were salvaged items such as a chipped ceramic pitcher that might have done double duty as a chamber pot, and the freakish anomaly of a dressmaker's dummy draped in a tallis and tefillin, with, God help us, a pair of French drawers stretched over its bottom. (When the old man saw Gershom staring at them, he lifted and let fall his scrawny shoulders with only the least hint of chagrin.) Otherwise there was nothing to distinguish the place from a hermit's cell, except for the teetering, waist-high stacks of books—their bindings warped from moisture, covers dappled in mold—that boxed in his living area like redoubts against the dark. Aladdin's cave this wasn't.

Without preamble Herr Nachum launched into his merchant's spiel. "Mayn dear Reb Fellow Book Maven," he began, flattering his prospective customer with the presumption of a shared passion, "will you like perhaps by the pen of the honorable Shomer Shaykevitch a thrilling what we call in the business a who-did-it?" Having taken a book from the top of a stack, he blew the dust from its cover and held up the lamp to read its title. "Here I got his famous *Glatt Kosher Murder*, which it's about a man that he tries to kill his wife only like Rasputin she don't die and . . . oops," stagily slapping a hand over his mouth, removing the hand, "I'm almost giving it away the ending." He grabbed another book. "And this one, *Mekhil, the Impure*, which it stirred up in Lvov a scandal."

Gershom emitted a comfortless sigh.

"Or maybe," the peddler began rifling another stack, causing books to tumble onto the cavern floor, "maybe you will prefer something a little more tickling-the-ribs? This one I got for you by Aksenfeld, his *Velvele Eats Compote*, a most popular entertainment that it makes everybody who reads it to plotz with laughing. No? You want maybe naughty? I got also," giving Gershom a lascivious wink, "his *Feyge, Tear Off Your Blouse*."

Gershom closed his eyes in lieu of covering his ears.

"Nisht zorg," assured the peddler, adjusting his tone to better suit what he assumed was the taste of his audience. "Don't worry, I got here as well your chaste and moral fables. Take this one," dislodging a dozen volumes in order to find it, "called *The*

Temptress, a righteous romance from Torah, only a *bisl* steamy, by the consecrated genius of Reb Isaac Meyer Dik . . ."

It was a bizarre performance to say the least, as "performance" was what the old man's hoopla amounted to. On the one hand, the peddler made his pitch as if soliciting his wares from a marketplace stall (instead of from a hideaway in a rock); while on the other, looking to all appearances like the very caricature of a stage Jew, the malformed old codger gave the impression of a seasoned actor playing the part of a peddler of books. And as for the inventory of which he was so proud—Gershom could have wept. Here, at the expense of what remained of his dignity, he'd traveled as good as to the underworld, and for what? A hoard of Yiddish *shund*, hackneyed melodramas and pulp fiction, the kind of sensational pap read by frustrated housewives and cheder boys behind their volumes of Midrash. How could Gershom have put himself in such an absurd situation? "Where is ordinary life?" he wondered. "Can I find my way back to it from here?" He was gripped by the beginnings of claustrophobia: His skin crawled; his already receding hair, he sensed, was rapidly retreating toward the back of his scalp. Clapping a hand over the crown of his head, Gershom nearly yelped, "I'm sure I'm much obliged for your time, Herr Nachum." Why did it pain him so to acknowledge the man's name? "But I must be going."

The hunchback ignored the farewell and again changed his tone. "I can tell you don't like what they read, the hoi polloi? This, believe me, I understand, a distinguished gentleman such as yourself. You want maybe for the gelernteh student in you a volume Rashi," stooping to run the lamp along the spines of a toppled stack, "which I don't seem to have got. But *here* is something special which only to my most refined clients I'm offering it."

Gershom had already turned to make his exit when, better judgment aside, he was checked by the covetousness that had grown obsessive in him over the months. These were after all Jewish books, and so had their place. But this wasn't a case of simply reclaiming stolen property; this fellow owned his goods and wanted gelt for them, and funds had not been allocated to Gershom for making purchases. Though even if there had been, the problem would have remained of how to transport this lowbrow cache to the proper archive; the boot of the Škoda could scarcely have accommodated it. Still, it seemed to Gershom, with what was quickly becoming hindsight, that this hapless, demented old oddity deserved some recompense for having somehow preserved, in his mole-like existence, both himself and his merchandise. So what priceless gem was he hawking now?

"A book that it contains from the ages their mysteries . . ."

Gershom exhaled the poor relation to a snigger. Here the old *kucker* was trying to fob off as unique—and before the world's preeminent expert in Jewish esoterica—one of those cheap medieval facsimiles of which there were already scores in the Offenbach Depot. This one, *The Book of Raziel*, a so-called magical grimoire, wasn't even in decent condition, its limp cloth binding partly unstitched, the snuff-brown pages bloated with damp. The weird diagrams, which the peddler revealed as he fanned the pages, were faded to indecipherability. The book had been a standard text among crackpot occultists for centuries, yet the scavenger in Gershom was often as avid a collector of such spurious artifacts as he was of authentic documents.

"How much?" he asked.

"Its price beyond rubies," replied the peddler, still working his jaw as if to keep its hinges pliant, "but for you . . ." Again Gershom rolled his eyes. ". . . fifty zloty?"

Highway robbery by any measure. Was the man selling books or demanding ransom? Of course, the inflated price was an invitation to bargain, but Gershom was never one for haggling, and besides, you could write off the expense as a down payment on reparations. God only knew what the fellow had suffered. Gershom handed him the fifty zloty note, then, on second thought, handed him another, which the peddler accepted with a slight lifting of the brows.

"If this much," he said instead of thank you, "why not more?"

Gershom took the book rather brusquely from the old man's hands, surprised by a heft that seemed out of proportion with its size. At that moment he was also aware of how the peddler's flickering lamp sent shadows chasing one another like scurrying salamanders about the rock-ribbed walls. Those shadows plus the air's dank pungency, and the figment of the hunchback himself, all conspired to give Gershom a feeling of even greater disorientation than he'd experienced thus far. He shut his eyes again, this time conjuring the image of his damask-cheeked Fanya, and for the first time since leaving Palestine, he desperately missed his wife. When the sensation passed enough to allow him to reopen his eyes, he was vexed by a question it had only just occurred to him to ask, if mostly to himself,

"How deep is this cave?"

Without waiting for an answer, Gershom was already halfway through the stunted portal, bursting back into daylight like one escaping the belly of a beast, when he heard the bookseller's strident voice.

"All the way, I think, to Jerusalem it goes."

ife continued in its ordinarily shopworn fashion, give or take the odd intrusion of terror. The leaflets with which the invaders had blanketed the town informed its gentile residents that the end of the reign of the Jews—"the Jews of Moses with his seven heavens, friends of Roosevelt, Churchill, and Stalin, who brought Bolshevism, abuse, and exploitation into the world"—was at hand. "We have come to liberate you from this unwanted element," the leaflets declared. The Poles who could read, read the flyers to the unlettered, who received the news in some bewilderment. Did they not have a long-standing dependence on the dirty *zhyds* for trade and mutual resentment? Though, come to think of it, weren't those same miserable pests a lot of well-poisoning, blaspheming Christ killers, who were seen to spit routinely when passing the church and rumored to piss on stolen communion wafers? To say nothing of the legend, still fresh these past five hundred years, of little Jerzy, the child the zhyds had murdered for the blood they baked into their unleavened bread. And so the Polish citizens of Zyldzce lent a willing hand in the persecution of their Jewish neighbors.

There were arbitrary beatings and humiliations, the worst of them received by the twelve men who had been pressured into volunteering for the Judenrat. Required to satisfy the Germans' incessant demands for chickens, eggs, butter, milk, cheese, tobacco, and barrels of beer, the council invariably came up short. For this they were punished in ways that graduated in cruelty over time from the comical to the inhumane. One day they might be made to line up in opposing rows and pull one another's beards, on another instructed to form similar lines and throttle one another with their fists. When they exchanged only timid pokes and slaps, the soldiers stepped in to demonstrate how a proper drubbing should be dealt. They were forced to jump in the river, where bets were placed as to who would sink or swim. They were ordered to take down a bronze statue of Marshal Pilsudski—once regarded (mistakenly) as a defender of the Jews—from its plinth near the horse market gate. Afterward, they were compelled to dig a crater-sized grave in which to bury the statue with all appropriate Hebrew obsequies.

The invaders, Amalekites and *mamzrim* (bastards) as they were referred to in whispered asides, made great sport of clipping the beards of the elders and angling with rod and reel to snag the patch wigs off their wives' shaven heads. Backhandedly honoring the Jewish tradition of *bar mitzvah*, the Germans mustered all males aged thirteen and over, able-bodied and otherwise, for the daily work details. (Exempt were skilled artisans such as carpenters and bespoke tailors, whose services were deemed essential to the Reich.) The work, which lasted from sunup till sundown, mainly involved heavy labor—repairing roads, chopping trees, converting public buildings into stables and warehouses; but often the delegated tasks were purely frivolous, such as scooping moss from between cobblestones and scouring the stones themselves with steel wool. Tasks conceived only for the purpose of degradation and amusing the occupiers. Jewish women were put to work cooking, cleaning, doing laundry for the Germans—work the dowdy Balabustas took on with a resolute fervor. Their hope was that their industry would divert the overlords from realizing that their daughters remained at home.

But the Germans were not easily deceived. They were provided by the coerced Judenrat—and the informers they'd begun to cultivate—with extensive lists of the richest merchants, the best tailors, *die Juden* with overseas relations sending money, the prettiest girls. As a consequence, the girls did their best to look unpretty, so that it became a game among the soldiers to snatch at the thick shawls the Jewish daughters muffled themselves in to conceal their charms.

Most of the town's Jewish population lived in a stupor of apprehension, since, to be fully conscious, was to be inconsolable. Some, however, remained stoical, or at least pretended to be. They took the long view: After all, such unjust violations of Zyldzce's society had a well-established history. The synagogue's *yitzkor* book overflowed with the names of the victims of Cossack mayhem and rioting hoodlums sanctioned by the government to remind the zhyds of the unforgivable crime of being themselves. So what if there was a curfew and no one allowed to leave town. The Zyldzcers had always been early to bed, and with the exception of a few travelers in fabrics and ladies' unmentionables, nobody journeyed beyond the Sabbath boundaries. If electricity was cut off during most of the day, electricity was anyway a luxury all but a few did without. And as for the scarcity of food and the recent interdict against trade, well, there had always been a fine distinction in the shtetl between the observance of fast days and periods of outright starvation. Moreover, the bright badge of the yellow star, as Menke Klepfisch so tactlessly pointed out, lent the townspeople's typically wintry garb a certain panache.

Blume would have told him to bite his tongue, but Blume was still not talking to him. She had avoided all his best efforts to put himself in her way, as if *he* were the enemy. Though maybe, he reasoned, it wasn't personal; maybe, like so many others, she'd chosen elusiveness as a prescription for survival. Once, he believed he caught sight of her from a distance, her comeliness hidden despite the warm weather beneath a wool babushka and layers of frocks to obscure her youthful form. Of course, thought Menke, she would have more reason than most to camouflage herself; a glimpse of her *shayneh* features in the shadow of her shawl would be tantalizing, and he feared some fiendish Nazi might be provoked into revealing the rest of her. God knew, he was well aware of the potential for such unrestrained urges.

Some of the market folk must have witnessed Menke's impertinent encounter with the Obersturmführer, because the tale had spread among the Jews. But rather than heroic, his arrogance was viewed as insanely foolish—as what had he ever done that wasn't considered foolish? But now his rash behavior could further jeopardize the security of the entire community. In consequence, he was generally shunned by his fellow citizens lest they acquire guilt by association. As for Menke himself, he couldn't quite believe that he'd gotten away with it: that the German commandant had simply walked away still sniggering, as did his subordinates who must have felt obliged to snigger as well. But even Menke felt he'd pushed his luck far enough. Thereafter he kept his head down and turned up obediently on time for the morning work detail he'd been assigned to. It was after all employment of a kind, though not the kind he would have sought had he been inclined to seek employment. Menke's particular party of laborers had been accorded the task of shoveling hot tar from the back of a dump truck to fill in the potholes along the Grodno Road, a road comprised more of holes than pavement. The toxic fumes from the tar caused the frailest among them—weak-kneed tailors and pallid Torah scholars—to swoon, if they hadn't already collapsed from the unaccustomed exertion. For their debility they were roundly trounced by their guards. Although muscles he'd never known he had were aflame, Menke managed to endure the drudgery, if only to escape the consequences of not enduring it. Then there was the fact that, like so many others, he had yet to be entirely convinced that what was happening was happening, despite having anticipated the coming disquiet these many months. In any event, having exhausted the supply of coal for making tar, the Germans had lately set Menke's detachment to digging ditches for no apparent purpose.

It was early morning, not quite daybreak, and the Jewish conscripts were assembled in the market square, whose dwindling mercantile activity had yet to begin. Today the raddled workers were being treated to a rare visit from the Obersturmführer von Graf und Trach, who had ordered them to line up with their shovels at shoulder-arms like regulation troops summoned for inspection. The blood orange sky was still graced by the faint meniscus of a moon, the air stinking as usual from rotten produce and horse dung. The Jews were yet only half-awake, slovenly attired and trying to stand erect in their formation. By contrast the Herr Oberst was lively, a picture of Teutonic vitality in his shining jet-black boots, his rope-braided tunic draped over his service shirt like an opera cloak. He made a show of formally reviewing the laborers, pausing before select individuals and awaiting their awkward salute, which he smartly returned with a suede-gloved hand. He halted in front Selo Mstislav, the hare-lipped synagogue beadle, to adjust his skewed skullcap, while the terrified man looked as if he expected his head to be spun about along with his yarmulke. The commandant uncurled the ragged lapel of Alter the grinder's sheepskin and patted it firmly into place, and chucked the chin of Pisher Benjy like the feeble-minded child he was. Exaggerating his satisfaction or lack thereof, the Obersturmführer was clearly enjoying the burlesque of his military appraisal. From the town hall's shingle roof a raucous dawn chorus of blackbirds seemed to join in the mockery.

Flanked by underlings, the commandant continued to pass down the shoddy row of laborers, pausing again in front of a spindly, bulbous-nosed youth with a large head of snaky black curls.

"Minky, is it?" he asked. His voice was shockingly amiable.

Menke thought it best not to correct him. He saluted, feeling somewhere between frightened and flattered to have been remembered, though he wondered if it was wise to be remembered.

"So, Minky," asked the Herr Oberst, "what good works will you and your brethren undertake today?" He pronounced his German slowly enough that the Jew might understand.

Menke blinked from the glint of the rising sun reflected in the officer's monocle, which flashed as if communicating in code. If he could decipher the message, thought Menke, it would probably tell him to keep a civil tongue in his head.

"If it please your honor," he ventured, speaking the *daytshmersh* conflation of German and Yiddish in which the Jews addressed the invaders, "we are digging for the Führer a tunnel to Moscow."

A groan was heard among the laborers within earshot of

Menke's response: The *goylem*, did he want to get them all hanged? But Menke had intended no disrespect, quite the contrary; it was just that the words often came forth from his mouth before his brain had an opportunity to process them. The commandant's cheek twitched just shy of a flutter and a passing cloud erased the gleam of his monocle, revealing an auger eye behind its lens. Then his lips, thin near to nonexistent, spread slowly into the approximation of a smile. He muttered something in the ears of the subalterns on either side of him, who, at his nod, stepped forward to take Menke by the arms and remove him from the ranks of the dragooned.

"Did I just bite my *toches* with my own teeth?" wondered Menke, as he was roughly escorted across the square and shoved through the wood-slab door of Shmulke Goiter's taproom, converted now into a mess hall for ranking and noncommissioned officers. It was the moment when the full unequivocal certitude of the occupation finally came home to the young bigmouth.

The hum of conversation among the breakfasting Germans dropped several decibels in volume as the Jew was ushered into the low-ceilinged room. All heads turned toward Menke; forks froze on the way to open mouths as he was left to stand unattended beside the dampered clay oven. He was under no illusions now: This was the lion's den. The Hitlerites in their spotless *feldgrau* sat, according to rank, at the long trestle table in the middle of that airless, inelegant space and at smaller tables around the periphery. The plates before them held generous helpings of blutwurst, potato pancakes, and sour cream, and Menke, who'd had only a raw onion for breakfast, felt his mouth beginning to water from the aromas. Hunger, however, was no match for his baleful trepidation. His knees knocked, his neck perspired from the conviction that he'd been brought here for a reckoning—if not for this morning's churlishness then as an overdue reward for his lack of respect on his first encounter with the commandant. He shuddered under the stares from so many unfriendly faces, one of which was the jowly puss of the proprietor himself—Shmulke, a big man in a soiled apron trying to look small behind the tarnished credenza that served as his bar. All appeared interested in whatever crime the intruder was about to be called to account for. Unable to bear their relentless scrutiny, Menke inclined his head, burying his chin in the hollow of his clavicle, studying his ill-shod feet.

There was a span of some minutes that may have been a decade before Menke felt his chin lifted by what turned out to be the business end of a blackthorn swagger stick. Again he found himself facing the imperial features of the Obersturmführer von Graf und Trach.

"Minky," the man addressed him as before with his acerbic hardiness. Menke started at the greeting but the commandant reassured him, "Calm yourself, *mein junge*, we wish only to invite you to join us in our modest repast."

Acutely conscious though he was of the threatening hush that had fallen over the room, Menke couldn't help thinking, "We should all partake of such modesty," though he had the sense not to say it out loud. The Herr Oberst had taken a seat—quickly vacated for him by an obsequious under lieutenant—at a nearby table, and beckoned Menke with a gesture to sit as well. A second officer at the table, signaled by his superior to give up his chair for the Jew, looked appalled, as did every other man in the tavern. This was erratic behavior even for a commanding officer known for his whimsical unpredictability. Menke, the object of such universally malign observation, suspected that his fate might well depend on his comportment during the next few moments; but while his hammering heart recommended extreme care, perhaps even a groveling for mercy, his thoughts asked heaven if he had anything left to lose.

"With respect, Herr Commandant," he replied, trying hard to suppress the quaver in his voice, "I don't think so. I ate one time Shmulke's kreplach but had to spit it out. Then a dog ate it up what I couldn't and had to lick his behind to get from out of his mouth the taste."

The silence in the taproom persisted, jaws fallen agape at the Jew's effrontery. All awaited their commanding officer's response, no doubt anticipating an angry invective. But the Oberst, shirtsleeved after turning to fold his tunic over the back of his chair, retained his relaxed attitude. He stretched his legs, began to fan himself with his peaked cap, and rather than spewing venom, gave himself up to a wheezing laughter. Then, with looks askance at one another, the soldiers of the Reich took the cue from their commander and followed suit.

Menke was cautiously encouraged. He dared to take hasty stock of the room, observing that Shmulke's wife, Fruma-Batia, was also present. She was placing glasses on a shelf behind her husband, who stood speechlessly fuming over the bold-faced wisenheimer's insult to his livelihood.

"Have you gentlemen met Shmulke's charming bride, Fruma-Batia?" Menke delicately inquired, for the innkeeper and his wife had only recently wed. At the mention of her name, the blowsy Fruma attempted to duck beneath the bar. "You should know," continued Menke, growing ever nervier, "that she has buried already three husbands before him, and two of them were only napping."

This time the room—with the exception of the beet red Shmulke, whose wife had vanished from sight—needed no permission to join their commander's robust laughter. Menke grinned also, his overlarge knit jumper its own comic statement amid the piped jodhpurs and whipcord tunics of the assembled. Had they forgotten that he was *jüdisch* filth? Instinct told him he should shut his trap now while his audience was still diverted, but the Obersturmführer continued to egg him on. Slouched leisurely in his chair, hands entwined behind his close-cropped, ash-blond hair, he asked, "Minky, such a dashing fellow as you, have you not got a wife of your own?"

Menke sighed theatrically. "All the good ones are spoken for, your honor. Cross-eyed Brayneh the matchmaker, she says to me, 'Have I got for you a girl!' But when I see the lady, I whisper to her, 'Brayneh-Ettl, she's old and ugly, she has bad teeth, a squint, and if I'm not mistaken, she limps.' 'Wiseguy,' says Cross-eyed Brayneh, 'you don't have to lower your voice. She's also deaf.'"

Belly laughs all around, one especially susceptible officer actually spitting out his food in his projectile mirth. This is too easy, worried Menke, who feared they might recall their loathing at any point. He wondered if he could slip discreetly out of the tavern under cover of what now seemed an officially licensed hilarity. He had endeavored to back up a few paces when a broad-shouldered, lantern-jawed warrior, clearly forgetting himself, slapped his back as if fraternizing with an ordinary Aryan citizen. Thus unable to escape the spotlight, Menke felt he had no choice but to carry on with his schtick. At the trestle table a podgy soldier with a shaved head like a large butterball was tucking into his sausage and Reibekuchen.

"Pardon me, your excellence," said Menke, sidling nearer, "but you got on your chin a smidgen smetana. No, not that chin but the third one down." Then, to a trim young officer with a well-oiled mustache: "I like what you do with your hair, Herr Captain," they were all captains to Menke, "but how did you get it to grow like that out of your nostrils?"

If any of the diners rankled at his raillery, they were apparently ashamed to show it in the face of their comrades' good spirits. They were further constrained by the wholehearted laughter of their commandant, under whose tacit protection Menke had become increasingly emboldened.

An enlisted man, emerging from the kitchen to clear the tables, dropped his tray at the spectacle of a *Kartoffel*-nosed Jew pulling the legs of his betters.

THE ZYLDZCERS QUAILED AT THE reports of Menke's *mishegoss*. They fluctuated between their open resentment of the privileged status he enjoyed among the invaders and their fear that his brand of buffoonery would antagonize the Amalekites even further. He should make himself scarce and leave them to their more time-tested methods of appeasement. For some these included informing (as in the case of the craven fur merchant Abba Rotbard, who manufactured incriminating secrets about his shiftless brother-in-law in exchange for work release) and bribes. These latter came mostly in the form of offerings of the gelt and heirloom jewelry they'd been able to salt away. The German brass used the jewelry to seduce the Polish girls, the Jewish girls having thus far managed to hide their allure. In any event, the few members of the community that did not actively cold-shoulder Menke Klepfisch, cautioned him that he was playing a dangerous game.

Among them was Blume, though she had not been eager to speak to him again. They'd crossed paths in Catch-Basin Street, for once by accident rather than through Menke's contrivance. She was hurrying home from the greengrocer's with a sack of weevilly potatoes as soft as putty. (The produce available in the shops that were still open was either overripe or illusory.) The girl should have been unrecognizable, bundled as she was in her shawls and thick fustian skirts, but the single helix of loose sable hair across her forehead was sufficient—when Menke glimpsed it—to give her away. He planted himself athwart her path, and when she attempted to dodge around him, moved to block her progress. They persisted a few more steps in this ungraceful dance until Blume gave up and stood still.

"Blume," said Menke, chuckling, "excuse me but you look like a banty hen." Though the face that peeked from under her cowl was as fetching as ever.

Her expression, however, was not kind. "So," she hissed—it wouldn't do to raise one's voice in public—"have you come from playing the pet Jew for your masters?"

Stung, Menke was about to mount a defense—did he have a defense? Instead, he assumed his customary chastened attitude, the one he adopted whenever he sought her forgiveness; there was always, it seemed, something to forgive. But the girl was having none of it. She made to move past him again, when Menke impulsively caught her wrist; then realizing his presumption, quickly let go. He fully expected her heightened irritation, but rather than walk on, she turned toward him and appeared slightly to relax her hostility.

"Menke," she admitted, "I'm worried for you."

Although her tone was still more annoyed than concerned,

Menke savored the sentiment. Since childhood he'd made a meal of any crumb of concern she might allow him. Not that she'd been particularly stingy with her affection; he had always believed he held a special place in her heart. But he'd also understood from an early age that he would never be entirely worthy of her. She deserved a person of substance like those who had paid suit to her in recent years, not-so-patiently suffering her respectful equivocation. Of course, everything was changed now: Her fate and that of her suitors was imperiled, and Menke knew better than to think he was the exclusive cause of her fretfulness. The fancy-pants Yoysef Blokzilber had been beaten to within an inch of his life by his fellow laborers, who'd suspected him of attempted collaboration. Moyshele the Prodigy, who'd vowed to conduct a marathon prayer vigil until peace was restored, had lost all of his pink-cheeked baby fat and was on the verge of perishing from hunger. Yitzkhok Sumac, he of the angelic countenance, had fled to join the rumor of a Jewish partisan alliance in the forest and had since been given up for lost. Still, Menke trusted that the girl kept in her troubled breast enough room to honor his unconditional devotion to her.

"Don't waste on me your worries, Blume," he assured her, with a confidence fortified in part by the schnapps he'd been treated to at Shmulke's inn. "The Oberwhatsit, he don't let nobody touch me."

His cockiness restoked her ire. "*Paskudnyak!*" she snapped, looking both ways, on guard after turning the head of an unfamiliar passerby. It was unsafe to linger there in the open, inviting witnesses. An unaccompanied woman (Menke scarcely qualified as an escort) might be dragged in for interrogation or worse. In truth, any human interaction was judged suspect and viewed as possible conspiracy, never mind the colluders and talebearers looking to curry favor with the enemy.

The girl yanked Menke by the collar into the shadow of an overhanging eave. Under her breath Blume told him sharply, "Funny man, you're playing with fire," and began to walk away. Always she was walking away.

Menke followed her a few steps, protesting, "Blume, when I do my monkey business I am making them forget to do theirs. It's a mitzvah!"

Without stopping, she looked about with her lustrous drowning eyes. "And this you believe?"

The question prompted him to pause and suck a tooth while considering. By the time he'd drawn his unsurprising conclusion, she was gone.

Gershom wouldn't have put it past his contrarian driver to have disappeared together with the car; his passenger had been away so long. But when he approached the waiting vehicle, there was Yitzhak leaning against the hood, a cigarette dangling from a fleshy lip, showing not the least sign of shock at his passenger's disheveled condition. Gershom suspected the man was past being shocked by anything on earth. Neither did Yitz express any impatience over Dr. Scholem's extended absence—which gave the still rattled Gershom to wonder if an encounter that had seemed to him to have lasted an age had actually transpired in a matter of minutes.

"You look like you seen a ghost," judged the driver, opening the rear door for him, a gesture for which Gershom was inordinately thankful. "I'm told they are in these parts thick on the ground."

Until he'd fully digested it himself, Gershom was disinclined to share any details of his exchange with the troglodyte book peddler. He examined the battered book he'd purchased as if it were an object retrieved from a dream, then tossed it aside. As they drove out of that lonely little town, Yitz offered him some boiled chickpeas from a greasy paper twist he'd bought in the market. Realizing he was famished, Gershom gratefully took a handful, and swallowing several at once, softly belched.

"The professor's got a appetite," Yitz appraised. "What else the professor got a appetite for?"

Was he needling "the professor" again? Gershom wondered if the man's asperity was reserved exclusively for him or for anyone who had not been where he'd been. In any case, he would not take the bait, nor did Yitz seem disposed to pursue the question. Gershom noted how the man's rolled-up sleeve revealed the pale skin sagging, in the absence of muscle, from his upper arm. He had seen the irregularity in so many of these people, how their once vital flesh, depleted of tissue, hung like loose bunting from their bones. While on the one hand he welcomed the driver's silence, on the other Gershom had an aberrant urge to break the ice all over again. Perhaps he just wanted to preempt anymore of Yitz's aggravating conversation, or did he suddenly feel compelled to prove to the jaded driver that he too had lived?

"I feigned madness to get out of the German army," he submitted. The driver adjusted the rearview mirror—perhaps the better to see his passenger? Gershom took it as an indication that he should continue.

"It was 1917 and I'd been called up for the third time. Twice before I'd been rejected for neurasthenia and asthma, but by the third year of the war everyone of age was being conscripted. During the six months' training I did everything I could to convince the drill sergeant I was *meshugah*. I fainted, sleepwalked, gibbered in Hebrew, and threw the odd fit, which got me sent to the company doctor. That bored gentleman took a look at me and decided that I suffered from 'insufficient libidinal discharge'; he told me to masturbate more. There was a great deal of flagrant masturbation among the recruits, along with revolting streams of indecency, much of it anti-Semitic and directed at me. What the doctor saw as malaise, the sergeant merely perceived as incompetence and insubordination, for which I was subjected to 'group correction.' This involved hazings that included brutality and an assignment to 'the supervision of toilet hygiene.'"

Gershom could see the red tip of Yitz's hand-rolled cigarette, which had yet to leave his lips, drop an ash into his lap; he was listening.

"One dim-witted cretin in particular would deliberately miss the urinal and call me every kind of kike *Fickfehler* and *Stinkfotz* when I went to mop it up. That is, until the day something did truly snap in me and I broke the mop over his head. I jumped on him, though he was much bigger than me, and boxed his ears until they pulled me off. Even then I remained hysterical. The thing is, I frightened myself into believing I really had gone mad. And my own conviction was strong enough to persuade my superiors to have me transferred to the military hospital, where I was diagnosed a lunatic and dismissed from the service. The kabbalists might say I was possessed by a demon, which I don't think has ever been properly exorcised."

Yitz remained quiet awhile, then asked, "Why do you tell me these things?"

"Because my past ought to count for something too," Gershom wanted to assert, but instead felt a twinge of intense discomfiture; the disclosure had been so wholly out of character.

"I was just making small talk," he replied, almost by way of an apology.

Then, if only from the thoughtful way the driver stubbed out his cigarette butt in the ashtray, Gershom believed the man *had* in some degree received his story; though why it mattered, he couldn't quite have said. At length, Yitz began to speak in his gravelly baritone.

"In the camp the people would also make believe. Some make-believed they're already dead. They're walking and talking but already they're dead. They think that, Kaynehoreh, when the Angel of Death passes over, he won't pay to them no attention. His work is already done. Myself, I think also it's already done."

At hazard of overstepping himself, Gershom asked, "What about you, Yitz? How did you survive?"

"Me? I think all the time of the *shtupping* I'm doing when comes the angel to set me free." But for all its bravado, his voice sounded as if the words themselves had been dragged through barbed wire.

"Have you got any family, Yitz?"

"Had."

After that, conversation lapsed, but when Gershom announced an urgent call of nature, Yitz pulled the car abruptly onto a shoulder; then both of them walked a few yards from the road and emptied their bladders in tandem into a mulberry bush.

By and by they were in Germany. Even without the annoying procedural fuss of the border crossing, it would have been apparent from the lay of the land. The cities might be debris-strewn lunar wastes: vestigial structures showing their innards, bathtubs suspended nonsensically from pipes in midair; but the forests and fields, even during those dog days, were saturated in brilliant shades of emerald and jade—a rich rolling counterpane spread over a multitude of sins. It's a sin to even appreciate such a landscape, thought Gershom, recalling the adage from *The Ethics of the Fathers*: "He who is studying but then breaks off to remark, 'How lovely is that tree, that fallow field!,' Scripture regards such a one as having injured his soul." What fanatics they were, the ancestors! But Gershom turned away from the breezy open window all the same.

At the Offenbach Depot he was given a small office with a glass-paned door, through which his colleagues had sometimes spied him resting his head atop a cluttered industrial desk. Most assumed Gershom was despondent, and they were right but only in part. When not actually (to his shame) catnapping, he was reviewing his achievements. He'd traveled far, expanding the parameters of the commission he'd been charged with along the way. Beyond merely taking stock of Jewish library collections and archives, he'd bargained for them with both the members of international organizations and the often abrasive agents of German cultural institutions. He'd followed informants who followed maps that led sometimes to hidden treasures, sometimes to forsaken dead ends. In his role as ambassador from Eretz Israel, he'd condoled with the "unpersons" in the holding cells of DP camps; he'd debated with their rabbis over the future of the Jews and their books. The graveyard of Europe, he'd insisted, was no place for the cultural and spiritual remains of the Jews, and it was imperative that the stateless survivors themselves be encouraged to emigrate; it was essential that all recoverable Judaica be sent along with them to wherever they went. Preferably to Mandate Palestine.

But what had he really accomplished? The alps of books and documents at the Offenbach Depot had grown ever higher during Gershom's wanderings; previously empty bays were heaped to the ceilings with Seder plates, Torah crowns, Hanukkah lamps, silver goblets, menorahs, embroidered tapestries—an abundance of spoils surpassing even the reliquary genizah at Cairo. They ought to have been guarded by Thell, the flame-breathing dragon from the *Sefer Yetzirah*, thought Gershom, who cringed at these instances of his imagination's overactivity, further evidence of his mortal fatigue. But he worried that, if the archive wasn't redistributed with prompt dispatch to the places it now belonged (and he knew precisely where it belonged), it was in danger of suffering the fate of its former proprietors.

A plan was already afoot, advanced by shortsighted officials, to melt down the damaged artifacts in a process that echoed the crematoria, and sell the resulting ingots to support welfare projects for immigrants. (A token portion of these pilfered items had been spirited by concerned depot staff to the banks of the Main, where they were buried with full liturgical rites.) Gershom had seen, in the ruined streets of Frankfurt, fish for sale wrapped in the pages of Talmud; Jewish gravestones were sold for building materials, illuminated Torah parchments clipped by stenographers for typewriter covers and some even made into carpet slippers. In the grip of his brittle self-pity Gershom identified with the contents of the depository to the point of fellowship: He was himself no better than some outworn relic suitable for liquidation along with the rest. The situation was so much more critical than anything he'd dreamed of from the serenity of his bowery home in Jerusalem, and Gershom gave himself up to exhaustion.

Again he berated himself for his youthful fantasies—how, a second Moses, he would lead the people to a revitalization of spirit through the return to their mythic origins. "Even the dead will not be safe from the enemy if he wins," Walter had written long before he knew exactly who the enemy was. Hannah Arendt, hardheaded Hannah, who'd shared Gershom's indulgent friendship with the splendid Benjamin, contended that the crimes of the Nazis could not be judged by conventional moral standards, since they had broken the continuity of Occidental history. "Their crimes explode the limits of the law and that is what constitutes their monstrousness," she wrote to Gershom. "For these crimes, no punishment is severe enough." She wanted to understand the universal meaning of such bestial events: How had the forms and elements of a nation's political organization become so "radically evil"?

"And you, Gershom, peerless decoder of mysteries," she asked pointedly in their sporadic correspondence, "are you not interested in explaining *di shechitah*, the slaughter, to yourself and the masses?"

"I am not by nature a political animal," he had maintained. He preferred to focus such energies as he had on reinforcing the notion that the genus "People of the Book" continued to define the lasting authenticity of the Jews. "Only by the appropriation and renewal of the different strands of their religious and spiritual tradition," and bupkes-bobkes, taunted a voice in his head, "can your 'existential rupture' be healed. By that and the foundation of the state of Israel."

"Seems to me," responded Hannah—he could hear her mocking laughter—"that the apolitical animal has become a militant Zionist."

If true, thought Gershom, then so be it. But whatever animal he might be now was feeling wounded and demoralized.

Meanwhile, the bureaucracy at Offenbach was still maddeningly byzantine, a controversy of rival acronyms: The JCR vied with the LBI and the CRIF for the lion's share of the goods, while the MFA&A obstructed, with its lingering indecision, every reasoned initiative. The latter, the Monuments, Fine Arts, and Archives Unit of the U.S. forces still hung on to the delusory idea of returning the collections to their original owners, most of whom were extinct. The Brits of the Leo Baeck Institute and the Conseil Représentatif des Institutions Juives de France made a forceful case for themselves as safe havens; while the Jewish Cultural Reconstruction organization insisted that the preponderance of the trove belonged where the Jewish population was greatest—that being America; or potentially, as Gershom persisted in arguing, Palestine. There was, however, no authorized legal entity that could speak in one representative voice for the Jews worldwide. And so the books and artifacts languished in the limbo of the onetime pharmaceutical factory. Some volumes had already been boxed for shipment in crates bearing the stenciled Hebrew inscription *Tekumah Latrabut Israel* (Resurrection of Jewish Culture), but nobody was yet able to agree on the primary locus of that new beginning, so their destination remained unknown.

Gershom's chief worry was that, if determinations were not made soon, the depot's choicest contents might fall into the grasping hands of the Germans and Russians, who were still making claims on the archive. The holdings were at risk of being displaced all over again. His concern was shared by Captain Bencowitz, the harried U.S. Army officer who had introduced him to the depository months before. His assistant, the short, scrappy Corporal Rouben Sami, a former flyweight boxer turned librarian, was also in accord with the need for transporting the archive out of Germany at the earliest opportunity. Another ally was Rabbi Herbert Friedman, a genteel but principled army chaplain who'd seen his share of combat; stationed at Frankfurt, he'd elected to make Offenbach the seat of his ministry. All subscribed to the urgency emphasized by Gershom for the timely distribution of the depot's cornucopia of riches; and even though their allegiance was theoretically to the United States, the mismatched trio were sympathetic to Gershom's argument that nowhere else could the goods fulfill their proper purpose so much as in the Altneuland (Theodor Herzl's designation) of Palestine.

For a while, Gershom was able to keep himself occupied with the work of the archive. He set about identifying and sorting the orphaned volumes from various collections. He pored over codices bearing the seared traces of the bombed warehouses, collieries, and brick kilns where they'd been stashed by owners and thieves. Some of the materials discovered in a bunker under the Wittelsbacher Allee in Frankfurt included valuable sixteenth-century Judaica along with rare brochures and journals. Some were mystical tomes from a blown-apart castle in Ratibor, scored and defaced now but once regarded by the learned as gateways to the sublime. Surprisingly though, Gershom was most taken up with his perusal of *pinkasim*, the unsophisticated and crudely printed pamphlets containing selective accounts of shtetl histories. In them were recorded events, both commonplace and exceptional, in the lives of ordinary shopkeepers, porters, peddlers, rabbis, mikveh attendants, madmen, and abandoned wives; they recounted occasions that marked particular calendar days as outstanding—the dates of holidays and funerals, a ritual murder accusation, the eagerly anticipated but finally disappointing visitation of a wonder rebbe, a "black wedding" wherein a pair of orphans were married in a cemetery to avert a plague. There was an Easter pogrom in Pshishke, against which the Jewish butchers and teamsters had mounted a stout defense; a children's strike against an abusive Talmud Torah teacher in the town of Brisk. So absorbed did Gershom become in cataloguing these texts that he'd have traded a volume of the prized Bomberg Gemara for one more tale of an uproarious, vodka-soaked circumcision celebration in Rimanov.

For all the bittersweetness of his current task, Gershom was nonetheless aware that it was in the nature of an avoidance.

Still, he was able to take comfort in the stolen moments of his return to scholarship, however pedestrian, and he resented any interruption—such as Captain Bencowitz's diffident tapping on the dirty glass pane of his office door. Gershom signaled for him to enter and the gloomy captain, bags like black crepe under his wire-rimmed eyes, stepped into the book-thronged little room with a cable in hand.

"Another communiqué from Frankfurt," he said, apologetically handing the cable to Gershom. "Seems the JCR and OMGUS are still at a stalemate."

Gershom, who'd become ever more partial to Yiddish-inflected expressions of disgust, uttered a subvocal "*Feh*," and dropped the cable into the wastebasket without reading it. He was sick of all this *administrivia* (Walter's word), wearied by these faceless organizations bound tight with red tape. The illustrious delegates of the Jewish Cultural Restitution agency had been negotiating for months with the Office of the Military Government in the U.S. zone over who would have ultimate authority in redistributing the looted Jewish cultural property. Thus far the Americans had conceded—subserviently, to Gershom's mind—to Soviet demands for sending the properties in question back to Poland, Czechoslovakia, and the Soviet Union, whence they'd originated. But the Jewish populations of those countries had been wiped from the map, and the Russians, who supposedly disparaged recognizing ethnicity, had only mercenary reasons for wanting the contested items. Meanwhile, the Kielce pogrom, inspired by a murdered gentile child whose death was blamed on the Jews, had flared in Poland. The event, which gained international headlines, promised more anti-Semitic aftershocks, which only compounded the absurdity of shipping the materials east.

"You can't send the books back to countries where they're still killing Jews!" declared Gershom, and the captain momentarily overcame his listlessness to concur. Not so listless was his dogged and forthright assistant, Corporal Sami, and the mannerly Rabbi Friedman, both of whom had also crowded into the office. It had become the men's custom to share their concerns round the lodestone of Dr. Scholem's desk, despite there being scarcely enough room to accommodate them all.

Gershom was testily reprising his hard-line position: that even the small, still extant congregations of what he called "de facto Jews" in Germany should not come into possession of the depot's stock—declaring which had energized him enough to get to his feet. "German Jewry either died in Auschwitz," he proclaimed, wiping sweat with a hankie from his freckled brow, "or lives on in the shape of its representatives in other countries, and above all in Eretz Israel!"

The burden of responsibility for the archive had aged Captain Bencowitz beyond his thirty-five years. The tonsure of his salmon pink scalp was evident amid his sparse, salt-and-pepper hair, his hangdog face a skirmish of nervous tics. He resembled—thought Gershom—one of those sorrowful synagogue sextons who had guarded the scrolls of the Law in some otherwise unattended synagogue for generations. "So what can we do?" he asked in a voice tantamount to a wringing of hands. Corporal Sami, who fretted over the health of his senior officer, constantly assailing him with supplements and laxatives, jutted his jaw in a gesture of defiance. (The same glass jaw whose shattering had propelled him back into the arena of books, his first love.) "We should petition the JWC and UNRRA," he staunchly contended.

"And so on," sighed Gershom. "This is how the People of the Book become the people of papers."

Rabbi Friedman had perhaps been the one most affected by the contagion of Gershom's growing impatience. He had visited Palestine in a liaison capacity during the previous year and been deeply moved by the fortitude of the people he witnessed in the Yishuv. There was a spirit in the land that seemed quickened almost in inverse proportion to the ghastly decimation of their coreligionists on the European continent. In his soft-spoken but implacable manner, the rabbi was a zealot, who sometimes gave the impression that he might be prepared to martyr himself for the sake of the cause. Albeit that cause had yet to find a name.

"I'm in agreement with Dr. Scholem," he stated, the hands at his sides curling into fists, "the time for waiting is over."

Which left the men standing in silent embarrassment over their toothless resolution, to say nothing of the cramped and unventilated circumstance of the tiny office they were somehow reluctant to vacate. Then, to further aggravate their situation, a fifth man insinuated himself into their midst, so that all were jostled to the point of losing their footing. The intruder was Gershom's now redundant driver Yitz Kabatcznik, who had perhaps been kibbitzing their conversation from the corridor. His cap was askew, furrowed cheeks unshaven, his rumpled person having just returned—Gershom would wager—from a circuit of the taverns and brothels along what remained of the Frankfurt waterfront. The escapade, judging from his moody countenance, had left him unsatisfied. In a voice still thick from his presumed consumption of black-market spirits, whose acrid odor (along with the taint of venery) pervaded the room, he asked,

"You gentlemen never heard from to smuggle?"

The wind picked up and acquired a whetted edge, scarlet leaves turned rust brown and fell, and the mamzrim remained. Who would have thought that little Zyldzce, a dust mote on the torn map of Europe, would merit such attention from the Thousand-Year Reich? Regardless of the occupation, though, the people continued to observe the Sabbath according to their means. But it was no longer so easy for them to convert Saturdays in time into Saturdays in eternity as Talmud prescribed; and the foretaste of paradise that the holy Shabbos promised had become vinegarish on the tongues of the piece tailors, pretzel mongers, and leech gatherers who were made to mend roads and dig ditches, and had now, at the behest of their overlords, to become lumberjacks as well, an occupation they were equally unfit for.

Pinkas Botwinik, however, thanks to tonsorial skills that were much in demand among the Amalekites, was allowed to pursue his barber's trade. One morning the Herr Major Dieter Pfeiffer came into his shop and asked for a haircut and shave. The spruce major was hardly in need of Pinkas's services, but the master barber, anxious to please, gave him the works in any case. He trimmed the major's embrocated black hair *a la mode* and then—his practiced right hand trembling despite its dexterity—gave him a hot-lather, straight razor neck shave. Afterward, he swiveled the red leather chair around so that the man might admire his handiwork in the mirror. Satisfied for the most part, Major Pfeiffer tilted his head to one side and suggested that his exquisitely waxed handlebar was looking a bit frayed at the edges.

Pinkas swallowed hard and set about improving the symmetry of a mustache that already appeared in perfect equipoise. He was tempted just to clip the air around the man's upper lip and leave it at that, but he felt obliged to make some miniscule alteration. But when he had delicately trimmed the mustache's left-most extremity, he realized that he'd slightly spoiled the thing's immaculate balance, and so snipped the right end to even it up. Judging that there was still the tiniest inequity, he repeated the process. Then, to his horror, he saw that in his nervousness he'd inched the major's magnificent handlebar closer to the width of the Führer's abridged toothbrush. Having relaxed after his scalp massage, Major Pfeiffer now opened his eyes to see that he'd been heinously disfigured.

"*Fotze Jude!*" he shouted, tearing off the haircloth bib as he sprang from his chair. He grabbed the ceremonial saber he was taking along to the knife grinder, drew it from its silver scabbard, and impaled the poor barber with his best Heidelberg lunge.

Szymen Munkacz, the clubfooted *shammas*, was shot by a German rifleman on his way back home after sweeping up and padlocking the Old New Synagogue for the night. The crouching brick and stone shul, with the octagonal *kappel* hat of its dome, was one of the few public buildings that had not yet been turned into a sheepfold or stable by the invaders.

"Why did you shoot him?" asked the rifleman's companion, mildly curious. "The curfew doesn't begin for some minutes yet."

"I know where he lives," answered the rifleman. "He would never have made it back in time."

(Or so their dialogue was shamelessly imagined by Menke Klepfisch.)

The haberdasher Muni Farb was caught trying to pass off a counterfeit imprint of the military-issued scrip at the post office. As a consequence, a paper bull's-eye was pinned to his back and he was ordered to run through the market. He took off scuttling across the cobbled square, giving the marksmen a laugh at the sight of his bandy-legged sprint, before they riddled the target with a salvo of "iron rations," as the Germans called their cartridges.

Tuvia Rogovoy, on appearing unnaturally full-figured for a woman with so small a head, was stopped when a black-market horseradish root fell to the ground from under her skirts.

"What peculiar turds a Jew bitch will drop," quipped the inspecting sergeant, who had her dragged to the command post in the hijacked tea merchant's house. There, upheld by her ankles so that kilos of contraband spilled out of her drawers, it was discovered that an aspect of her girth was due to the fact that she was also pregnant. Despite the gruesome retribution visited upon her for her crime, Tuvia somehow survived, but her unborn child was tossed into the river where an idle soldier tried to spear it with his bayonet. No one in town, including her husband Chaim Yankel, was ever again able to look her in the eye.

With little encouragement from the occupiers, the Polish boys threw stones at the Jewish scholars as they passed in front of Saint Jadwiga's Church on their way to the children's cheder. The school was still maintained in its decrepit, kennel-like edifice by the sexton Reb Yahke Dubitski, called Yahke the Cough for his chronic consumption; though the place functioned more now as a triage for boys who came in with bleeding abrasions and fractured skulls. In the synagogue and in their crowded houses—doubly crowded since the addition of families evicted from other houses—the people prayed; they dusted off ancient prayers against the savage abuses of Crusaders, Inquisitors, and Cossacks; and when those pleading devotions showed no signs of having altered their dismal situation, they resorted to other remedies to preserve themselves from harm.

Magical thinking ruled the day. Men nailed knife blades for luck to their steep-pitched rooftops and slept with their phylacteries on; women rubbed their bodies and the bodies of their children with brining salts and wore their undergarments turned inside out. The opportunistic pharmacist Gershke Lichtig, seizing the opportunity, turned mountebank overnight; he began peddling charms, amulets, and colored rocks, which he fobbed off as precious gems (jacinth, carbuncle) with unusual safeguarding properties. People stuffed their *mezuzot*, in place of the obligatory Deuteronomic verses, with the names of avenging angels and fastened them to every doorpost. Some slathered their doorposts with the blood of slaughtered roosters and did everything they could think of short of constructing a golden calf to ward off an outcome that seemed more and more inevitable. It was unsurprising, then, that a delegation of Jews should turn in their desperation to the ordinarily derided wisdom of old Rabbi Vaynipl, who still clung to his faith in miracles.

After meditating on the issue, the doddery sage recommended that, absent the advent of Messiah, the shtetl might conduct a *shwartze chasseneh*, a black wedding, over which he was prepared to personally preside. Held by custom in a cemetery under a dark canopy, such weddings were an age-old if largely outmoded practice observed during times of plague and dire crises. In accord with tradition the community would arrange for a pair of poor orphans (sometimes regardless of the orphans' wishes) to be wed. A suitably outcast and downtrodden bachelor and spinster were found, then donations were collected to fund the costs of the ceremony and the feast to follow. It was believed that, with this act of charity, the people could purchase their protection and ultimate God-given liberation from the troubles that afflicted them.

Of course the community's executive council, the *kahal*, would never have sanctioned such ill-founded folly, but the kahal had been disbanded by the occupation. In its place was the Judenrat, whose only authority lay in passing on the orders of its German masters. The proposal wasn't exactly trumpeted throughout the shtetl, but neither was Rabbi Vaynipl known for keeping his own counsel; so whisperings about the projected ceremony soon reached the ears of every attentive Jew. It was a straw that even the freethinkers were ready to clutch at.

After only a few days a prospective bride was found and duly led by solicitous citizens to the rabbi's "chambers," which consisted of a curtained alcove at one end of his antiquated house. (His former study house had been annexed for an armory.) Her name was Tsippe-Itsl, and beyond being an apparently simple-minded orphan with no dowry, she would have been judged unmarriageable by any reasonable criteria. For the docile Tsippe was that rarest of curiosities, an albino Jew. Her hair was a fine white gosling-like plumage; her perpetually blinking eyes primrose pink; visible blue veins branched beneath her nearly translucent skin. She was a tiny bird-boned thing of an undetermined age, though her spare anatomy in its plain *schmutter* shift showed signs of an incipient ripening. Her father was unknown and her beggared, cast-aside mother, a stranger from even farther off the beaten track than Zyldzce, had died giving birth to her daughter— though some said her death was from her shock at having first set eyes on what she'd conceived. Since infancy Tsippe had been passed along from family to family, sleeping on sacks in storage lofts and compartments under stairs, performing domestic chores for her keep. But while the girl was said to be generally quiet and obedient (and sometimes even remarkably resourceful), few households seemed willing to abide her presence for long. No very specific complaints were ever attributed to her behavior, only that her inscrutable, ghostlike countenance could be somewhat disturbing. Mordke Feyfl, the miller and sometime philosopher, put it this way: "It's like she never got all the way born."

When asked respectfully by the rabbi if she would care to be married, Tsippe replied after much consideration, "Will they let me to sleep in a bed?" An apprehensive witness to the girl's conscription, the rabbi's own daughter hung her head. It wasn't that Blume was unused to curious types passing in and out of their house—wasn't their humble habitation already a way station for every vagrant and bindle stiff her father took in from the streets each Shabbos? Tsippe-Itsl was not such a far cry from those. But Blume wondered if the poor creature even understood what matrimony meant; she grieved at the thought of the girl's fate at the hands of some equally defective bridegroom. Then she was appalled beyond measure to learn that the designated *chassan*, the groom, was to be none other than the impenitent ne'er-do-well Menke Klepfisch.

At first no young men had volunteered. This was not from

a shortage of orphans: Owing to the toll of exhaustion that forced labor had taken on the already weakened workers, plus the occasional indiscriminate execution, children had begun to lose parents with some regularity. But there was an injunction against any kind of unofficial public assembly and no telling what consequences such a bizarre ceremony might incur. Bribes and various sops notwithstanding, none of the field of available youths were eager to take on the burden of a wife in such uncertain times, least of all one as untypical as Tsippe-Itsl. But when Menke heard about the proposed black wedding, he thought that such an extraordinary event might be a romp. (He fancied himself perhaps the only Jew left in Zyldzce still capable of having a good time.) Not to mention that his participation in the sham nuptials was likely to reap certain rewards from his grateful neighbors. Moreover, humoring her father in his delusions might help redeem him to some extent in the eyes of the rabbi's daughter. As for the invaders: So what if they got wind of the affair? He had no doubt they would waive the minor transgression of such a picturesque provincial entertainment, especially when that entertainment featured a star turn by the commandant's favorite Jew. Such was Menke's logic when he presented himself to the old rabbi as a candidate for standing under the *chupeh*.

He counted on the rabbi's dim memory to have already befogged the travesty Menke had made of his earlier attempt to summon heavenly assistance. But even if the holy man did recall the incident, his forgiving nature would assuredly absolve the scapegrace of his guilt. Besides, Rabbi Vaynipl was in no position to appoint a bridegroom of his choosing, and so he welcomed Menke's self-nomination.

"A *rekhfartik yungerman*," the rabbi affirmed, actually taking hold of Menke's hand with his desiccated fingers. A righteous lad.

Others, Blume included, had longer memories, and were less receptive to Menke's offering of himself as chassan; he must be up to something, was the general assumption. Of course, the rabbi's daughter had worries enough of her own without fretting over Menke's tomfoolery. Since her mother's early death some years before from an ossified heart, Blume had been left in charge of housekeeping and managing her elderly father's affairs. This involved collecting tuition from those of the rabbi's students whose families could afford to contribute to their teacher's threadbare existence—a thankless task since her father's cheder drew only the neediest scholars. She kept their cottage relatively free of rodents and dust, cooked their paltry evening meals, washed their clothes in the Bug in all seasons, darned socks and knitted others, knitted as well the mittens and glove puppets she sold from a cart at the monthly trade fairs. Duties aside, she was also the confidante of half a dozen girls her age, who respected her for her brains and beauty; as opposed to those who resented her for her brains and beauty, and for spurning the perfectly serviceable suitors that they would have gladly embraced.

Why *had* she spurned them? Just what (or who) did she think she was saving herself for? Did she delight too much in playing the coy maiden? Shame on her! Didn't she want (and wanted still) what the others desired?—though the time of expecting to get what one wanted may already have passed. How they pestered her with their regrets, the other girls, keeping her from her tasks and the books that were her refuge from unpleasant truths. Lately they confided in her things they would never before have ventured to express; they carried tales of those who, in the extremity of their predicament, had done what they themselves would never contemplate, or even dare to dream of. Then they admitted that they too had dreams. Angered somehow by their unburdenings, Blume wanted to call them all cowards, a category from which she could not exclude herself. For didn't she still retreat, whenever leisure allowed, into the guilty pleasures of the medieval *Bovo bukh* or Yankev Dinezon's Yiddish romances, novels bought from passing peddlers with groschen better spent on essentials and hidden under her bed? (She had used to relate their extravagantly contrived plots to her fond if intractable friend Menke Klepfisch, who poked fun at her indulgent pastime, though he listened intently to her renderings of the exotic narratives.) But mainly she was consumed by her efforts to compensate for her father's penury, while the godly old man, immune to material deprivation, gave credit not to his daughter's industriousness but to the good Lord's providence.

With regard to the rabbi's latest ploy, however, Blume supposed that such innocuous frivolity could hardly worsen a situation that was already so grim. Besides, when you thought of it, they were in many ways an ideal match, Menke and Tsippe, since he was easily as unmarriageable as she. That said, Blume couldn't help feeling a pang of melancholy at the thought of her Menke marrying anyone—though since when had he ever been *her* Menke?

THE WEDDING CEREMONY WAS SCHEDULED to coincide with the full moon that signaled the end of the Days of Awe, a period during which the Jews gave themselves license to weep without cessation. The affair was meant to be conducted in the strictest secrecy, with only a few select witnesses, but word had spread among the hopeful, and a sizable number of citizens showed themselves willing to risk collective punishment in order to be present in the cemetery on that October night. Viewed through the tangled branches of a yew tree, the brimful moon spilled its cascading light over the tilted gravestones and the mounds of earth that had yet to be marked. (Burials were still allowed but formal funerals outlawed.) Sheltered from the moonlight under the black crepe de chine canopy stood Menke Klepfisch, looking a little like a down-at-heel impresario in a borrowed top hat and gabardine capote. Facing him in his moth-eaten fur hat and silk *bekishe*, supported by scholars who would also double as groomsmen, the taper-thin Rabbi Vaynipl swayed in prayer. The gathering itself was reverent, muted in their respect for the unconventional observance, though what may not have been apparent to the rabbi and the wedding guests was how the groom, in the shadow of the chupeh, was grinning to beat the band.

The band was Velvl Szulkin's klezmer ensemble (fiddle, bass, and flügelhorn) stationed at the edge of the congregation, playing a lively air whose volume put at additional risk the clandestine nature of the nuptials. Buoyed by the music, however—and heedless of the voices cautioning the musicians to pipe down— Menke waited in anticipation of instigating his bit of mischief. Wasn't that the part he'd been officially assigned by the authority of the Reich commander himself, when that sanguine gentleman had rapped his head and shoulders with the swagger stick? "I hereby dub you," he'd proclaimed before his sniggering officers, "der Kaiser von Judenspass." The chief (and sole member) of the Council for Jewish Fun. In that capacity Menke looked forward to what opportunities the occasion might present for turning ritual into farce. That was at heart his calling, was it not? And in its pursuit, he esteemed himself as something of a sacrificial lamb; he was after all furthering his own disgrace in the service of diverting a troubled community, while at the same time distracting its occupiers from the business of dispensing dread. So if, in the process, he betrayed the credulous old rabbi once again, all would be pardoned in the end.

He had as yet no real idea as to how he might subvert the ceremony after his fashion. Maybe he could pretend to be possessed by the spirit of a dead *badkhn*, a wedding jester, and scandalize the attendees with a volley of rude jokes: *I gave one time a shikse a bowl of soup. "What's this?" she asks. "Matzoh balls," I tell her. "Isn't there," she asks, "another part of the matzoh you can eat?"* Or maybe he needn't bother: The half-baked ceremony was its own parody.

Then the rabbi motioned to the klezmerim to subdue their serenade, which they obligingly modulated to a strangled rendition of *Chatzkale! Chatzkale! Shpeel mir a kazatzkale!*—their chosen processional. At that the guests stepped aside to make room for the advance of the bride, escorted down the aisle by a pair of dour, heavyset housewives, each of them a head taller than their charge. Her face was veiled, her loose white linen gown like the composite of a pillow slip and a shroud. Menke had not given much thought to the bride until now. Of course there would have to be one, but she would be no more than a stage prop in the prevailing comedy. He had neither asked for nor been given any knowledge of her pedigree; and since there were no families to attend the wedding, there had been no signing of a marriage contract, a formality during which chassan and kallah might have met. But there she was, approaching him to the accompaniment of the incongruous

music like some graveyard apparition; and Menke, who hadn't—
he insisted—a superstitious bone in his body, felt the goose
pimples begin to erupt all over his skin.

Once the bride had arrived beneath the chupeh, she was gently
instructed by Rabbi Vaynipl to encircle the groom seven times.
(The congregation enumerated each of her circuits aloud in case it
turned out she couldn't count to seven.) The orchestra had finally
ceased playing and the atmosphere seemed to Menke to have
grown heavier, while the girl—he'd been told her graceless name:
Tsippe-Itsl—moved about him as if she were trudging upstream.
Menke followed her with his eyes, his head turning nearly full
circle like an owl's to watch her. But rather than representing
the traditional intertwining of souls (horrid thought!), the ritual
appeared to him more in keeping with the casting of a spell: She
might be describing a circle within whose circumference the
surface of the earth would collapse, plunging the bridegroom into
the abyss of Gehenna where he doubtless belonged. The pit of
Menke's stomach seemed to echo that thought, and the ceremony
no longer appeared to him an object of ridicule. Now that the
rabbi had positioned the girl so that she was standing toe-to-toe
with the groom, Menke lost all sense of the occasion's potential
for humor.

Didn't they understand, that huddled assembly, that if Menke
Klepfisch was the chassan, then the whole affair must be some
manner of send-up? The Jews were not holding candles as tradition
enjoined them to do, for fear of the attention the lights might
attract to their supposedly surreptitious gathering—though the
brazen moon, having freed itself from the yew tree, more than
compensated for the absence of candles. Then, all of a sudden, a
cloud passed in front of the moon and the darkened sky seemed

to intensify the solemnity of the moment when the rabbi handed Menke the glass goblet; the old man uttered a croupy blessing over the wine and bade the groom take a sip. Menke obeyed—it was sour—then passed the cup to the bride. Although there'd been no rehearsal, he'd witnessed enough weddings to know that this was the part where custom dictated he lift the bride's muslin veil. He hesitated in the action, however: First, because the whole affair seemed to have proceeded beyond his ability to influence it; and second, because he'd spied, past the bride and the rabbi's retinue, the rabbi's only daughter, Blume. She was standing cowled and alone beside an eroded marble headstone, biting her nails and fixing Menke with the gaze of her anxious eyes.

The rabbi prompted him and Menke repeated as in a trance, "*Ani dodi ve dodi li . . .*" "I am my beloved's," he said, pronouncing the customary invocation just above a whisper, "and my beloved is mine . . ." But he was looking over the head of his diminutive betrothed.

Holding the cup with both hands, the bride lifted it under her veil and drained its contents with noisy adenoidal gulps. Meanwhile, one of Rabbi Vaynipl's scholars, the pudding-faced Peshke Ezjyszki, shoved something cold into Menke's left palm. It was, when he looked, a small steel ring of the kind one hooked through a calf's nose to wean it from its mothers' milk. At the same time the rabbi, with his own palsied hand, was extending the bride's chalky forefinger toward the groom, warbling as he did so the *sheva brachot*, the seven blessings: "*Sameiach tesamach reim ha-ahuvim . . .*" These are the blessings that conclude the sacrament of marriage. The bride's veil still remained in place, as did the cloud that veiled the face of the moon, though the billowing cloud was growing opaque like thickening smoke. Then the darkness was nearly absolute, the surrounding company reduced to a gallery of silhouettes, and a sepulchral rumble of thunder was heard. From somewhere a second glass of wine was placed in Menke's free hand, which, as the scene was suddenly emblazoned by a bolt of lightning forked like a serpent's tongue, he promptly dropped.

"*Gevalt!*" he cried, because the lightning had illumined, among other things, the face of his bride, who must have removed the veil herself. It was the face of a wax doll, without eyebrows, hair like thistledown—a phantom.

The wedding guests cried out as well, because the lightning had also revealed, standing at the margin of the burial ground, a complement of German officers, the very beasts the ritual had been conceived to eradicate. They had donned their parade dress for the spectacle, complete with high boots and brass buttons, and were laughing fit to be tied.

Abruptly, the downpour commenced and the wedding party began to scatter. It took him a moment to come to his senses; then swept up in the general panic, Menke also absconded, crushing the fallen goblet to splinters beneath his foot in his flight. He joined the headlong exodus across the groaning footbridge, charging toward the hodgepodge of the shtetl streets; while some, avoiding the bottleneck, splashed directly into the river (whose waters notably did not part). Menke had crossed the bridge and was sprinting up Casimir the Great Alley amid his stampeding neighbors, when he felt someone prying apart the fingers of the hand that still held the ring. He turned to see through the curtain of torrential rain the bare head of the girl Tsippe-Itsl, his spouse, lifting her skirts as she galumphed in her clodhopping brogans alongside him. But rather than snatch away the worthless ring, she persisted in holding on to his hand, which she gave no indication of letting go.

They should have known the enterprise was doomed from the outset, but for all their good intentions none of those involved had any special talent for subterfuge. Not that their plan wasn't theoretically sound: Yitz had brought to the table much credible information gleaned from his days in the Föhrenwald DP camp—a clearing house for shady rackets and illicit schemes—in Bavaria. There was, he imparted, an underground network called *Aliyah Bet* sponsored by an arm of the Haganah commandos, which facilitated the illegal immigration of Jews to Mandatory Palestine. Their far-ranging agents helped shepherd refugees across Europe to secret ports of embarkation on the Mediterranean coast, where they boarded ships to ferry them to Eretz Israel. Of the armada of tin-can vessels that were launched for the Holy Land, most had unfortunately been intercepted by the British naval blockade, their passengers taken to guarded detention camps on the island of Cyprus. Many of the vastly over-crowded boats had sunk, thousands were drowned, and only a handful of asylum seekers had made it safely to Palestine. But so intoxicated were the self-styled conspirators with their fledgling plan that they heedlessly discounted the odds against its success.

In sharing his covert knowledge, Yitz seemed, at least for

the time being, to have overcome his case-hardened attitude; his wan, creased face acquired color, his logy eyes opened wide. He even appeared to rise in stature, as did the others as they warmed to their plan. The ex-palooka Corporal Sami, in his exuberance, repeatedly slapped the back of his sad-sack captain, who coughed at these muscular expressions of affection but was actually seen to grin. Rabbi Friedman was positively inflated by what he perceived as the rectitude of the project, comparing the *Ha'apala*, the Ascension (as the illegal immigration of Jews was termed) to the Underground Railroad of the fugitive slaves in the States. It was generally agreed that if ingatherings of human beings could be smuggled to the Yishuv, then how much easier would it be to smuggle books. Caught up as well in the initial enthusiasm, Gershom nevertheless felt called upon to remind his colleagues that the distinction between books and people was finally moot, since each depended on the other for their ultimate redemption. All paid a courteous lip service to this credo, then continued to congratulate one another on their inspired undertaking—that is, until Captain Bencowitz asked with a mindful delicacy, "So how do we proceed?"

The question prompted a unanimous hush.

Eventually Yitz remembered that, while in a *nafkeh byass* on the seamy wharf-side Wenzelstrasse in Frankfurt, he'd met a man who knew a man.

"Nafkeh byass?"

"A whorehouse."

Then nearly a week passed during which Yitz was nowhere to be found. Awaiting news from him, the company's excitement over their speculative project began to wane, along with their trust in the driver's dependability. Captain Bencowitz, in a fit of nerves, questioned why all this cloak-and-dagger was even necessary. Couldn't the books simply be sent together with the trickle of Jews whose emigration was approved within the British quota? He was reminded of what he knew better than most, that without authorization from the Joint Distribution Committee and its accompanying alphabet agencies, no goods would be permitted to pass through customs. Among the conspirators it was the bluff Corporal Sami who tried his best to keep spirits up. An avid devotee of Dickens and Dumas, he recommended various audacious strategies for transporting the contraband. They could send the books in caskets that, they would claim, contained dead Jews whose final wish was to be buried in the Promised Land. Told that the caskets would surely be opened for inspection at their port of departure, the impetuous corporal suggested that they might rob graves in order to conceal the books beneath actual bodies. It was stunning to see how readily the rabbi responded to this extravagance; he seemed, in fact, game for anything—until Captain Bencowitz, recovering some scrap of reason, pronounced the plan finally impractical; the bodies, telltale stench aside, would usurp the space required for the books.

At last Yitz reappeared, stubbled, unwashed, and reeking of schnapps, but "reporting," as he proclaimed, "for duty." He even made a facetious salute. He said he'd made contact with a member of the maritime branch of Haganah, who, after much liquid persuasion and the promise (on pain of his tongue's amputation) of strict confidentiality, had agreed to provide the smugglers with a sub-rosa route to the sea. The man had wavered at first, protesting that the books would take up room that might be better apportioned to passengers. "But to him I explain," said Yitz, eyeing Gershom with an infuriating smugness, "how the professor says that the heritage we got to preserve it a *nechtiger tog* . . ." At length the stealthy fellow traveler had produced a much-folded map as flimsy as a chamois cloth. He regretted that no militia members could be spared to escort their convoy (Yitz had imagined a convoy), but the driver had assured him they could fend for themselves; all they needed was the itinerary and perhaps a little cautionary advice. Then rudely brushing aside the books and papers on Gershom's desk, Yitz spread out the tattered map.

The route would take them south past the collection post at Leipheim near the disputed Saar Protectorate, where he was told the soldiers, comprising as they did a babel of diverse nationalities, tended to turn a blind eye to refugees. "If they don't arrest the Jews themselves," Yitz maintained, "then why they going to arrest Jewish books?" The journey over the camel-backed Jura Mountains, though indirect, was less hazardous than the alpine alternative, and the remainder of the trip through Alsace down into sunny Provence should be "a piece of piss"—as Yitz guaranteed them. (His speech, since his arrival at the depot, had grown rich in American idioms.) It should take, barring the unforeseen, no more than three or four days. If the smugglers left Offenbach with their cargo within the week, they would find a boat—a previously mothballed Italian paddle steamer, the *Victor Emanuel*, renamed for its current engagement the *Alfred Dreyfus*—waiting at the Mediterranean port of Sète. With God's help or the devil's luck, the boat would sail the sea, elude the immigrant embargo, and enter the harbor at Haifa without incident.

Gershom eyed his scruffy driver and, in a rare moment of lapsed intellection, imagined him as the prophet Elijah. In the mystical tales it was often the undying prophet who appeared to aid those in distress. He commuted between paradise and earth, turning up in a sundry array of disguises to dictate transcendent texts to illiterate cobblers or endow poor families with a heaven-sent prosperity. Then the very thought of the dissolute Yitz as an avatar of Elijah evoked from Gershom a furtive laugh at his own expense. Ignorant of its source but delighted by Dr. Scholem's good humor, his fellows laughed along with him.

Now it was time to work out the details in earnest. At first they proposed sending an impossibly large shipment of books before reality set in, and after weighing the risk they were forced to scale back their ambition: They might safely transport, say, a modest six crates.

Captain Bencowitz signed the proper forms for requisitioning a vehicle and sent them via Corporal Sami to the motor pool. The forms requested a flatbed Oshkosh cargo van, one of the depot's three aging but available vehicles, for the purpose of delivering materials to the inmates of the DP camp at Bad Reichenhall. It was a routine assignment of the type the Offenbach Depot had carried out time and again. As to what books would be included in the endeavor, all agreed that Dr. Scholem should make the "selection"—a word that had acquired infamous connotations, though in this case it was in the service of the good.

Gershom pried open and inspected the crates that had already been packed for shipment to unresolved destinations; he eliminated the books he regarded as nonessential, substituting them primarily with classic rabbinical literature. His choices comprised valuable seventeenth- and eighteenth-century Talmud commentaries and responsa along with prayer and legal texts, kabbalistic manuals, death registers dating back to the Middle Ages, and of course the timeworn parochial pinkasim. No mother ever placed an infant in its cradle more tenderly than Gershom loaded the books into their wooden containers.

While he was busy with this task, the others debated over who would have the honor of accompanying the books in the van. It was understood that Yitz would drive, but he would need a companion to help with the navigation and logistics (and moreover to ensure Yitz's reliability). Corporal Sami was quick to volunteer, but his prudent captain submitted "with all due respect to my indispensable right hand" that the chaperone ought to hold a position of some authority. Thus it fell to Rabbi Friedman—who would have wept had he been denied the opportunity—to ride shotgun, so to speak, alongside the driver.

They drove away from the loading dock on the fifth day of September at the first light of dawn, as befitted their unofficial mission, with the captain, the corporal, and the professor all on hand to see them off. The six plywood crates took up the entirety of the small van's canvas-covered bed. Corporal Sami had suggested further camouflaging the boxes, but there was really no point; the papers that declared the books on loan to the displaced persons facility were perfectly in order and ought to raise no suspicions. Still, Captain Bencowitz had prepared an authenticated receipt for the goods and bade Rabbi Friedman sign it in the captain's own name: that way the rabbi would be protected against any possible forgery accusations he might face down the road. All were satisfied with the thorough measures they'd taken; there were a score of other staff members at the Offenbach Depot who could be sticklers for policy and should by no means be alerted to their operation.

So the truck rattled off into a carnelian sunrise and the waiting began.

There were brief messages—three in six days to be exact—in the form of telegrams delivered expressly to Captain Bencowitz, which he read to the co-conspirators then promptly destroyed. The first was to apprise their anxious colleagues that the travelers had successfully negotiated the Leipheim checkpoint. The second was sent from the French border on the downward slope of the Jura range just north of Basel, where they had apparently been compelled to grease some palms in order to pass through. BAKSHEESH AT BORDER was all their cable said, which was worrisome, since the conspirators had managed to scrape together little more than petty cash to underwrite the journey. (Though each had contributed more than he could reasonably afford.) Several nail-biting days ensued while the Offenbach confederates followed the travelers' progress conjecturally on a roadmap of France. Then came word that they had reached the sea: ARRIVED IN SÈTE STOP SHIP A RUSTY TUB.

But after that, silence.

Days passed, then a whole week without news from the rabbi and Yitz. This was to be expected, the colleagues told themselves, all of them insomniac in their suspense: The lull was simply indicative of the smugglers' single-minded absorption in their task. Besides, wouldn't communication by cable be insecure during the Mediterranean crossing—and perhaps costly if not unadvisable from the Holy Land?

Still they feared the worst, and sometime into the third week since the smugglers' departure, their fears were confirmed. Unannounced, Rabbi Friedman was suddenly back among them—"A bad penny" as he offered in a voice of toneless contrition.

The ordinarily impeccably groomed chaplain was bleary-eyed and haggard, his beard untended, his beribboned uniform

in neglected disarray. His pleated brow bore the imprint of his
hatband like a vanished halo, and his irreplaceable yarmulke—
knitted by his wife and resembling a beige tea cozy—was nowhere
in sight.

He was immediately assaulted by a battery of questions,
which the rabbi, slumping from the weight of a heavy heart,
attempted to address in the order of their priority. "The books
have been returned along with myself," he confessed, "and reside
on the loading dock again, while Mr. Kabatcznik"—after whose
whereabouts the men had finally remembered to ask—"remains in
Palestine." Protesting his own disgrace throughout the recital of
their failed exploit, Rabbi Friedman unriddled the tale.

The journey south had been more arduous than their laconic
telegrams revealed. They had in fact breezed through Leipheim
and the subsequent checkpoints, manned by mostly indifferent
recruits, but their battle-weary van struggled with difficulty—
"Sisyphus-like" was the rabbi's phrase—over the mountains. More
than once the engine had overheated near the crest of some cloud-
girded pass; then the stalled-out vehicle, due to a faulty emergency
brake, would begin to roll backward down the incline, while the
two companions wore out their heels attempting to halt the thing
in its career. It was only by the grace of a passing U.S. troop
transport, and later a friendly gypsy caravan, that they had cadged
enough water to rebaptize their steaming radiator and proceed.
Not so friendly, however, were the guards at the French border,
where the excuse of a DP destination (no such camps remained
in France) no longer gave them carte blanche. But the guards'
reservations were not based so much on procedure as naked
greed, and they refused to remove the striped barrier without the
requisite remuneration.

"It was wonderful," allowed Rabbi Friedman, "how swiftly the sweetener altered their mood."

But the transaction had significantly diminished the smugglers' negligible funds, so that they had to subsist on jailhouse rations of zwieback and tinned milk for the remainder of the trip.

"If I complained," said the rabbi almost wistfully, "Yitz reminded me that the rusks were less likely to stick in your craw than the beetles they feasted on in the *lager.*"

The rest of the journey to the coast had been relatively uneventful. Their route paralleled the old Canal du Midi, which was lined with plane trees in the shade of which the rabbi and Yitz took their trifling noonday refreshment. "Yitz would state his regret that we had no fishing tackle, then content himself with making an inventory of past sexual encounters in disturbingly graphic detail. Once I tried to change the subject, reminding him of the gravity of our mission, upon which he looked at me almost pityingly and said, 'Books are drek.' A very strange man."

As they drove out onto the long sandy spit of land that connected the town of Sète to the rest of the continent, they found that they had joined a lumbering cavalcade of paneled vehicles. It seemed that the seafaring Palyam wing of Aliyah Bet had taken advantage of a French teamsters' strike to hire a fleet of redundant diesel trucks. In this way they managed to spirit more than fifteen hundred refugees, who had checked out of their respective purgatories, to the small, canal-riven Mediterranean port. The wharves, beaches, and dockside streets of that parti-colored town swarmed with the nationless survivors of cataclysm ambling about in their discomposure like rundown windup toys. They came in all shapes and ages, every category of wandering Jew, as various as the animals that boarded the ark: the woeful remnants of families harassed by screeching seabirds and laboring to walk upright under their burden of hampers, bedrolls, and bawling children.

At its mooring the steamship *Dreyfus* looked to have been out of commission since the Gallic Wars: Its smokestacks were seamed in corrosion and bound in captive guy wires to keep them from toppling, its iron hull scalloped in barnacles. It sat low in its berth even before the passengers—only a fraction of whom it was meant to carry—had come on board, practically submerging the hull and lowering its main deck to the waterline. There had of course been no way to keep a lid on such a momentous operation, but rather than a source of disruption, the ship's imminent departure had become a grand public spectacle. The citizens of the town—a quantity of them had been Maquis resistance fighters during the war—were largely sympathetic, and the authorities did nothing to obstruct the proceedings. Indeed, conscience prompted many to bring needed provisions to the oyster-eyed nonpersons on the pier.

"There were the anticipated objections to taking on the crates from the multinational Palyam crew," said Rabbi Friedman, "but we were ready with our affidavit." This was the document the co-conspirators had regarded as their crowning achievement: a certificate jointly composed and printed on a legal form festooned with a bouquet of phony regulatory stamps. It confirmed that the crates contained the contents of the library belonging to Dr. Chaim Weizmann, the biochemist turned ambassador-at-large and foremost campaigner for Israeli statehood. The form bore the signature of Chaim Weizmann himself, inscribed by Dr. Scholem, who'd never set eyes on the great man's autograph.

Impressed in spite of their lingering qualms, the ship's officers ultimately agreed to consign the bulky crates and their escort to the cargo hold—where, since there was no other freight than the refugees, the two smugglers were far from alone. Every spare inch of the vessel belowdecks had been fitted out with two-tiered 'immigrants. These suffocating souls did not view with favor the six crates of books—no matter who they belonged to—which deprived them of both accommodations and additional room to breathe.

So infernal were the conditions in the ship's hold that some began to call the boat "a floating lager." But then, for the refugees, the lager was a migratory thing that accompanied them wherever they went, sometimes superseding the unfamiliar places they found themselves in. They might pray fervently in the narrow spaces between berths or sing an inharmonious rendering of the *Hatikvah* anthem; a twig of a girl in a coarse hessian smock might challenge the hold's close quarters in an attempt to dance her interpretation of hopefulness—but in the end the prayers and songs fizzled due to a common shortness of breath, and the girl tripped over her shadow, twisted her ankle, and hobbled back to her bunk. Nor was the situation much improved above them on the corrugated weather deck, where the passengers were camped out with the density of a lidless tin of sardines.

"You could say," mused the rabbi cheerlessly, "that, on the good ship *Alfred Dreyfus*, mortality was never in danger of becoming an abstraction." Because, for one thing, its inanimate representative was ever present in the form of a metal box sequestered under a bulkhead, its plunger raised like the legendary sword in the stone. For it was tacitly agreed among the adult passengers that they would choose *kiddush ha Shem*—they would blow themselves up together with their children rather than be boarded and taken prisoner by the British Navy.

At night, when the hurricane lanterns were extinguished, the darkness was impenetrable. Various sounds took turns at holding dominion: sobs and hacking coughs, the elegiac chords of a fiddle, the groans of the infirm that were sometimes indistinguishable from the plaintive moans of couples making love, the prayers. They swelled throughout the night, those noises, into a communal banshee drone that persisted in defiance of the shushing of the ship's oscillating engines, precluding sleep. With the hatch sealed against turbulent seas, there was no clear demarcation below-decks between night and day; though in what was presumed to be morning, the lamps would flicker back on and the general abjection become public again. Those that had brought food of their own—a rock-hard roll, raw herrings in brine—would eat, while the rest awaited the delivery of the galvanized soup pails from a galley somewhere in the bowels of the boat. The mysterious soup, ladled by choleric men in hairnets, was alleged to have been ruled kosher by a party of shipboard rabbis. It was a mouse-gray broth of a brackish consistency, tasting of paint thinner, which the voyagers spooned with shared utensils into the same gullets that would later give it up, contributing to the regurgitation in which the floor planks were awash.

The ship rolled and pitched and the people convulsed and lost their breakfasts; they staggered fore and aft to suffer the humiliation of the overflowing troughs that served as privies. The available oxygen in their confinement was in large part displaced by foul gases, and some preferred starvation to attempting to eat in that miasmic atmosphere. The sick were made sicker and some among the elderly passed quietly away. Toddlers, weaned in merciless environments, were now too enfeebled to play, and made nests out of coils of rope to curl up in.

The crew did what they could to relieve the misery. A

physician who could hardly recall his practice, moved among the immigrants with a syringe, inoculating them with some unavailing palliative against rampant diseases. "I heard one poor unfortunate ask the doctor if he had an inoculation against memory," said the bone-weary rabbi, who had taken without argument the office chair Dr. Scholem relinquished to him. But mostly the voyagers were left to care for themselves. There were those among them, primarily sinewy women in headscarves with rough hands and faraway eyes, who had risen above their common ordeal to give comfort to fellow sufferers: They should remember that they were on their way to the Promised Land— and Yitz Kabatcznik, said Rabbi Friedman, Yitz, the fatalist and self-professed libertine, had joined their company.

"We fared no better than anyone else," said the rabbi. "I had a spell of dysentery and Yitz boiled the undrinkable water on a spirit burner to make me tea. When he saw I was better, he left his post to intermingle with his kind."

At first the rabbi thought that, in his stated ambition to make up for lost time, Yitz was actually flirting, but he engaged with men as well as the ladies, both young and old. From his convalescent vigil beside their precious cargo, Rabbi Friedman was unable to hear his conversations—he couldn't have followed the Yiddish anyway—but he observed that those Yitz addressed often wagged their heads spiritedly in the affirmative, and one old babushka even risked subjecting her flinty face to the trauma of a tight-lipped smile.

"When I teased him that he was becoming a humanitarian, he became irritated, then boasted how he'd copped a pinch here, a nudge there . . ."

Then one evening the ship gave a shudder like a dreaming

mastiff and was still. British patrol boats might be in the vicinity; perhaps they'd been spotted. The engines had ceased their throbbing, the boilers stopped belching, and the breathing (or what passed for it) of the passengers in the hold was universally suspended. A child whimpered, a stomach growled, the winch-driven hatch was cranked gratingly open above them, and there was the moon.

"'A Jaffa orange!' cried one dumbstruck old man."

What followed was a chaos that had yet to sort itself into a coherent narrative in the rabbi's pained recollection. He pinched his temples with his thumb and forefinger as if to squeeze some clarity out of the succeeding events. Word quickly spread among the immigrants, along with the rush of fresh air that invaded their quarters, that the ship had successfully breached the blockade. They had defied the odds and entered Haifa Bay undetected. With that news there was no keeping the people hunkered below any longer, and the entire population of the cargo hold began a mad scramble to gain access via the single ladder to the upper deck. Unable to resist the tidal movement of that feverishly impatient body, Rabbi Friedman and Yitz took their turn at the hatch, climbing over those—God forgive them—who climbed over others to view what was transpiring above.

Crowded far beyond its capacity, the deck was a bedlam of refugees pushing and shoving for space, and generally ignoring the efforts of the crew to keep order. Cries of elation were mixed with the cries of mothers attempting to protect their children from being injured in that delirious crush. There were the shrieks of those pressed hard against the rail, and of the one or two who tumbled overboard. Some even jumped into the water voluntarily and began to swim toward the shore.

"They were maybe lured in their recklessness," the rabbi speculated in his dreamy enervation, "by the moonlight on the bay, which looked like a kind of quicksilver highway leading to a glittering city on the slope of Mount Carmel."

A flotilla of fishing trawlers had been launched from an isolated cove to collect the immigrants and ferry them to the beach. Deafening cheers went up among the passengers despite their straitened circumstance and the calls from officers and crew for silence; they weren't safe yet—British patrols were everywhere. Thrilled along with the rest and satisfied that the operation had now reached its climactic stage, the smugglers returned to the vacated hold to begin wrestling the crates toward the hatch. They were aided in this labor by a couple of Palyam sailors in a hurry to get them and their lading off the vessel—expedition was all. "In the process we were unaware of what was happening to the immigrants who'd already begun to disembark from the fishing boats onto the beach."

Initially, as they later learned, all had gone deceptively well: The newly arrived were welcomed by a contingent of Haganah, plus an auxiliary of ordinary citizens there to offer refreshment and counsel. Some among that mass of human flotsam swooned in the arms of their greeters; some fell to their knees and kissed the wet sand. They were assured by all that their coming had been methodically prepared for; vehicles were standing nearby to convey them to safe houses, waiting relations, kibbutzim. Then, even as they received those pledges, searchlights abruptly flashed on, blinding in their brightness, and a unit of British regulars issued forth from the dunes, charging the dazzled throng with weapons drawn. In the resulting melee many scattered and some must have managed to escape; but the soldiers—their sporty pith helmets and tropical khakis at variance with their fixed bayonets—penned in the crowd, arbitrarily rounding up both illegal immigrants and those citizens of the Yishuv come to receive them. The Haganah members among them, greatly outnumbered, chose not to resist; armed resistance would have further endangered the non-combatants. Vengeance would have to wait.

Meanwhile, just off the coast, a British insect-class gunboat had pulled alongside the *Alfred Dreyfus* at its anchorage and announced through a bullhorn, "You, illegal ship, stand by to be boarded!"

"You, British swine," shouted back one of the steamer's remaining seamen, *"pishn zolstu mit verem!"* May you piss green worms.

The skeleton crew of the *Dreyfus* had begun unrolling accordions of barbed wire to impede the boarding party; they aimed the high-powered jet of a pressure hose at the naval vessel, only to be answered by a more virulent spray of machine-gun fire. Exploding canisters of tear gas followed, and in the attendant confusion a complement of British marines, wearing gas masks and carrying small arms, clambered over the side of the ship on grappling ladders. Through a scrim of blue smoke they stormed the captain's bridge and the wheelhouse into which the handful of Palyam sailors had been driven, and descended into the hold where Rabbi Friedman and Yitz had some vague notion of defending the books.

"We were taken into custody at gunpoint along with the sailors, several of whom were seriously injured, while the six crates were hoisted by a derrick onto the deck and suspected at first glance of containing arms." Rabbi Friedman fingered the bald spot where his missing kippah had been as if it were as vulnerable now as a baby's fontanel. "Once they'd broken into the boxes, though, the marines were told to treat the books with the same penal severity as they would have a cache of trafficked weapons." After all, like the immigrants, the books had exceeded a quota and were unlawful. The Weizmann excuse got no more traction with the Brits than it did later with the American consulate, which had apparently received a report that a valuable shipment of materials had been purloined from the Offenbach archive. Once seized, the cargo should be immediately returned.

During their brief fettered passage on the gunboat from the ship to the beach, a thunderous blast was heard behind them. All heads turned to see that a great gaping fire-rimmed hole had been blown in the port side of the *Alfred Dreyfus*; water boiled all about the wounded steamship as it began to sink slowly into the sea. Evidently not all of the Palyam crewmen had been captured.

At the quayside mooring Rabbi Friedman and Yitz, still with his eternally insouciant expression, shook hands as best they could in their restraints before they were separated. "After that," said the rabbi, "I never saw him again." Unsure of what to do with an American officer, let alone an army chaplain, the Brits turned the rabbi over to the U.S. Consular Agency in Haifa. There, he was met by a horse-faced consular-general who, in his role as advisor to the military governor of Jewish affairs, was obliged to give the rabbi a stern dressing down. Despite the reprimand, however, the much put-upon administrator was practically apologetic when he ordered the renegade chaplain to be bundled off—along with his contraband—under armed escort and placed on board a British destroyer bound for Marseilles. The *Dreyfus*, the rabbi was told, was to have been converted into a prison ship to transport the ensnared refugees to DP camps on either Cyprus or the more remote Indian Ocean island of Mauritius. But since the ship now lay among the sharks at the bottom of Haifa harbor, the captured Jews had been imprisoned ("detained" was the operative word) at the recently reopened Atlit camp on the coastal plain south of Acre. Rabbi Friedman assumed that the countryless Yitz Kabatcznik had also been interned there.

Gershom could picture his former chauffeur shuffling still shackled through the gates, hands cuffed and fingers fidgeting, a dog-end dangling from a fleering lip. He would take stock of the watchtowers and concertina wire, perhaps survey an oasis of date palms just beyond the fence, and say to himself, "Home again."

"**M**inky, tell us a joke," said the Obersturmführer von Graf und Trach.

He was seated in his unbuttoned tunic and top boots in need of a shine, at his usual table in the tavern-turned-officers' mess that was Shmulke's Hotel. (Shmulke and his wife had since been sent packing from the premises.) As the occupation wore on, the commandant had become less fastidious in his dress, and also less strict in overseeing the deportment of his officers, who were in turn less scrupulous in monitoring the behavior of their men. Menke stood skittishly before the Herr Oberst, not knowing what to do with his hands. Since the night of the black wedding, he'd steered clear of the Hitlerites' haunts; despite having been anointed "Czar of Jewish Fun," a dubious title at best, even he knew enough not to overplay his hand. There had as yet been no special repercussions stemming from the histrionics in the graveyard, and he feared this summons to the taproom might involve a delayed comeuppance. Perhaps they meant to make his retribution an example to the town.

Though his German was less than rudimentary, Menke was familiar by now with the commandant's standard request; he knew what was expected of him.

"Froy Retzkin's son Hirshke," he began in the daytshmersh that was passably intelligible to his audience. "Froy Retzkin's son Hirshke comes back to Zyldzce after ten years in America. His sidelocks are gone and he's wearing a smart new suit. 'Hirshkele,' asks his mother, 'where is your beard?' 'My name is Harry now,' he says, 'and nobody in America wears a beard.' 'But my boy,' she asks, 'do you still keep the Sabbath?' 'In America,' he says, 'everybody works on Saturdays.' 'What about the food?' she asks, still hopeful, but Harry tells her you can't get in America good kosher food. Froy Retzkin wipes from her eye a tear and whispers, very confidential, 'My son, you can tell your old mama, are you still circumcised?'"

As was customary, the other officers waited for the commandant to laugh before joining in. He was mercurial, their commanding officer, frequently given to jovial outbursts then just as abruptly withdrawing into a self-contained reserve more befitting his rank. Ultimately he did condescend to chuckle, if with no more heartiness than he might have expended on a cough. Was he already tiring of Menke's warmed-over repertoire? Did such quaint, frankly jüdisch material finally inspire less joviality than disgust? Or was the Obersturmführer's lack of a forthright appreciation due to his distraction by the creature—coral eyed and tallow pale, like the negative of a shadow—that had trailed the Jew into the taproom?

Menke turned to see that the object of the commandant's amused gaze was the girl Tsippe-Itsl, who had followed him into that viper's nest. At his startled surprise—which he dissembled for the purpose of inviting a humorous response from the room—the genuine laughter commenced. Since the night of their bogus nuptials, and despite his concerted efforts to elude her, the girl had followed him about like a motherless lamb; that is, when she wasn't scrounging for food or tending to his household (which, owing to the infestation of refugees, had grown substantially) or performing the myriad unsolicited tasks she'd taken it upon herself to assume. Capable as she was, Menke would have much preferred to do without her wraithlike attachment to himself. She seemed to him scarcely mortal, more like some fey organism conjured by a *kishef-macher*, a magician, than an authentic female human being. It had never crossed his mind that the hocus-pocus of that aborted ceremony should count for an actual marriage, though you wouldn't have known it by the girl, whom Menke had been unable to lose ever since.

What's more, Blume, his precious Blume, had accosted him near the wagonyard (now a parade ground) not long after that ill-omened night to put him on notice. Despite the shapeless amplitude of her layered garments and the head covering that shaded all but her aquiline nose, she was instantly recognizable to her admirer by the liquid resonance of her voice.

"You should, please God, take good care of her," she cautioned him just this side of a threat. They were the first words she'd spoken to Menke in weeks.

"But Blume," he protested, "I didn't expect . . .," giving a nod toward the peculiar, whey-faced slip of a thing standing placidly behind him—though exactly what he *had* expected when he put himself forward as bridegroom, he couldn't have said. In any event, the reverse of Blume's imperative was more to the case, since Tsippe, though unbidden, was doing her painstaking best to look after her ostensible husband.

Menke had fallen silent in the face of Blume's admonition, which seemed to imply that, having made his bed, he must now lie in it. Had she not so swiftly departed, he could have assured her that he had in fact abandoned his bed. He'd surrendered it after that first exceedingly awkward night, when Tsippe-Itsl had followed him home in the rain. He wished he could have mustered the hardness of heart to turn her out, but instead, he had tried to ignore her; he'd donned a nightshirt over his wet clothes and lay down upon the flock mattress in the hope she would simply take the hint and leave him alone. But in obedience to her wifely duty, the girl had climbed wordlessly into the bed beside the groom. When he felt her animal warmth nestled against him, Menke bolted without forethought from that unwonted intimacy. Afterward, he convinced himself that she was as relieved as he, and it was finally merely the bed the girl coveted. At any rate, Menke had taken to sleeping atop the unlit stove. Floor space was limited since the bedding of the Bialovsky family occupied the greater part of it. They were a family—husband, wife, and yet-to-be-housebroken toddler—who'd fled their ravaged town to seek a less precarious shelter in Zyldzce, and Tsippe-Itsl had taken pity on them when Menke's back was turned.

In the taproom, the commandant leaned forward to poke Tsippe in her belly with his baton as if to determine if she were real. ("Oof," she said.) Reclining again in his chair, he offered almost avuncularly, "It occurs to us, Minky, that we have yet to congratulate you on your marriage. Let us wish you a *herzlichen glückwunsch*, or should we say with your people *mazel tov*." Then he did the unthinkable; he led his idle officers in a less than rousing chorus of "Mazel tovs!" A phrase which, in that forum, chilled Menke's spine.

Which is not to say that he was unaware of Tsippe's potential for comic exploitation. When she wasn't a cause for unease in the formless white smock that served to enhance her unearthly presence, she was perceived by most as a figure of fun. The bored soldiers of the Reich hooted and even those among Menke's neighbors not yet prostrated by hopelessness managed a joyless smile at the sight of the no-goodnik and his pasty hanger-on. Since it was clear he couldn't shake her, Menke thought that, if the opportunity arose, he might make use of her as a kind of dim-witted foil to his gags. At first he'd tried to teach her a pratfall or two, or the trick of pretending to walk down stairs behind a low wall, but it was obvious that she had no aptitude for slapstick. Though she seldom spoke (except to mutter the incomprehensible syllables that comprised her daily prayers), she was not a mute, and might therefore function as straight person to Menke's schtick.

He attempted to coach her: "When I ask you, 'What's green, hangs on the wall, and whistles?' you say . . . ," beckoning her with a forefinger to reply.

"I forget," she uttered at length in her expressionless monotone.

He sighed. "You say, 'I dunno.'"

"I dunno."

"Good," encouraged Menke. He had perched her, a featherweight, on the edge of the stove beneath the sagging ceiling of the room euphemistically called the parlor. Their trial audience, the broad-bottomed Mama Bialovsky and her rake-thin husband Itche, sat at the table munching the boiled chestnuts that were their primary repast; while their little Yanki, in a loaded diaper, trod wantonly upon a cockroach.

"Now," said Menke, calling upon untapped reserves of patience, "I say, 'A whitefish,' and you . . . ," prompting her with a nod.

"A whitefish . . ." She looked to him for the words.

"A whitefish isn't . . . ," he supplied.

"Purple?" she ventured.

"Bravo! Then I say, 'You could paint it purple . . . ,'" wagging his head to urge her further response.

And so went her catechism, sometimes trying Menke's forbearance to the brink of hysteria. But after interminable repetitions, while the Bialovskys impassively chewed their chestnuts and their little one sat down on a column of ants, the girl learned her part.

So, on that late afternoon in Shmulke Goiter's tavern, having judged her ready, Menke turned to Tsippe and asked her (in what was to be their debut and farewell performance as a comic duo),

"Tsippe-Itsl, what's green, hangs on a wall, and whistles?"

Tsippe: "I dunno."

Menke: "A whitefish."

Tsippe (mechanically): "A whitefish isn't purple."

Menke: "You could paint it purple."

Tsippe: "But a whitefish doesn't hang on the wall."

Menke: "This one does."

Tsippe: "But since when does it whistle, a whitefish?"

Menke: "Nu, so it doesn't whistle." Clicking his heels in the air to highlight the punch line.

When the laughter came, it was hard to know whether it was occasioned by the joke or the singular contrast between the very idea of levity and the ectoplasmic figment of the girl.

"Hear, hear!" applauded the Obersturmführer von Graf und Trach, actually rising to his feet. With his high cheekbones, cleft chin, azure eyes, and straw-colored hair (in need of a trim since the absence of the murdered barber), he might have posed for the "Blond Beast" of the propaganda posters. My protector and benefactor, thought Menke with wavering conviction. "In our gratitude," continued the commandant in the arch tone that informed his every breath, "for lifting our weary spirits in these trying times . . ." Menke strained to catch the gist of the German words. "We wish to return the favor." The Herr Oberst signaled to his adjutant with a wink and whispered something in the man's ear, upon which the adjutant called over a bullnecked *feldwebel*, a staff sergeant, in whose ear he also whispered. The sergeant then bade a couple of enlisted men to set down their serving trays. "And so," added the commandant with an unctuous bonhomie, "we have prepared a little cottage as a honeymoon retreat for you and your new bride."

At his nod Menke and Tsippe-Itsl were straightaway strongarmed and frog-marched from the mess hall out into the squalid yard behind Shmulke's, where they were thrust unceremoniously through the open door of the decaying wooden privy. The door was then locked from the outside by the sergeant, turning a key in a shackle padlock that had been placed on the facility since it was declared too revolting for use. This was because the waste had accumulated in the pit beneath the outhouse until it had risen above the rims of the double seats. The place now induced nausea and bred disease.

Shut up in that noisome darkness only slightly relieved by the slivers of light that eked between the slats, Menke had to concede that the prankster had been pranked. The commandant was clearly having his own kind of fun at Menke's expense. Did this mean that Menke's brand of foolery had begun to wear thin? Had his status as special Jew been revoked? Menke kicked at the door of the outhouse and shouted, "Thank you, your honors, but we had already our *honik-koydish*, our honeymoon!" But no one came to free them and the lock held despite the moldering door.

Then he and Tsippe sat in silence at either end of the hard bench, separated by the twin mounds of excrement. Stewing over the foulness of their enclosure, Menke was possessed of a mordant thought: The commandant had inadvertently played the part of a rabbi in recommending their confinement, their *yichud*. This was the tradition that prescribed the closeting of newlyweds after the wedding ceremony, so they should have some time alone—often for the first time in their lives—before attending the feast. Risible as was the notion, Menke took no solace from it. The girl, whose outline was becoming clearer as his eyes began to adjust to the dark, was trembling with an intensity beyond what the dank atmosphere warranted. Menke begrudged her the concern for her welfare that her discomfort aroused in him, but nevertheless asked brusquely, "What's the matter with you?"

Words never came easily for her, and her voice, always surprising in its huskiness, juddered from her shaking. "The outhouse," she tendered, "is home to Alukah the horse leech and Shirika the toilet demon." It was the longest sentence he had ever heard her speak.

The son of a gullible mother, Menke was familiar with the legends of evil spirits whose favorite haunts were root cellars, bogs, and privies. Of course, only shmegegges believed in such hokum, which made him feel all the more chagrined to find that he'd contracted somewhat the contagion of Tsippe's trembling. He wanted to slap her guileless face and squeeze her until she was still, though he shrank from the prospect of having to touch her. Instead, he contented himself with fuming aloud over the injustice of their incarceration.

"Menke," she breathed—had she ever before uttered his name? "I have to tinkle."

"You have to what? . . . Oh." He felt suddenly sorrier for her than himself. "But you can't do that in here," he snapped, and was struck by the unthinking irony of his alarm. "Don't look," she cautioned, and he turned away, then cringed at the sound of her dismal stream as it moistened the far hill of filth and further awakened the god-awful stink. When he hazarded a glance in her direction, she was fussily straightening her smock, and while the pale light that penetrated the outhouse gave faint proof of her corporeality, Menke could still make out the girl's tears and the fine, dun-white floss of her hair. If I blew on it, he wondered, would it scatter like dandelion fluff and leave her bald?

"So," he began companionably, "the Rabbi asks Getzl why he walked out of his sermon. 'I needed a haircut,' says Getzl. 'So why you didn't get a haircut before the sermon?' Says Getzl, 'I didn't need one.'" Nothing, not even a snicker. He tried again, selecting from among his least salty anecdotes: the one about the waiter who asks the table of Jewish ladies if anything is all right, the one about the designated worrier from the village of Chelm, the peddler who sells a peasant a pint of elbow grease. He stuck his hand in his pants pocket and waved at her out of the cuff. Neither a simper nor a smirk. Humor was clearly wasted on her, and Menke wondered if Tsippe-Itsl even knew how to laugh.

When the sun had set, the darkness of the privy deepened to pitch black. They were being punished, thought Menke, for his crime of having had the brass to do what he'd been invited to do. There were of course worse punishments for lesser crimes administered every day. Take, for instance, the one dealt to Yekutiel the bookbinder.

It happened shortly after Menke and Tsippe-Itsl's release from captivity, when the Obersturmführer von Graf und Trach's wife—his presumptive wife anyway—arrived for a visit. This was highly irregular. But Zyldzce, like so many out-of-the-way *shtetlach*, was not an especially significant post, and the commandant was secure in the authority he'd put in place. So long as the Jews remained appropriately brutalized and degraded, a certain latitude might be afforded himself and the soldiers under his command. But lest the laxity of his administration be confused with liberality, he made sure that deference was paid to even the Reich's dereliction of their own protocol. When his "wife" slid out of the zinc-green limousine that brought her—showing as she did a deal of silk-stockinged calf, the calf no doubt attached to a shapely thigh hidden by the fabric of the skirt that caressed her well-turned figure—Yekutiel Yerkantski, who'd never before seen such a glamorous lady, stood ogling her from in front of his shop. For his offense the Herr Oberst had him held still while he scooped a fishy eye from Yekutiel's head with the penknife he used to pare his nails. The gouged-out orb drooled down the bookbinder's cheek and hung there by a sinew, while Yekutiel let loose a hyena shriek that could be heard, wagered the Zyldzcers, as far away as Lodz.

"I leave you your other eye," said the commandant reassuringly, "which should serve you well enough in this one-blink town."

After that, having left his second-in-command, the Hauptsturmführer Horst Ziegler, in charge of policing the town, Herr von Graf und Trach became preoccupied with his conjugal dalliance. The Hauptmann, however, tended to follow the example of his distracted commander when it came to the conscientious execution of his duties. As a consequence, the regiment was left to act largely upon its own initiative. Such negligent oversight of their martial project naturally had conflicting results. On the one hand, it gave the more reckless types among the Jews new opportunities for their smuggling and black marketeering activities, and even for running away; though it was generally acknowledged there might be nowhere else to run to. On the other hand, without stringent supervision, the under officers competed in the ingenuity of the penalties they inflicted on transgressors, or on those unlucky souls for whom they invented transgressions. Take the example of the stitcher Mottl Klepak, who was caught on a ladder trying to reach into a robin's nest for eggs, an act not previously stipulated a crime. But in the name of further enabling Mottl's reach, the soldiers were advised to pull his arms from their sockets, leaving his knuckles practically to drag the leaf-strewn ground.

Heard playing a scratchy disc of wedding songs on the gramophone she'd concealed from looters in her family's attic, the young Mina Lustig was hung by her uncommonly abundant hair. She dangled naked from a rafter in the slaughterhouse, now a stable, until the hair detached itself from her scalp and she dropped to the ground, the crown of her head resembling a bloody skullcap. A creative young grenadier untied the hair and stuffed it like a horse's tail into the crack between the girl's bare buttocks. Dissatisfied with Benish Spektor's repair of his bridle-leather boots, the Oberleutnant Manfred Böhm claimed he could read on his brow the seditious thoughts the shoemaker harbored in his mind. Benish was strapped in due course to the waterwheel on the Bug, where bets were placed as to how many rotations it would take until he drowned. Grown weary with counting, however, the military spectators wandered off, leaving the shoemaker's bloated carcass to ride the wooden wheel in perpetuity.

Also taking advantage of those undisciplined days was the deputy mayor Ignatz Wisniewski, who used his newly appointed office to conduct his own petty reign of terror. Either personally or by proxy, he superintended the avenging of the (often fabricated) sins of his zhydy neighbors. He egged on Januscz Nowak's evisceration of his boss, the tannery manager Ratner, in whose employ Januscz had worked for thirty years. The mayor also took possession of any keepsakes and bibelots the occupiers may have overlooked in the homes of the greedy Jews.

For each of these iniquities there were ever-widening circles of friends and relations whose hearts were forever torn asunder.

For all that, collective punitive actions were infrequent in Zyldzce, which is why it was still regarded as a comparatively benign destination by refugees from the surrounding towns. They continued to pour into the shtetl, whose warren of houses was mobbed to capacity, their inhabitants in some cases squeezed out of their own homes. The population of Menke's own dwelling had grown denser as well, since, during Menke and Tsippe's long night in the privy, the Bialovskys had reunited with some of their extended family. Still, while the Messiah and the commandant tarried, ordinary occasions like anniversaries and bar mitzvot persisted in the interstices of the German scourge; holidays—the New Year, the Day of Atonement, the Feast of Tabernacles—came and went, and were observed to the best of the people's abilities; though every holiday now seemed a version of Tisha B'Av, the day when all the calamities that had befallen the children of Israel are mourned and the Book of Lamentations read.

As if to commemorate the season's first frost, the midwife Zlateh Kochleffel delivered to Shifra and Leibke Kook a child with a caul, an event that she avowed, augured dark times. Her prophecy prompted the shtetl's single instance of communal mirth, since how could the times become any darker?

Now, thanks to the sparseness of food and adequate accommodation, every Jew had become a species of luftmensch, everyone living more or less on air. The Zyldzcer Yehudim had always dwelled virtually on top of one another, their houses so huddled together that they appeared from a distance as one large rambling structure of many rooms. So it wasn't difficult for the Germans to keep the Jews quarantined in their own neighborhoods, corralled in quarters now labeled "the ghetto." It was nearly November, the rime already forming arabesques on the early morning windows, but heating coal was in short supply, and the occupiers had hoarded most of the firewood for themselves. The ghetto dwellers had begun to feed their stoves with their few remaining sticks of furniture and to eye as tinder whatever books were left in their possession. There had been valuable books— ancient morocco-bound volumes of Judaica preserved on the study house shelves, books for which some might have sacrificed themselves rather than see burned. But those had already been impounded by a traveling Waffen-SS unit of legalized pillagers specially commissioned to despoil the occupied towns of their treasures. As a result, the only books remaining to the Jews that might serve as heating fuel were cheap Yiddish novels, children's Hebrew primers, women's *Tsene-rene* bibles, and the like.

Around that time the little hunchbacked book peddler, Nachum by name, still making the rounds of the villages in his horse-drawn cart, turned up again in Zyldzce. Now he was offering to buy back the books he'd sold to the townspeople in the past. This seemed a losing proposition on all counts. For one thing, it was not a time when a lone Jew was free to ramble about the countryside (though maybe such a harmless anachronism as Nachum could travel under the enemy's radar). But instead of *hondling* his second-rate library, old Nachum proposed purchasing such books as the Jews might yet have on hand. What's more, he had no hard groschen to exchange for what he so illogically sought, though his cart was loaded—in place of printed matter—with a miscellany of rag-and-bone merchandise. For a scrub brush or a can opener, a person might be willing to forego the momentary warmth a burning book could provide. So the trading transpired, no one really questioning the unreason of the transactions, since reason was a thing the people were learning not to expect. Even the artless Rabbi Vaynipl swapped his conjuror's grimoire, which was clearly bankrupt of magical properties, for a slightly mangled garlic press, though his household had not seen a garlic clove for months. Thus had the old peddler, *der macher*, become *der zamler sephorim*, a redeemer of books. On completion of his backward enterprise, he vanished as abruptly as he'd appeared.

"He takes them away, the books, like a Yid Pied Piper," observed Mordke Feyfl, the village deep thinker. "Too bad he can't rescue *der kinder* as well."

IT WAS MORNING BEFORE MENKE and Tsippe were liberated from their "honeymoon cottage." In fact, no one had even thought to release them. But a dumpy, off-duty lance corporal, having ingested a tin of bad anchovies, found himself in urgent need of a facility, and the padlocked outhouse in Shmulke Goiter's yard was the closest to hand. Having dropped his pants in anticipation of emptying his guts, he broke the lock with the butt of his rifle and yanked open the rattletrap door, where he discovered the commandant's clown and his albino baggage wrapped in an embrace over a mound of shit to stave off the cold.

To his colleagues Rabbi Friedman expressed his profound regret over not having laid down his life for their venture. All assured him this was nonsense, he'd done everything anyone could have, gone beyond the call of duty in point of fact; and besides—this from a transparently cheerful Corporal Sami—the failure of their endeavor was no great disaster in the scheme of things.

"I mean, where's the tragedy? At least the books were returned to us safely, whereas the refugees," and here his voice dropped an octave upon realizing where his logic was headed, "were sent back to the camps."

His captain hung his head in sympathy with his assistant's chapfallen attempt to put a good face on things. The uncertain fate of the boomeranged books only corroborated the unending confinement of the dispossessed. Would their liberation never come?

After the brief reunion he was allowed with his fellow conspirators, Rabbi Friedman was arrested and restricted to quarters until his arraignment for the charge of larceny. But when news of the indictment reached the war-weary ear of General Lucius Clay, head of the American Military Government in Germany, he felt charitable toward the heartsick (if unrepentant) rabbi and saw to it that the charges were finally dismissed. Rabbi Friedman was let off with a frosty, by-the-book upbraiding, and shortly thereafter resigned his commission; he returned to the States where he worked for the United Jewish Appeal and wrote a much praised but largely ignored memoir about his time at Offenbach. Captain Bencowitz and Corporal Sami were also called before a tribunal of higher-ups, and there was even talk of a court-martial. Himself in bad odor, Dr. Scholem spoke at a hearing on their behalf, insisting that they had "acted in good faith and in the best interest as to the preservation of valuable documents of the Jewish past."

"It would have been dangerous to leave these documents for a longer period in the hands of a German staff," he explained, to the aggrieved dissent of the Germans in attendance, "and so I urged removal at the first possible moment."

He tried to take sole responsibility for the whole abortive affair, though his loyal partners in crime disputed his testimony; all, they affirmed, were complicit in the misappropriation of the books. It's debatable as to whether Gershom's advocacy helped remit the unhappy archivist and his assistant from a harsher punishment; military regulations had always been lax at the depot. Neither of the men were cashiered from the forces, though they were informed that their services would no longer be required at Offenbach. Captain Bencowitz was offered reassignment to a mindless stateside desk job but chose instead—since his term of enlistment was nearly up—to part ways with the army, an organization for which he'd never had much affection. (He was replaced as director of the Offenbach Archival Depot by Major Bernard Grober, a squeaky-clean career officer formerly in charge of the conservation and restoration of documents—and incidentally the one whom the conspirators suspected of having blown the whistle on their scheme.) Without the option of following his boss's lead, Corporal Sami, rather than serve out his hitch, went AWOL everlastingly, waving goodbye with his middle finger on his way out the door.

Owing to the American consulate's involvement, the intrigue surrounding the unauthorized books was made known to the Otzrot HaGolah committee in Jerusalem.

"Understand, dear Scholem," Chancellor Magnes had stressed in his communication recalling Gershom to the Holy Land, "that your colleagues here were not unsympathetic to your 'outlaw' endeavor. (On the contrary, any one of us might have done the same in your place.) None would dispute the yeoman service you have done for our cause. But since the affair has brought undue attention of an adverse nature to the Archive's methods, and to yours in particular, we're left with no recourse but to relieve you of your present duties . . ."

Magnes also alluded delicately to Gershom's own recent letters, in which he had candidly confessed that he was reaching the end of his tether, and assured him he might now enjoy a much needed, well-earned leave of absence. His able university colleague Abraham Yaari would be assuming the appointment ("carrying the torch, as it were") in his stead. The committee had only one final request of him: that he return to Palestine via the city of Prague, where he might make a last attempt at negotiation with that body calling itself the Jewish Museum; they had more than their share of high-value holdings in their possession.

So ended Dr. Gershom Scholem's tenure as chaser after wayward books. At least he'd escaped—undeservedly, he thought—the public humiliations of his fellow connivers. But despite a few minimal successes, what had his year-long retrieval efforts really amounted to? *Gornisht,* he brooded, nothing, when compared to the wholesale failure of his attempt to transport books to the Yishuv. He excoriated himself for the hubris of his grand designs. Of his misguided identification of the books with *am haJehudi,* the people themselves, he was mortally ashamed. The books ("Books are drek") were finally not people, and in his fanatical desire to recover them at any cost, he'd lost sight of the immeasurable human toll of the carnage. That fact was before him inexorably now.

"The Jewish people has been murdered," he wrote Fanya from his sleeping quarters in the depot's Quonset dormitory; "it has ceased to exist; only smoldering stumps are left, with no strength or direction. Their source of nourishment no longer exists, the people has been cut off at the root." To Hannah Arendt, with whom he'd never before been so unfiltered, he wrote, "Everything is sad and becoming sadder." It was a sadness without end—then, it seemed to end and Gershom felt nothing at all.

"**BESIDE A DRAGONFLY LAMP IN** the lobby of the Hotel Europa," he would reflect in years to come, "Gershom sat down, and there he wept when he remembered Zion." But at the time, his grief precluded any nostalgia; it superseded all but the reawakened pain for which he was staggeringly grateful.

The Otzrot committee had booked a puddle-jumping flight for him back to Jerusalem, via Milan, Zagreb, Istanbul, and Aleppo. It was scheduled to depart from Paris on October 29, which left Gershom the better part of a week to spend in profitless discussions with the so-called Jewish Museum. On the overcast morning after his arrival in Prague, he took the short trolley ride from the hotel to the address he'd been given in Dusni Street. The Museum proper was housed in the first story of a former hospital, but its collection of documents and artifacts had swelled to overflowing during the War; afterward its possessions had been distributed among the defunct old synagogues of the Josefov district, the prior Jewish ghetto. The dispersal was due to the Nazis having designated Prague as a storehouse for the bulk of their stolen Judaica, with a view toward—it was rumored—creating a Museum of an Extinct Race.

"Which is of course what you are," Gershom told the curators and custodians gathered at one end of a long conference table. They were in a boardroom of the Ceremonial Hall, one of the vine-battened Italianate buildings now under the state-run administration of their bootleg museum. Gershom was speaking from the opposite end of the table in a flat and unemphatic voice after resting his case once again. That his arguments for the transferal of a major portion of their archive to Palestine had fallen on deaf ears, came as no surprise. The assembled government servants remained adamant in their insistence that the Jewish community of Prague—to which none of them incidentally belonged—was more than the "de facto body" that Gershom had characterized it as. No matter that there were fewer than ten Jews left in the city who could even read Hebrew. He'd anticipated their crepe-hanging suits and institutional obstinacy, which was why he'd been less than passionate in making his demands; he was only going through motions to satisfy the behest of the Yishuv. As for all the museum's precious plunder, it could rot in the mortuaries of their empty shuls for all he cared. Sick of pursuing a fruitless cause, Gershom was already on his way back to the Holy Land in his mind.

"Don't you realize," he asked in an afterthought, "that you and your holdings have no interest beyond the archeological for anyone here?" Then he gathered up his briefcase and departed without waiting for an answer that was not in any event forthcoming.

He'd decided that a walk back to the hotel might help settle his nerves, but on the way Gershom got lost. It was easy to get lost in Prague at the best of times; the labyrinthine congeries of its streets and narrow lanes, the squat houses with their canted walls and rolling red-tiled roofs, had prompted one writer to compare the city's geography to the convolutions of the human brain. His own brain being more or less spent, Gershom was especially prone to losing his way. Once he might have accounted his confusion a pleasure. Prague was a palimpsest of architectures—Baroque upon Gothic upon Romanesque—and to explore it was to experience the heady vertigo of traveling back and forth in time. You passed through latitudes freed from sequential chronology, a condition validated by the clock in the tower of the old Jewish quarter, whose hands with their Hebrew numerals ran backward. It was in that quarter, long before its tenements and sordid courtyards had been cleared to make way for opulent art nouveau apartments, that the sorcerer rabbi Judah Loew had created his golem. This was the monster formed from river mud to defend the ghetto Jews of previous centuries from violent pogroms. Gershom had always relished the legend with its kabbalistic associations; he'd even delighted in the idea that the remains of the deactivated monster still lay dormant in the attic of the ancient Altneuschul, preserved there until it was needed again. So what if the need had come and gone without the golem's intercession. The city had always oscillated pendulum-like for Gershom between the fabled aura of its past and the drab unlit chanceries of Kafka's cosmos, where no speck of magic could be found. But there was no question as to which Prague he had currently lost his bearings in.

During previous visits Kafka's houses had been Gershom's coordinates; he'd located their addresses on a map and been excited to find that most were still standing. There were the houses where Franz and his family had dwelled in or just off of the sprawling Old Town Square: the dreary address on Celetná Street, where Kafka's bedroom window had looked into the chapel of the Tyn Church; the U Minuty house with its sgraffito'd walls and the pitch of its roof like a tented book; there was the small apartment in the outsized Oppelthouse on the corner of Parizka and Neruda Streets; and the apartment in the House of the Golden Pike with its bay window like a ship's prow. There were outliers beyond the river: the high-ceilinged rooms in the Schönborn Palace, the tiny cottage like a painted toadstool in a row of others running downhill from the Castle in Golden Lane. Kafka had been nomadic in the city of his birth, and Gershom had set his compass by the various sites of the writer's abodes. But he must have taken a wrong turn somewhere, because in the absence of those familiar landmarks, which had once seemed so ubiquitous, the city was an alien place; it was an unrecognizable mare's nest of streets in a country that, since the fall of the Nazi Protectorate, was technically no longer a country at all. So there was Gershom in a strange municipality in a country that was effectively nowhere, wondering if he could even regard himself an authentic person anymore.

He tried to remember how he and Walter had bandied back and forth, over the years of their correspondence, their ideas concerning the prophet they'd made of Franz Kafka. It was Walter who first described his work in the language of Torah (which Gershom viewed as a trespass on Walter's part into his own domain): Kafka was a creator of Aggadah, of parables and lore, as opposed to Halakhah, or legalities. His stories were parables without paraphrasable morals. Gershom agreed: The writer was "a heretical kabbalist" whose work—he professed in support of his friend's thesis—exemplified the proverb, "Aggadah has a laughing face."

"Do you really mean that, Gerhard?" pressed Walter, perhaps distrusting his friend's somewhat facile avowal. Then he took the sentiment a step further, insisting that humor was in fact the ultimate secret of Kafka's uncanny fictions. And later, as they sat under the awning of the Closerie des Lilas in the Paris of 1927, Walter proclaimed that only one who was able to extract the comic aspects of Jewish theology could grasp the key to Kafka's work. After which he'd issued the haunting challenge to his friend: "Has there been such a man? Would you be man enough to be that man?"

"Oh yes," said Gershom, glibly sidestepping the question, "the Hebrew Bible is a barrel of laughs."

Walter looked puckishly over the rims of his glasses, which had slid halfway down the slope of his beaky nose. "You didn't laugh when Elisha sics the bears on those slanderous youths for making fun of his bald pate?"

"Hilarious," sneered Gershom, who resented Walter's constantly testing the strength of his convictions.

"And the plague of frogs? And the moment when Naomi asks Ruth, 'So, how was he hung?' after her night with Boaz on the threshing floor?"

Gershom harrumphed.

"And what about that old battle-ax Sarah, who guffaws when the angels tell her she's expecting?" pursued Walter. "You didn't find it infectious, her laughter?"

Gershom was still smirking: "And I suppose you think that the child she bore was the original *l'homme qui rit.*"

"Precisely!"

They had continued their epistolary quid pro quo throughout the next decade, thrusting and parrying in what seemed to them a heroic effort to salvage some necessary truths from the world before it toppled into the abyss. Meanwhile, beyond the walls of Gershom's private library, the Arabs rose up in homicidal opposition to the invasion of the Yehudim, and the British Mandate shut down Jewish immigration to Palestine. At Walter's ever-retreating heels the concentration camps (into which both his brother and Gershom's disappeared) were inaugurated, *Kristallnacht* happened, and soon after, the war began; while the two scholars, sedentary and peripatetic, had no doubts as to the critical urgency of their exchange. But now Walter was dead and Gershom felt practically as good as, and the abyss had swallowed up, well, everything. How inadequate and self-congratulatory seemed their fateful dialogues now. Gershom writhed at the memory of how implicitly he'd come to embrace Walter's assertion that Kafka had "plucked from the center of dread the possibility of humor."

"Humor!" Gershom groaned aloud. Where Walter had seen Quixote and Charlie Chaplin, Gershom saw Job.

"Understand," he'd written conclusively to his indispensable friend, "that Kafka's is a revelation without meaning; the work has validity but no significance." In making this contradictory pronouncement Gershom had brought to bear the entire weight of the kabbalistic cosmogony, explaining that the Infinite, the *Eyn Sof,* transposes itself into the created world through the mediation of the *Ayin,* the divine primordial nothingness. Kafka's revelation was finally Job's: He had "transcribed a voice from the whirlwind and bore witness to a vision of a sheer cosmic power that shattered all human categories—and that included the Bible's own framework of anthropocentric creation."

"Validity without meaning!" exclaimed Gershom. "Don't you see, Walter? Kafka's revelation must be viewed from that perspective in which revelation is returned to its own fundamental nothingness."

Which had put Walter in mind of a joke: "On the altar the rabbi throws up his hands before the congregation and cries out to his Creator, 'Lord, before You I am nothing!' The cantor, moved by the rabbi's humility, also shouts, 'Lord, before You *I* am nothing!' Reb Panke, the nebbish on the back bench, also inspired by this show of mortification, cries out, 'Before You, Lord, *I* too am nothing!' The rabbi elbows the cantor and says, 'Look who thinks he's nothing.'"

Gershom hadn't laughed.

He'd been wandering about now for an indefinite period, had walked off the map of the known city, or so it seemed, into a zone where the membrane between the living and the dead was very thin. Everywhere he looked under that leaden sky there were mementos mori: the tower clock in which death's effigy tugged the bellpull to chime the hour, the puppeteer on the bridge manipulating a skeleton at the keys of a ragtime piano, a vendor peddling sweets called "little coffins," the tombs and cenotaphs and monuments to the Black Death. Every portal seemed to invite you into an underworld of crypts and catacombs. The city itself, with its crooked houses and umbrageous arteries no wider than snails' paths, appeared half-enamored of death, and Gershom felt himself falling under its spell. Then it was twilight and he realized he'd come full circle; he'd arrived back at the Ceremonial Hall that bordered the old Jewish cemetery, its jagged tablets like a congregation turned to stone by a Vesuvius of centuries. This was the chicory-stippled, elder-scented *beyt olam* that contained the tilted gravestone of the golem-maker Rabbi Loew. It was said that the revered sage had eluded his own end until he accepted his granddaughter's birthday gift of a red rose, wherein death was hiding. Death had long since come out of hiding and was in some fashion, thought Gershom, a welcoming presence. Perhaps Walter had had the right idea. At any rate Gershom had found his bearings again.

He had spent much of that noxious night in the outhouse wasting some of his best jokes in an effort to make Tsippe laugh. It had become a point of honor to crack her benighted absence of expression, but long before dawn Menke conceded defeat. That's when it occurred to him that the girl, with only a tatty shawl to cover her shoulders, might be trembling less from fear than from the cold. Shivering himself, Menke at last overcame his acute distaste for their proximity to opt in favor of their mutual warmth. He sidled past the near heap of night soil, reducing the distance between them enough to fold his arms around Tsippe-Itsl; then, gingerly, he pulled her toward him. They had only just begun to fall asleep when the door was jerked open and there stood the lumpish lance corporal, rifle in hand, pants dropped around hairy ankles, putz shriveled to the size of a dried gooseberry from the chill. Only then did the girl, having opened her drowsy eyes to the incongruous vision, give herself up to laughter. It was an unusual, even alarming laugh for such a nebulous creature, a sound like a braying donkey.

AFTER THEIR RELEASE FROM THE privy, it became apparent to Menke that the terms of his situation were somehow irrevocably changed. He felt as if they'd been held captive not just for one but for a month of nights. He recalled the tale of the saint Honi Hamaagel, who fell asleep beneath his freshly planted fig tree for a period of seventy years. Upon waking, Honi found the tree fully grown and laden with fruit. Of course, Zyldzce's bitter late autumn was hardly a fruitful season; the Germans had not departed nor had the Jews—many of whom were now driven beyond despair—discovered any miraculous means of resistance. Before that fetid night alongside the girl, Menke had thought himself capable of dodging the evils the occupation had wrought. Now he wasn't so sure; maybe the evil had infected him as well and he was in need of an antidote. In the past there would have been the occasional stroll with Blume among the wildflowers along the riverbank to allay for a spell his darker instincts. But Blume had her own hands full with negotiating the deathly climate for both her father and herself, while Menke, who had believed he needed no help from any quarter, felt himself never so friendless and alone.

To be sure, there was Tsippe-Itsl, though it was she he blamed for his current agitation. The bothersome thing had become for better or worse his burden to bear, and he deeply resented the encumbrance. He also worried for her safety, a sentiment he had not invited. Why should he waste his concern on such a clinging, misbegotten creature? Then he remembered that he had only himself to blame for her unasked-for presence. Moreover, Blume Vaynipl, his sometimes conscience—*his* Blume, who would never belong to him—had admonished Menke to look out for the girl, and some aspect of her infernal vulnerability had in fact gotten under his skin.

He was further vexed by the humbling episode of his overnight detention: The joke was on the joker. Had he finally fallen from grace, his role of favored Jew rescinded? Had his foolishness, rather than mitigating them, made matters in Zyldzce even worse? Could things be any worse? With the declaration that their country was now a ward of the Reich, the abuse of the Yids was, if possible, compounded. Not that their commandant would have restrained them, but since he'd temporarily removed himself from active duty, his subordinates had shown themselves ever more inventive in their methods for humiliating and terrorizing those under their governance.

The Judenrat remained the primary target of persecution. Their treatment was advertised as a kind of preview of what was in store for the rest of the Jews if they were uncooperative. Daily, members of the ineffectual council were assigned impossible errands, for which, if they failed, they were severely punished. They were continuously tasked with requisitioning unrealistic quotas of supplies and valuables from the destitute ghetto; they were ordered to seize from friends and neighbors their mythical hoards of gold, silver, fur coats, fine linens, and foreign currencies. In this way they became despised by their own community. When the brothers Kaganowicz, Haikl, and Zvi, turned up at the Wehrmacht's firehouse headquarters with an inadequate quantity of chickens and eggs, they were made to climb onto the roof where they were subjected to a gale-force spray from a fire hose. Haikl was shot when he lost his grip and fell from the ice-glazed eaves, while Zvi, who managed to hang on to a chimney, lost his fingers and toes from frostbite.

A particularly original penalty was imposed on Oyser Nussbaum, the teamster, who'd had the temerity not to surrender the sidewalk to a sergeant major. He was buried up to his neck in the soft river mud with a bucket placed over his head; then local lads were challenged by the soldiers to see who could kick the bucket farthest.

Most of the mamzrim's punitive measures, however, were less innovative, consisting mainly of arbitrary beatings and summary executions. Some of their ill-usage of the townspeople was delegated to the *Volksdeutschen*, the German-speaking Poles, who were keen to prove their loyalty to the Reich by functioning as surrogate torturers. Following the example of the occupiers, they also participated in isolated violations of Jewish girls, whose efforts to hide their attributes had eventually been exposed.

Several of the Judenrat members, if not murdered outright, were rendered useless from overwork and chronic maltreatment, and were replaced—the Germans specified that there always be at least ten men, as in a minyan—with others drawn from another lottery. This time the moonstruck Rabbi Vaynipl was conscripted, despite his declining health, into their number. Though he hadn't seen her for a while, Menke knew that Blume would be beside herself with fear for her father's well-being. For her sake he wished he could do something to help the old man—though what, in the midst of the Hitlerites' stepped-up campaign of depravity, could he really do? Especially now that the Obersturmführer had taken himself from the field of endeavor. The other officers and enlisted men, if they remarked on him at all, acknowledged Menke with an indifference bordering on contempt—their standard posture toward everyone. It was an attitude that had little patience for Menke's trademark *narishkeit*. His asininity.

Out of favor as he judged himself to be, Menke thought it advisable to keep as much as possible out of sight. Life revolved now about subsistence, a thing Tsippe-Itsl showed an unexpected talent for maintaining. She had appointed herself mistress of the Klepfisch menage, which—with the addition of Reb Itche Bialovsky's twin nephews and his wife's half sisters, one widowed and one maiden—had grown to what should have been unsustainable proportions. But Tsippe proved herself to be an able provider. Beyond foraging, she could also apparently bargain, acquiring goods from the fly-by-night black markets that never appeared in the same ghetto courtyard twice. She secured for the household their muddy lentils and the rare scrawny pullet with currency extracted from the refugees she'd admitted to Menke's residence—despite his hope that her uncanny countenance might have scared them off. But even Menke understood that it would have been a crime to turn such needy folk away.

In the meantime he was as willing as the rest to reap the benefits of Tsippe's resourcefulness and to let her run the risks involved in keeping them fed. The schmaltz she obtained for their soup might taste of bilge; the potatoes she made her latkes with were soft as pincushions and the flour for the Sabbath challah crawling with mealworms; but where others hungered, Menke and his houseguests could rely on the girl for their board. How she managed all this seemed almost preternatural: The once prosperous Bialovskys, having landed so cozily after their perilous flight from Zhitomir, suspected her of being a *makhshayfeh*, a witch. Still, it had become an article of faith among them that she would continue to find the means to provide for them. (One of Froy Bialovsky's half-siblings—"the frail sisters" as Menke perceived them—hinted that she maybe traded base favors for provisions, as some were reduced to doing; while the other sister, the maiden, wondered who would accept such favors even if offered.) Leaving little Yanki's mother to her progressive inertia, Tsippe-Itsl even changed the infant's diapers and gave him the bugs with hard carapaces that he liked to chew. No one thanked her for her efforts—which they seemed to accept as their due—nor did the girl appear to expect any commendation, servitude being her natural condition. Besides, it was obvious to the household that, while she labored for them all, her exertions were essentially for the sake of only one.

Menke was of course aware of her slavish adoration. He'd done nothing to earn it and could do nothing, it seemed, to get shed of it. Still, he knew from adoration owing to the years of his unrequited longing for Blume, and he found himself as touched as he was unnerved by the girl's devotion. Naturally there was no question of returning it in kind, but ever since their night together in the privy, punctuated by her hee-hawing laughter, Menke had developed a tender spot, like an ulcer of the mind, for the chimerical creature.

His occasional attempts to engage her in ordinary discourse, however, were frustrating, as her answers seldom corresponded to the questions asked. Often she responded with mystifying monosyllables. Once, observing her tireless industry, Menke exhorted her, "Tsippe, take already a rest, you work yourself to the bone."

"She works herself to the bone," she parroted, tasting the phrase as if it belonged in a nursery rhyme.

Eavesdropping on her devotions at the washtub, Menke suspected that she might be babbling nonsense. "What tongue is that you pray in?" he asked her. "It doesn't sound like any Hebrew I ever heard."

She looked at him askance and explained, as if any ninny would know. "It's the language of praying."

He wouldn't have put it past her to be warbling like Solomon in the language of birds.

Taciturn though she was, she surprised him from time to time with some sudden spontaneous offering. Once, having left off gutting a malodorous carp to follow him around, she chirped, "Menke," though she seldom addressed him by his given name, "Menke, I dreamed that at our wedding feast," which had occurred only in her dream, "you gave to me the gift of a bicycle, and also a pretty lace *stanik*."

He stared at her. All bicycles had naturally been seized by the invaders, and a stanik, a brassiere—Menke blushed hotly at the word—was a thing the bird-breasted girl had no earthly use for. For a brief instant he pictured himself riding home to her on a bicycle with a flowery brassiere hanging from the handlebars. To puncture the sympathy she'd evoked in him, he yielded to a contrary, even malicious, impulse.

"Tsippe," he said, as if to jolt her out of her infatuation, "you do know that our days here are numbered?"

Her blinking eyes fluttered like breathed-upon petals. "Teach us to number our days," she voiced mechanically, "that we may get a heart of wisdom."

Menke felt the chill bumps prickling his skin. Was the girl finally some type of conduit for divine ventriloquism?

"Tsippe-Itsl," he asked without expecting an answer, "what are you?"

"An orphan like you," came her ready reply, allowing herself the inkling of a smile.

Accustomed as he was to his own double-talk, Menke could

almost believe she was having him on. He peered into the girl's stark-staring, roseate eyes, and thought that behind them lay a province unavailable to mere mortals. It was then he had an urge, unfelt since their night in the outhouse, to touch her. But instead of caressing a cheek or squeezing a shoulder, he reached out to stroke the lint-white tow of her hair. It was a patronizing gesture that seemed all the more maladroit when he thought he heard her emit a sound like a purr.

Some of the mamzer soldiers at Shmulke Goiter's had done the same, alleging it was good luck to rub the head of an albino. Tsippe had suffered their petting forbearingly as she did almost everything else. As for luck, Menke thought it must still exist somewhere, just not in Zyldzce, not for the Jews. These days the ghetto's population shuffled about in their matted sheepskins, raggedy blankets, and torn gabardines, some looking so much like spooks that they were asked by their neighbors in all honesty if they were still alive. And it was true that many seemed to occupy a latitude somewhere between this world and another, which they were already well on their way to. Some retained enough residue of spirit to devise escapes, though their preparations seldom got past the planning, so grievous was the news from beyond their town. A couple of families—among them the Glombotskis, with their three children and a grandfather deranged from his decades in the Russian army—did manage to flee into the forest, which swallowed them without a hiccup. Rumors later reached the shtetl that they had been safely hidden by the baron of a Polish estate, and while the people knew better than to believe in rumors, they feasted upon any morsel of good news they could garner.

The RAF were outmaneuvering the Luftwaffe over Britain, the Germans were being driven back from the Russian Front, the

United States had finally entered the war—their radios confiscated, the Zyldzcers took such wishful thinking on faith. They had all become masters of denial. Since the scope of their circumstances had no logical historical precedent, then logic had it the whole implausible nightmare must soon be over. If they simply remained obedient to the demands of the invaders, they could hang on for the duration; the Hitlerites would soon be vanquished.

"*Halileh*," thought Menke, "God forbid that the war will last as long as the Jews are capable of enduring."

He too had bent to the general subordination. He pinned the yellow star prominently to the breast of his draggled sack coat, and when the pin didn't hold, allowed Tsippe-Itsl to sew it back on again. "Sporty, no?" he remarked, suggesting that the stars were so attractive they ought to be hung as ornaments from the branches of junipers and around the necks of starveling dogs. No need, though, to decorate the night sky with them, since the entire stellar firmament was already tagged as Jewish. Menke observed the curfew and attended the mandated Judenrat assemblies in the Old New Synagogue, where the gathered were informed of new ordinances beyond their ability to carry out. (If nothing else, such convocations afforded Menke a rare glimpse of Blume Vaynipl, who was otherwise seldom seen at-large.) Like everyone, he kept as much as possible to the shadows, an effort made more difficult by the conspicuous reverse shadow of his chalk-pale follower.

Not that Menke had much occasion to loiter in the December streets. He persisted in his truancy from the killing work details, reasoning that the provisional reprieve granted him by the Obersturmführer was still in effect. It was a notion he was not eager to test. Also, it was cold outside: The winds scoured the lanes and raked your bones with icy talons, a further harassment which the Jews took personally. The winds penetrated as well the cracks and crannies of Menke's house, whose shingled walls the ill-mannered twins from Zhitomir had begun, oblivious to their host's protestations, to tear off and feed to the stove. Now that the occupancy of the little house approached standing room only, the guests never ceased their tedious complaints. As a result, Menke, fed up with their kvetching and boorish behavior, was periodically driven from their midst—especially when Tsippe's back was turned. Then he would prowl the quarter, stumbling among the milling population who stumbled against one another without apology in their unrelieved quest for some means of sustenance. It was their single vocation: keeping the body in one piece for reasons the depleted soul was hard-pressed to recall.

Menke told himself he was looking for something too. Perhaps an unattended bicycle or a discarded item of lady's lingerie? Toward that end he happened to pass the shanty, really a glorified lean-to, of Lemel Hutzpit, the joiner, who'd lost a leg at Ypres during the last war. (In view of Poland's ambiguous situation, Reb Lemel had never been sure of which side he was fighting for.) In his yard Menke spied, hanging by a leather strap from a clothesline whipped by the wind, the joiner's homemade prosthetic limb. The apparatus had been artfully fashioned from metal, wood, and barrel staves, with hinged joints at the knee and ankle and even articulated wooden toes. Needless to say, the crusty old artisan was quite proud of it, but the rigor of its usage required airing it out now and again.

Despite his newly minted commitment to stealth, Menke felt the tug of his *yetser hora*, his evil impulse, which he was ultimately helpless to overcome. He surrendered to the beginnings of a grin, painful due to his frozen cheeks or maybe the fact that he had not smiled for so long. The joiner, he determined, was nowhere in sight and the few mufflered pedestrians abroad in Chicken Feet Street appeared virtually insensible. Stepping into the yard, Menke unfastened the hollow limb from the line as swiftly as his stiff fingers allowed, and hid it inside his buttoned coat. With a few wriggling contortions he managed to slide his arms out of his coat sleeves and take hold of the artificial leg, positioning it between his own. He wound the straps attached to its rim around his fingers so that he was able to manipulate the prosthesis as he pitched forward, thus giving the impression to anyone watching of an armless man with three legs.

He lurched forth in this manner through the waste of the tanners' yard, suppressing his grin lest he spoil the effect. He paraded the spectacle of himself down along the avenue lined with the clapboard dwellings of tailors and schleppers; past the log house of Reb Lipkunski, the kahal's chief elector, which looked as rundown as the others from the outside but was sumptuous in its sunken interior—at least until it was stripped of its furnishings by vandals and overrun with refugees. Continuing his convulsive progress, Menke shunted past the shulhoyf courtyard and the old beit hamidrash, its windows filled with the saucer-eyed faces of cheder boys. He emerged from a skein of alleys to clump around the peppermint pole outside the barber shop now belonging to Dudye Gimblett, Pinkas Botwinik's nervous successor; and on across the market square as far as Ropemaker's Row, where barbed wire marked the western boundary of the area apportioned for the ghetto. Then, as a few sparse snowflakes settled onto his shoulders, mingling with the cotton batting that foamed through the seams of his coat, Menke turned around and retraced his staggering steps.

Early in his circuit he'd encountered some off-duty soldiers warming their hands over a fire in a steel drum. Perhaps recognizing Menke as their commandant's clown, up to his tricks again, they snorted a sinister excuse for laughter, which Menke nevertheless took as a ringing appreciation. That endorsement, however, was short-lived, given that the Jews who witnessed his transit were most assuredly not entertained: For them his horseplay was a resounding horror. If they dared regard him at all, it was with doleful, frightened eyes, which had already seen too many ineradicable sights. Froy Golda Karpov, backing into a doorway, had seen her nine-year-old son Ephroyem, who in his hunger had eaten a deadly jack-o'-lantern mushroom, heave his insides into her lap. Little Batsheva Zemz, hiding behind her fleshless mama, had seen what befell her brother Shmuel when a marksman missed the apple he'd placed atop the boy's head. For them, and an abundance of others, a three-legged man only called to mind even more ghoulish prodigies.

Their reactions to his performance began to trigger in Menke a sense of shame that aroused in turn a resentment toward those that inspired it—which left him feeling at length an aversion toward himself and the world. Besides, the stunt was wearing him out, causing him to sweat profusely despite the biting cold. The auxiliary limb chafed his thighs, and as his crotch was situated in the hollow of the prosthesis, it occurred to him that the third leg might be perceived as some grotesque extension of his *shmekl*. He resolved to return the thing forthwith to Lemel Hutzpit's abode.

At his first opportunity he would open his coat and tuck the leg as discreetly as possible under an arm; but no sooner had he turned a corner into the Naphtha Passage than Menke came upon Rabbi Vaynipl's daughter approaching from the opposite direction. She was one of a trio of young women cocooned in their layers of garments, though her wimpled face was unmistakable as ever—albeit its perfection, upon confronting the monstrosity that was Menke, bore the wound of a grave disappointment. All three of the girls were bearing cholent pots, presumably on their way to Boynbaum's to borrow his oven for heating the Shabbos meal. (A largely symbolic if not bootless errand, since there was no meat for cholent, no fuel for the bakery oven, and no telling what dogs' dinner their stoneware pots contained; but old customs died hard.) The other girls, in their agitation at the sight of Menke's deformity, gave him a wide berth as they hurried on, but Blume stood fast.

Menke fumbled to extract the leg from under his coat, a clumsy operation due to the difficulty of unbuttoning the jacket from the inside. Blume held her ground and made no move to assist him. Finally he managed to wrest the leg from the tangle of his coat, which had slipped, still partially buttoned, down around his waist like a kilt. He held up the leg in front of him as if to prove its harmlessness, a gesture that seemed idiotic even to him. Opening his mouth to explain, Menke realized that he had no real defense. No matter, the girl would get over her disapproval as she always did; she would see the joke for what it was and laugh her silvery laugh in spite of herself. But Blume's hurt expression remained unchanged.

"Nu," said Menke, hoping to dispel the tension between them, "so how's your father?"

"He's making a golem," Blume submitted without judgment.

"Oh."

"Menke," her tone still somber, "this is no place for your *shtus*. Haven't we been belittled enough without . . ." She indicated with her glance the ludicrous totality of his presence.

"I know that," said Menke, though the accessory he was cradling in his arms argued to the contrary. "But it's my nature to make fun."

As if she wasn't aware of it. As if Blume hadn't been an audience to his hijinks since childhood. Long ago she'd conceived a fondness for the unregenerate prodigal with his overlarge head, a feeling similar to the affection she might have bestowed on a rambunctious puppy. It helped that his fawning over her took the form of skylarking and teasing jests, rather than the cloying blandishments she received from the other boys. But she and Menke were grown now, and the future they had shared as children extended no further than the occupiers' next unreasonable directive; the only fit humor now was gallows humor and the only faith left was (like her papa's) blind. How she worried about the doting old man, who, when not eating his heart out over the last ultimatum issued to the Judenrat, was reshuffling the letters of Torah to prove that this very month, or the one after, was the one in which Messiah would come. And now he was trying in his dementia to create a superman out of clay to defend them from their enemies.

Meanwhile, there stood Menke whose buffoonery was, in plain language, a form of pandering to the oppressor. Who knew but such mischief was even an affront to God? Though God had clearly hidden His face to keep from seeing how men had defiled his creation. And Menke, holding Reb Lemel's dummy leg like a nursing infant, was still up to his monkey tricks. The shtetl was shipwrecked on an ice floe in hell and Menke was still at his escapades. Her exasperation with him was equaled only by her pity. But demure though she was, Blume understood that she wielded a certain power over the boy, indeed over boys in general, and with that power came a measure of responsibility; and so she unbent enough to confer upon Menke a weary smile.

The snow had begun to fall harder, blown about like the blizzards of feathers generated by the women flicking chickens in the rear of Dlugach's butcher shop, before it was closed. But the blustery weather was supplanted by the warmth in Menke's chest. So relieved was he by the benediction of Blume's smile that he made no attempt to contain the ill-kept secret of his ardor.

"Blume," he blurted, "I wish I could take you away from here, to Zanzibar maybe or America."

"Or beyond the River Sambatyon to the land of the Red-Headed Jews?" she offered.

Said Menke, "Why not?"

Her eyes grew wistful. "Those places are very far away."

Menke knitted his brow, considering, then asked, "Far from what?"

But Blume was looking past him, and Menke turned to see what she saw: Tsippe-Itsl was standing there in the middle distance, mantled in a holey blanket and looking, for all her flake-white affiliation with the falling snow, as wilted as the lettuce leaves she held in her hands.

Menke turned back around. "Judith with the head of Holofernes," he quipped, pleased with his biblical reference; such allusions from his cheder days seemed more readily available to him of late. But Blume's face had grown deeply sorrowful again.

Back in his hotel room, utterly dispirited, Gershom rifled his suitcase for the indigo bottle of phenobarbital capsules that would help him sleep. He'd recently been using the prescribed drug to the point of abuse, but there was no other way to turn off his brain. Emerged from its lethargy, it hammered and throbbed, that weighty organ, and nothing short of a sleep beyond the annoyance of dreams could give him relief. He had an irreconcilable sense of having come to the end of something, not merely his assignment but rather—shaking a pill, then another, then a whole fistful into his open palm— something you might call simply "the end." Dropping the nearly empty bottle back into his suitcase, Gershom happened to notice, almost concealed under several dress shirts in need of laundering, a book. So he *had* brought a book with him, although he didn't at first recognize this one. Then he remembered: It was the rain-bloated, knockoff edition of *The Book of Raziel* he'd purchased out of charity from that poor schnorrer of a peddler in his solitary burrow. He had all but forgotten that bizarre happenstance, which seemed now to have occurred outside the bounds of reality.

Of course there was no "outside" of reality. Gershom, whose life's work had been the study of religious mysteries, had kept his objective distance from the speculative "realities" that his study entailed: the worlds upon worlds, four of them to be exact, each one stacked on top of the other in descending order, from the purely spiritual to the entirely material—which is ours, "the World of Action," at the bottom of the heap. Though the axiom "as above, so below" applied to them all.

"Humbug is humbug," Gershom's detractors had chided him, "but they call the history of humbug scholarship."

Tentatively, he retrieved the bottle from the suitcase and allowed the pills to spill out of his hand back into their container. Then, from among the packed clothes, he removed the book. It was an apocryphal book, to be sure, with the usual mythic and pseudepigraphic lineage attached: It had been given to Adam by the Angel Raziel, and so forth; a curiosity, but a book nonetheless, and it was Gershom's lifelong instinctive response to open a book whenever he met one. He fell back with that time-worn volume into the thick-cushioned chesterfield armchair. An "armchair believer," that was Dr. Scholem, the religious anarchist, a believer whose faith was balanced by his orthodox nihilism. That was how he'd styled himself, with a sly smile, to anyone who asked. He enjoyed the enigma with which he surrounded himself, the clever language with which he cultivated his air of a man keeping some immense secret. Language, as he and Walter had determined, was unquestionably of divine origin, making revelation itself a linguistic event. But language was also the armature that had always protected him from experiencing the unutterable essence of the mysteries he had the audacity to interpret. For that was Gershom's great secret: He was frightened of those mysteries, and only now, in his desolation, was he cast down enough to admit it to himself.

"Do I even believe in God?" he wondered.

He loosened his necktie, shucked off his suit jacket, even kicked off his shoes in a pantomime of relaxation; then he opened the book. Its undulant pages were replete with the now familiar language—*loshen koydesh*, the holy tongue—that had so transported him when he'd first encountered it all those decades ago. Pages with the taint of taboo, their contents defying all the classical wisdom of a religion that declared God to be unknowable—"Thou canst not see My Face!" Texts that sought not only to define the Godhead and measure its multitudinous dimensions but to confront it through a consciousness beyond what the intellect could apprehend. The field of inquiry was all old hat to him now. "Historiosophy" he called it, history distilled through metaphysics. Through a rigorous scientific methodology he had made logical the irrational; he had domesticated the heretical in order to make it fit for popular consumption, and in so doing—as his sinking gut informed him—betrayed the very tradition he'd hoped to redeem.

This particular book was a grab bag of diverse sources, all of which he instantly recognized. There were passages culled from the *Bahir*, the first text to be categorized as authentic Kabbalah, as well as the second-century *Sefer Yetzirah*. The latter was the earliest known mystical document in Judaism, and it included such transgressive formulae as the ultimate *imitatio dei*—that is, the creation of a man (albeit minus a soul). Mixed with the mélange of zodiacal symbols and diagrams of the opposing branches of the Tree of Life, were inscriptions for inserting in amulets against the evil eye; there were folk remedies for curing impotence, infertility, snakebite, and bed-wetting alongside techniques for invoking supernatural beings. As if the procedures for summoning a demon or guardian angel were as natural as braiding dough for a loaf of challah.

Angels, sniffed Gershom. Walter had had a fetish for them (or anyway the idea of them) that Gershom, for all his intimate acquaintance with angelology, had never shared; though he did cherish the original oil painting by Paul Klee, the *Angelus Novus,* that Walter had bequeathed him. It hung in a place of honor in his study, the only wall space not obscured by books. This was Walter's image of "the angel of history," with its face turned backward toward a past it perceives as a single bleak catastrophe, while a storm blows it irresistibly into the future and the pile of debris in its wake grows ever skyward.

"The wind at its back blows from the nethermost regions of death," Walter had assured his friend in the unconvincingly eerie voice he liked to affect. Gershom recognized the line from Kafka, whose own angelic vision the writer had recorded in his diary: a thing "in bluish-violet robes girt with gold cords descending on great white silken-shining wings"—which proved in the end to be "only a painted wooden figurehead off the bow of some ship . . ."

"*Yud . . . He . . . Vov . . . Heh,*" Gershom heard himself pronounce almost derisively into the stuffy air of that posh hotel room. These were the Hebrew letters of Tetragrammaton. They were the first syllables one uttered in a chant preliminary to acquiring the proper consciousness for summoning a heavenly spirit.

Despite his solitude Gershom felt an acute embarrassment. But when he examined the source of it, he realized that the embarrassment was not so much due to the erudite Dr. Scholem's having blurred for a moment the line between theory and practice, but rather on account of a suddenly acknowledged need—as shameful as it was compelling—to experience some glimmer of magic.

He closed his eyes. He knew all the rituals by heart, all the various measures for preparing oneself to perform some wizardly act. One must first, according to the storied rabbis Judah the Pious and Isaac the Blind, enter the state known as *hitbodedut,* the isolation preceding *kavanah,* the deep concentration, and *devekut,* a cleaving to the substance of the sacred. Gershom knew the cardinal techniques of meditation as espoused by the wonder-workers Abulafia (1240–129?) and Chaim Vital (1547 –1620), and had even trifled with them once or twice, only to feel the exertion unseemly. He knew that, in order to achieve a condition preparatory to receiving a celestial visitation, one must empty oneself of one's self; you must evict the intrusive ego to make room for illumination, just as *ha Shem* had enacted the *tzimtzum,* shrinking Himself to a flyspeck so that the universe would have limitless space to happen in. Gershom knew the prerequisite combinations and permutations of the Hebrew alphabet, the visualizations of the symbols that invited God's divine messengers to manifest themselves. He knew, he knew, and understood that the knowing must be subsumed in the doing.

"AoYo, AoYa, AoYe," he intoned in the singsong of praying Jews. He, the confirmed secularist for whom prayer had always been theater. "AoYi, AoYu . . . ," chanting according to Abulafia's system, the one inspired by the circle of Iyyun clairvoyants influenced by the medieval Sufis, wherein each syllable of the Tetragrammaton is processed through every possible combination of vowel sounds. The aspirant after transmundane splendor must proceed in this repetition until all skepticism and doubt have been banished by an inrushing of the breath of the *ruah ha kodesh,* the holy spirit. "AoHo, AoHa, AoHe . . ." Gershom murmured the combinations until he began to have the sense that his mind was starting to operate on an unfamiliar frequency. A corner of his brain remained aware, of course, that the exercise was foolish, even mad—the mystical lore was full of caveats, profuse with tales of seekers who lost themselves in ethereal dimensions from which they never returned. With all this he was well acquainted, and yet such consequences seemed incidental, as did the prodigious breadth of his learning. What, after all, was the Kabbalah and its orphic web of intricate devices but a vast word-cloaked scaffolding erected to conceal a terrible emptiness?

Yet he persisted: "*YoAi, YoAu* . . ."

And in his thoughts a catalog of God's "deputies" involuntarily unscrolled itself: Metatron, the recording angel, who had once been the cobbler Enoch, later translated alive into heaven for his piety; and the angel Zadkiel who rules over memory. There was Pahadron, the angel of terror, and Mefathiel, called "the opener of doors," a favorite angel of thieves; there was Moreal, the angel of awe, and Ezekiel's four-faced seraph, all of whose faces one perceived simultaneously . . . Gershom could recite the entire beatific roll call, though none of those spiritual beings managed to find any credible purchase in his consciousness. In truth, the names lacked an elemental currency, and all Gershom's formidable knowledge of an oceanic tradition stood for nothing; it had evaporated into a residue of simple expectation, like that of a child anticipating miracles.

"*HoAo, HoAa, HoAe* . . ."

He persevered in his recitation of the syllables until his voice had become strange to his own ears, a kind of raspy susurration, listening to which made him shudder. His heart registered his quaking as not from fear but from something else he could not assign a name to. The eldritch sound of his voice had its complementary sensation in the seam of light that seeped from under his clenched-shut eyelids. That sensation had no name either, though his follicles and nerve endings, intestines and testicles, declared it the pure light of faith. An apotheosis of light, displacing time and history, supplanting identity, and illuminating the core of his being like a hearth. Gershom had only to open his eyes and the light would stream in, filling existence to the brim with the nectar of unalloyed belief—or it would scald his retinas and reduce his mortal frame to ashes. Either would do. So long as revelation was at hand.

Gershom opened his eyes, and the light was dispelled. He was sitting alone in an unlit hotel room on a wet October night—it had begun to rain—in an evil age. Faith had fled along with the hope that Kafka said existed in infinite abundance, only not for us. The rain tattooed the high windows; Gershom switched on the table lamp beside the armchair and experienced himself as a complete vacancy.

By and by there came a knock at the door. Or had the knocking persisted for a while before Gershom was alerted to it? His first impulse was to ignore it, but as it resolutely continued he uttered a perfunctory "Come in" before remembering that the door was locked. "A moment," he said a little louder, rising slowly amid a creaking of joints. He was in his stocking feet, jacketless, his waistcoat unbuttoned, his four-in-hand untied, which was not the way Dr. Scholem was accustomed to greeting the public, but he couldn't be bothered to alter his dress. He steered his unsteady legs toward the door, turned the key, and cracked it open. Before he could respond—how should he respond?—he was forced to step back as the door swung wide, admitting a room service steward. This one was a sawed-off stump of a fellow, not the same one who'd carried up his bag, wheeling a trolley breezily into the room and parking it in front of the armchair.

"I don't remember ordering anything," protested Gershom in confusion.

"Room 301?" inquired the bellboy, checking the number he'd inscribed on the back of his hand to make sure it tallied with the one on the door.

Gershom winced at the gesture, having developed an intense sensitivity to numbers written on the skin.

"I was told Room 301, sir," said the boy, his voice as squeaky as the wheels of his trolley, which he'd taken hold of by the handle and begun to remove. "But since you don't care for the dinner . . ."

Gershom vaguely confirmed that there must have been some mistake, but as the boy was rolling the cart once more toward the door, he made to bar his way. "Wait!" he blurted, actually taking hold of the cart; because the aromas from the dome-covered dishes were tantalizing, and Gershom realized that he was quite hungry, ravenous even. "What sort of food have you there?"

The boy shrugged slightly, without bothering to reveal the contents of the covered dishes, and replied, "Chicken, I believe."

Failing to detect the note of arrogance, Gershom thought he ought to ask, "How is it prepared?"

"Well," the boy deliberated a moment, "we simply tell the chicken straight out that it's going to die."

Gershom's jaw dropped open. That's when he observed that the "boy" was not a boy at all but a pint-sized adult, his scarlet pillbox strapped like a shallow chimney to his oversized head. Despite his high-pitched, pubescent voice, his puckered face was crosshatched with wrinkles from which his froggy eyes bulged. In his trim uniform, its breast studded in a lyre-shaped arrangement of brass buttons, his limbs were proportionate if diminutive and compact, like a jockey's. Despite his cheeky response, his manner showed no hint of incivility or crack in his deferential attitude. "Shall I take it or leave it?" he asked, appending a belated "sir." Still off-balance, Gershom received the query as if he'd been handed some sweeping ultimatum, until he remembered that the fellow was merely referring to the food.

"Leave it," said Gershom, the statement half a question, "I suppose."

"Very good, sir," said the bellhop, though he made no move to vacate the room. He was clearly awaiting his pourboire. Not ordinarily stinting, Gershom stood wondering why he should give a tip for a meal he had not asked for, and to an impudent servant at that. On the other hand there seemed no alternative for getting rid of the runty intruder. He fished a coin from his trouser pocket and handed it to the fellow, who examined it as if it were some foreign object. Gershom sighed and added another crown, which elicited from the bellhop a toothy grin. Then the perverse little fellow did an extraordinary thing. He wedged one of the coins into his left eye like a monocle, then did the same with the second coin in his other eye. Saluting, he began to grope his way for the door in a progress as spasmodic as a marionette on strings.

As he lurched from the room, an altogether nonplussed Gershom thought he'd perceived a faint contour at the back of the bellhop's blazer, a curvature the merest suggestion of a hump. Not quite a hunchback but enough of a semblance of one to classify him an honorary member of their tribe.

"I am beset by hunchbacks and garden gnomes," uttered Gershom, who'd encountered exactly one such spinal aberration in his travels. Still, the image of the old stooped book peddler had

its taunting echo in the bellhop, once again evoking for Gershom
Walter's discomfiting nursery rhyme.

> When I kneel upon my stool
> And I want to pray
> A hunchbacked man is in the room
> And he starts to say:
> My dear child, I beg of you,
> Pray for the little hunchback too.

The recollection further deepened his palpitating sense of unease.

In addition, he was bone-tired and reeling from the events of
the day, a condition not usually favorable to a healthy appetite, but
he couldn't remember when he'd last eaten, and his stomach was
growling balefully. He was spurred as well by a mounting curiosity
as to what lay beneath the silver-domed dishes crowding the cart
like a miniature Arabian skyline.

He nudged the trolley back toward the armchair, sat
down again, and uncovered a platter of what turned out to be
an ambrosially scented, butter-browned chicken paprikash.
He raised another lid to reveal a flaky golden Jägerschnitzel
swimming in a creamy pearl-gray mushroom sauce, no less
appealing for the forbidden ingredient of pork. There was a
plate of steaming spaetzle and mouth-watering, meat-stuffed
Maultaschen with fried onions, plump white asparagus in a moat
of lemony hollandaise, rollmops curled round a savory filling,
lustrous red cabbage, and crispy Kartoffelpuffer topped with
apple sauce. A tall stein of sloe-black Kostritzer beer streaming
tears of condensation was the unlikely companion to a tureen of
matzoh ball soup, its broth afloat with copper medallions of fat.

There was a pot of fragrant Viennese coffee warming over the blue flame of a spirit burner, beside which sat a triple-tiered slice of Sacher torte crowned with a vertiginous spiral of whipped Schlag. Clearly the meal had been intended for the palate of some gluttonous epicure. For all that, Gershom felt like a character in a household tale, who'd wandered through a dark forest to stumble upon an enchanted place where a sumptuous feast had been laid out especially for him.

Of course, in the tales there was always a danger in consuming such a banquet. The food might itself be the catalyst for some harmful spell; you might be transformed into, say, a monkey or a jackass. "Ha," thought Gershom, amazed at how the spread before him had so swiftly altered his state of mind, "so bring on the transformation!" He scooted to the edge of his chair, folded the napkin into his collar, and tucked in. True, this was the fare of the Master Race (matzoh balls excluded), but it was also the cuisine of his childhood home, back before that home became oppressive. What's more, Gershom hadn't had a proper meal since his return to the Continent. He'd eaten on the run all these months—a nosh from a street vendor, rations from food banks and soup kitchens, irregular repasts in the Offenbach commissary or some nearby flyblown café. All of which had contributed to an ongoing gastric distress. But tonight he fell to with a wolfish will.

He sampled each dish in no special order, mixing sweet and spicy with every luscious bite; he chased a sip of coffee with a swig of beer, shoveled forkfuls of noodles and herb-seasoned meat onto his tongue before he'd finished chewing the previous mouthful. *Manna*, he thought, having recalled that their extraterrestrial bounty in the desert was said to have been received by each itinerant Israelite as both comfortingly familiar and wondrously strange. The providential food was also reported to have been experienced, throughout its ingestion, as sublime.

Consummately sated, Gershom dabbed his lips with the napkin, belched prodigally, and exhaled a luxurious sigh. "You are old, Professor Scholem," he confessed to no one, as if he'd reached in his forty-nine years an astronomical age, "and you haven't learned a bloody thing." It was remarkable how the thought soothed him.

He wanted for nothing now—oh, maybe a cigar, though he'd never smoked one in his life.

He was on the verge of falling blissfully asleep in his chair when he heard another knock at the door. "Go away," he said in a voice too drowsy to carry conviction. But as he'd neglected to lock the door after the bellboy's exit, it opened to admit an hallucination. What else could she be, the arrestingly well-endowed woman in the fluffy pink sweater, its top buttons unbuttoned to reveal the delectable twin globes of her breasts, bobbling beneath the sweater's thin material? Her waist, cinched tight with a large-buckled belt, was of an impossibly waspish circumference, the slit Apache-dancer's skirt hugging her curves, her silk-stockinged calves flashing below the skirt's hobbling hem. Her lashes overshadowed her feline eyes like awnings; her high cheekbones were garishly rouged, her shingled hair a fiery shade of red that Gershom had never before seen on earth.

"Lilith," he breathed. A succubus, but not just any succubus: the queen of demons, consort of the arch-demon Samael, collector of nocturnal emissions from which she fashioned an army of fiends. It was unlike Gershom to doubt the evidence of his senses, but so manufactured did the creature appear that she lacked any verisimilitude. For that matter, nothing about this evening seemed real. In the overpowering attar of jasmine that had filled the room at her entrance, Gershom sniffed for some trace of sulfur.

She tottered across the carpet on stiletto heels and took up a pose (hand on canted hip) that was almost a parody of provocative. Her pouting, raspberry lips were parted as if she were about to speak, but she had yet to say a word.

"You must have the wrong room!" insisted Gershom, his tranquility having instantly dissolved into panic.

She led with her hip as she took a step toward him. "*Milácku*," she crooned, "cuddle pumpkin, are you lonely?" She shoved the food cart out of her way so that no obstacle stood between her and Gershom. He made an effort to rise but she leaned forward to press him gently but firmly back into the chair. "What do you like, little beetle?" she asked, her Czech accent giving the German words a winsome lilt. When she smiled, her cosmetic mask assumed a quizzical, almost touchingly human expression. "Let Hedvicka make better where you hurt." Kittenishly, she lifted her skirt to kneel before him, undoing his already loosened necktie and flinging it over her shoulder. "*Mufinek*, my muffin," she murmured, her hot breath tickling his ear, "you got maybe five hundred koruny ceske for party?"

In his consternation, Gershom questioned whether, in some semiconscious fugue state, he had ordered both the dinner and the strumpet. Unthinkable! "I'm a married man!" he exclaimed, hopelessly cornered against the back of the armchair.

"Good on you," said the woman, her doughy breasts crushed against his trembling knees as she began to unbutton his shirt.

There had been many times during the onerous months of his quest for stolen treasures when Gershom had deeply missed his good wife Fanya—but this was not one of them. His longing for her had been in any case of an emotional rather than physical nature. Truth be told, the fleshly allure of his dumpling spouse had for some time been intermittent, and on the occasions when they were intimate, his performance was frankly hit-or-miss. Besides, his tour of the slaughterhouse of Europe had hardly been conducive to libidinous thoughts. Not that Gershom, with his wanton passion for textual hermeneutics, was much given to ordinary concupiscence. The life of the senses had not figured largely among his priorities; he'd never been what you'd call a lady's man. Still, he wasn't exactly shy. Hadn't he wooed his first wife Escha with a genuine ardor, which she'd likewise returned? And when their marriage had run its rocky course, hadn't he felt an unfeigned desire for the more malleable Fanya? Nevertheless, it was with rapt astonishment that he found himself amorously excited by this caricature seductress, this Hedwicka, if that was indeed her name.

She'd begun now to work at the buttons of his trousers, while Gershom realized, to his immense chagrin, that he was aroused, and that the woman's mischievous smile suggested she was aware of it as well. But when it came to asking forgiveness for his wholehearted surrender, it wasn't to Fanya he appealed.

"Walter, are you satisfied?" he inquired soundlessly, as the lady led him shuffling out of his fallen trousers toward the bed. "Do you see the schlemiel I have become?"

There were scarcely any gaps left in the general terror wherein one might play the fool. But who in such a climate would have been inclined to do so? It was true that the morale of the occupying Wehrmacht troops was low, but that in no way redounded to the benefit of the Jews of Zyldzce. If anything, the unrelenting winter had contributed to the Hitlerites' further bedeviling of their perennial victims. The commanding officer's public appearances were still infrequent and his immediate subordinate, often debauched, had delegated much of the authority vested in him by the Obersturmführer to a lieutenant colonel, Schulz by name. Oberstleutnant Schulz had then taken it upon himself to instill a greater sense of *esprit* in the restless men, which he attempted to do in part by involving them in acts of collective retaliation.

Most of the Jews no longer had the impetus to make more than token gestures toward observing the holidays (excepting those devoted solely to lamentation); the very idea of celebration seemed an insult to heaven. But Purim was different; Purim was a carnival holiday that catered especially to children, and God knew *di kinder* needed some small respite from the unabating gloom. So the families made costumes for them out of whatever scraps of fabric they could find. The invaders were at first bewildered by the sight of so many tiny Queen Esthers in hopsacking gowns and paper crowns, and hollow-eyed little Mordecais in patched bathrobes with lint beards pasted to their chins. They were suspicious at seeing a convergence of harlequin tykes (some of whom were actually laughing) escorted by their parents to the Old New Synagogue, where their gathering was tolerated only under armed guard. Nothing stirred the suspicions of the mamzrim so much as laughter.

Disturbed, Oberstleutnant Schulz, a starchy pedagogue in his former life, investigated the relevant biblical text and discovered that it commemorated a time when the Jews had been saved from destruction—after which they commenced to slaughter the enemy who would have otherwise slaughtered them. The Oberstleutnant took particular offense at the ritual that encouraged the children to flog a rag-stuffed effigy of Haman, the would-be annihilator of their race; he saw monstrous injustice in the *Megillah*'s account of the murder of Haman's ten sons. This wouldn't do; vengeance belonged to the Reich.

Resolved to reverse that mutinous narrative, he ordered the construction of a scaffold on the market platz with a crossbeam broad enough to accommodate ten victims. (A minyan, he noted.) The exacting Oberstleutnant then instructed the Judenrat to select the candidates for the gallows, and left them to construe what a refusal might mean. Under such duress, the council, composed primarily of merchants and artisans, chose a slate of victims from among the most expendable ghetto inhabitants—schnorrers, cripples, known thieves. To their relative credit, the council agonized over every decision, but only one of their members abstained altogether from voting. That was Blume's father, the increasingly frail Rabbi Vaynipl, who instead volunteered himself as a potential martyr. When his offer was dismissed by the others as self-righteous grandstanding, the pious old man, who'd been expecting a universal redemption any day, wept inconsolably.

"I think," he later told his daughter, while standing next to a washtub containing a lump of clay that had resisted his best attempts to animate it, "that Messiah came already too late and went back to his Bird's Nest in the Tree of Life."

"The Bird's Nest" was the aerie in which the Messiah was known to be dwelling until his descent to earth. When his daughter pleaded with him to cease what looked to be a terminal weeping, he explained that he was practicing the holy Abulafia's crying meditation.

The girl read aloud to him the psalm allowing that crying might extend through the night but joy comes with the morning.

"So let me know," said the rabbi in one of his more balanced rejoinders, "if ever comes morning again."

After the hanging, which all were called to witness, the ground was too hard to bury the bodies. The martyrs were laid side by side in the *hekdish*, the poorhouse since converted to a charnel house, together with the bodies that had preceded them during that frigid season. The Germans, in their pack rat mania, had stripped them of their clothing, and without available linen for graveclothes, they were laid naked alongside the rest. Sprinkled with quicklime to cut the stench, their bodies would lie that way among the multiplying dead (from suicide, disease, and murder) until the spring thaw. Their condition was an incentive for those still breathing to stay alive at least until April.

The suicides came in several varieties. Because the houses of Zyldzce were built near to the ground, those who attempted to fling themselves into the afterlife from the rooftops usually found themselves still alive, though often disfigured from broken bones. (With typical Nazi logic, unsuccessful suicides were deemed punishable by death.) A more expedient method of ending one's life was by hanging or slitting the wrists, though both involved much inconvenience to others. Least troublesome was swallowing a fistful of the stupefacient tablets the apothecary Tafshunski hoarded and distributed for an extortionate fee. Those who chose self-murder were not limited to any special age group: Recently orphaned children, however new to the world, were as likely to take their own lives as their elders who'd seen enough of it. Bimko, the bootblack's little boy, was seen holding his pants up about his wasted frame before throwing himself down the marketplace well, which made the water undrinkable for a time. Grunam Mintz, a young journeyman carpenter, separated from his fiancée due to a labor transport, walked the seventy kilometers back from Slupsk to rejoin her for an *aleynmord* pact. He chopped a hole in the ice of the Bug and tenderly lowered his betrothed into it before following himself.

The shtetl had always been a breeding ground for every strain of disease that poverty was heir to: Viruses, influenzas, scurvy, and parasites were its daily fare. Moreover, every affliction was exacerbated by the abysmally close quarters the occupation had brought about; every infection was swiftly transmitted. So far, however, the ghetto had been spared the dread pestilence of typhus. But with the inflated population had come an exponential rise in the proliferation of the lice and rats that carried the disease. The egg lady Malka Halpern was the first to show symptoms, which the Judenrat dutifully reported to the German command. Fearing the disease would spread to the troops, the Obersteutnant

Schulz—after conferring with the Obersturmführer (who did not appreciate the interruption to his protracted leisure)—declared that a general disinfection (what the Jews called a *paruvke*) be immediately implemented. Never mind that Malka had fully recovered and there were no more detected instances of that particular illness.

To augment the operation's potential for entertainment, the Oberstleutnant took it upon himself to enlist a gang of Polish roughnecks and their women to administer the fumigation. After a long wait in the cold outside the bathhouse, the Jews were made to strip naked in the vestibule; then, sufficiently humiliated, they were thrust—men and women alike—into the once separate chambers from which the partitions had been removed. There they were met by rowdies and harridans whose taunts rivaled the drone of the portable engines strapped to their backs. With these devices they sprayed an atomized vapor that engulfed their victims in a stinging mephitic fog, out of which emerged more fiends wielding electrical shears. Only those with coins to spare were able to salvage a bit of beard or, in the case of the girls, an ebony braid. Shorn and decontaminated, they were hustled from the bathhouse through a gauntlet of derision back out into the snow-encrusted street—where their wracked countenances inspired, if possible, more anguish among those still waiting their turn to enter.

The men who'd managed to save their beards lost them soon after by dint of an edict declaring facial hair to be an adornment. (Jews were not allowed adornments other than their yellow stars.) This gave the invaders more cause to stop the recalcitrant Hasids in the street and clip their beards—abuses the Hasidim could not preempt with the depilatories that might have spared them the use of a razor. Razors, also forbidden, were in any case no longer available. The bald and glabrous citizens of Zyldzce now hardly recognized one another, or themselves for that matter, or the place where they were born. It was a condition aggravated by a hunger and fear only one step removed from perdition, though many had run out of ways to be afraid.

Spring did eventually arrive. The surface ice came apart in the Bug and the yellow cowslips and purple orchid flowers burst forth on its banks, but the thaw promised no ease for the Jews. There was no special satisfaction in having survived the punishing winter, and most lacked even the vitality to resent the hope of renewal presaged by the warmer season. Without sufficient flour for making matzohs, Passover went largely unheeded. (The scamp Menke Klepfisch tepidly proposed that, given the spilled food from bygone seders caked on his family Haggadah, they might boil the pages up for a holiday soup.) The Obersturmführer von Graf und Trach had finally come out of hibernation, looking somewhat thinner and less hale despite his sabbatical. He packed off his hypothetical wife in the same limousine that had brought her, though this time no Zyldzcer dared to watch her silk-stockinged lineaments sliding into the backseat of the Mercedes. With a touch of sarcasm, the commandant commended his subalterns for having maintained a rigorous atmosphere of blight and inhumanity while he was otherwise disposed. Then, reassuming the baton from the Hauptsturmführer who had repossessed it from the unsung Oberstleutnant, he took up his duties again. He took them up, following his lady's expeditious departure, with a reinvigorated commitment that coincided with the arrival of a cohort of Geheime Staatspolizei recently detached to the town.

He saw to it that the corpses were removed from the hekdish, stacked on the splintered boards of the freight wagons, and hauled by teams of plodding Juden to a forest clearing where they were tossed into a mass grave. (The gases released from the thawed bodies later caused the ground to heave and burble above them.) The Herr Oberst, tightening the reins of his control, outlawed foraging for "salad" in the military garbage bins and prohibited the dismantling of wooden buildings for use as fuel. Street singers were forbidden by his dictate as were children peddling the "candies" made from wax boiled in molasses. He also disbanded the doll-making workshop the Jews had established to occupy their children and had their motley creations sent to Germany. He oversaw the prompt execution of smugglers and attempted escapees, real or perceived, and even ordered, for the convenience of his Gestapo "guests," that the privy behind the officer's mess at Shmulke Goiter's Hotel be restored to functionality again.

Only once, during one of the commandant's renewed tours of the ghetto, did he and his erstwhile jester clap eyes on each another. This was on an afternoon when Menke was returning from having failed to earn a few zlotys at jobs that no longer existed. Rounding into Zyrke's *gessl*, he came face-to-face with the Obersturmführer, strolling in the company of his lieutenants and aide-de-camp. Menke braced himself for the man's standard mock-gallant greeting, which never came. The commandant passed him by in the sludgy street without a nod of recognition. Pausing to watch him walk away, Menke felt at once relief and a pang of regret at the realization that he was no longer the commanding officer's blue-eyed (his eyes were olive brown) Jew. Then he saw that the Herr Oberst, hands clasped behind his back, had stopped and abruptly about-faced.

"Minky der Spassmacher," he exclaimed with a simpering

smile. "I didn't recognize you without your raven curls. Gentlemen, look who's still among the living. Minky, my friend, say something funny."

Unpracticed as he was of late, Menke's "gag reflex" was always ready with a dependable if somewhat uninspired groaner. "Two Jews are at the circus," he began obligingly, "they're watching a trapeze artist hanging by his toes playing the violin . . . ," when the Obersturmführer interrupted.

"Ah, *mein trottel*, my lickspittle" he sighed, ruefully shaking his head, "you begin to repeat yourself." Then allowing the clown a measured laugh anyway, he moved on.

Under his breath Menke muttered at the officer's departing back, "One says to the other, 'Mischa Elman he's not.'"

His preferred status having apparently expired, Menke could safely assume he no longer enjoyed the impunity he'd formerly known. Still, he would have been the first to admit that he was better off than most, thanks mainly to Tsippe-Itsl's good offices. Throughout that merciless winter she had managed to maintain Menke's household, notwithstanding the whinging grievances of its guests, with an astonishing capability. She wielded her broom with the finesse of a partner in a macabre waltz, and from the peels of mealy potatoes made babkas that tasted eggy and sweet. While the rest of Zyldzce survived on bilious soups concocted from bones and the veins of nameless animals, Tsippe made surprisingly tasty salads from radish and carrot leaves tossed in an oil rendered from melted tallow; she made tzimmes from ingredients about whose origins no one dared inquire. (The Bialovskys might question the kosherness of her meals, but they had no problem with invoking *pikuach nefesh*, the law that allowed one to eat *treyf*, or filth, to save one's life.) In addition she assuaged the tantrums of the toddler

Yanki with preposterous tales that either calmed him or frightened him into silence. While he reserved the right to continue thinking of her as a needless encumbrance, there were times Menke was compelled to regard her as something of a treasure as well. For all Tsippe-Itsl's ministrations, however, Menke's house remained, like every other in the ghetto, a tinderbox of tensions. The Bialovsky family were camped out unhappily on pallets and bedrolls spread over the hard puncheon floor. The widowed and maiden sisters, anemic of body and impoverished of spirit, were more or less resigned to their disconsolate lot; but the skeletal Reb Itche and his fubsy spouse felt they were entitled to better accommodations; they coveted the bed, narrow as it was, that Menke had abandoned to his self-avowed bride. Though the Bialovskys, man and wife, were too leery of the strange girl to openly express their envy, their dull-witted twin nephews, Shloymke and Gedalya, spoke up for them. Out of some sense of tribal allegiance, or merely for the sake of bullying their host, the nephews argued aggressively that their Aunt Dobke and Uncle Itche deserved the bed by virtue of their debilitated seniority.

"Over my dead body!" declared Menke, scaring himself by his headstrong response. Then he thought he could read in the nephews' eyes, glaring from under their beetling brows, that his rapid dispatch might well be an option. The deprivation of all things previously regarded as necessary had driven ordinary people to murderous extremes, and Menke feared the surly twins might not have far to be driven.

But lest the guests try to usurp Tsippe's bed by strength of numbers, Menke stationed himself at its foot as she slept. He sat behind the canvas curtain with his back to the iron frame, listening to the girl babbling moonshine to the toddler, who'd taken to crawling into bed with her at night. Reticent throughout most of the day, Tsippe could be practically garrulous after dark, uninhibited in prattling to the snuggling child her catalog of nocturnal monsters. She described to him the chicken-footed demons of common ancestry along with ghosts and flying serpents—"and I myself have seen one time in the forest, riding on her blood-sucking dragon which she calls it Ishi-benob, the demon queen Lilith. I saw also the Re'em, which it's an ox so big that its drek could dam up the River Bug . . ."

Menke wondered if she was deliberately trying to scare the little pisher out of his wits; or was it that, where some counted sheep, Tsippe-Itsl lulled herself and the child to sleep with her litany of hideous phantasms? It was a kind of homeopathy, as if she thought the grown-up fears that besieged them by day were trumped (and thus diminished) by invoking a child's fears of things that went bump in the night. After all, what daylight atrocities could compete with the carnage wreaked by the giant silver-scaled Rahab, who could wipe away whole nations with a swipe of its tail? Somewhere during the conjuring of *naytmerim* that comprised Tsippe's lullabies, she and Yanki fell soundly asleep, while Menke was left awake with a spinning brain, entertaining fantasies of his own. One of which was that the girl in the bed was another, with whom he lay spooned beneath the blanket as if in a chrysalis that kept them safe from all external wickedness.

He returned to "defend" Tsippe-Itsl the next night, and the one after that, a pointless act since Reb Itche and his wife had settled their bedding atop the broad expanse of the enamel-tiled stove. They had taken possession of the stove in Menke's absence, which left him little choice but to make up his dustcloth pallet in the available space between the canvas curtain and the foot of the bed. The discomfort of his situation did not lend itself to easeful slumber, but Menke nevertheless found the girl's nightly roster of bugbears and bogeys to be in the end a not unjoyful noise. The rumors of resettlement, according to recent arrivals in the shtetl, were not rumors, and the Jews of Zyldzce, despite residual pockets of denial, seemed to sense what deportation meant without really knowing. Since the coming of the Gestapo officers— menacing black leather trench coats in grim disaccord with their bland bookkeepers' faces—any loose ends in the organization of the ghetto had been drawn tight. The commandant countenanced no margin of error in regulating the rules of conduct: As regarded the Judenrat's supervision of the workshops and labor details, the soup kitchen and the infirmary, the housing assignments, ration cards, and burial detachment, the least suspicion of double-dealing or bribery would result in robustly disproportionate consequences. Blanket punishments were meted out on the most venial of pretenses, and the seams through which the people might slip into memories of a prior time were securely stitched up.

Naturally the doctrinaire trench coats frowned upon any exceptions to the general contempt due the local Juden. Subtle operatives in their crow-like attire, they were aware of the practice among certain officers of adopting individual Jews for vaguely sentimental reasons. As if, by preserving a single Itzig from harm, they were free to subject the rest to the grossest barbarities. It had come to the attention of the Gestapo worthies that the Obersturmführer himself, a man known to be of a somewhat original stripe, had been guilty of such imprudent behavior. He was also answerable, they were aware, for a blithe dereliction of duty that left him under a cloud of probationary incertitude in their eyes. Needless to say, there were no more summonses for the clown Menke Klepfisch to come to Shmulke Goiter's for the purpose of enlivening the officer's mess.

Menke had long since ceased expecting such invitations, which he looked back upon now with a queasy stab of conscience. He no longer imagined reducing the occupiers to fits of helpless hysterics, under cover of which the Jews of Zyldzce could take flight. There was no levity, he understood, that could lift the heavy weather of their plight. Besides, what did Menke have left in his arsenal but a handful of stale chestnuts, the type of played-out old saws that kept Blume and everyone else, himself included, from taking him seriously? When what was needed was a joke so ferociously barbed that the laughter it provoked would tear the insides out of its audience and leave them foundered in their own bloody entrails. Still, in these days of harrowing *sitzfleisch*, of waiting for nothing, Menke sometimes missed his old nimbus of untouchability; he remarked with interest that, during those times when he'd managed to give Tsippe-Itsl the slip, his steps tended toward the scene of his former shenanigans. Such was anyway the case on an unusually sweltering afternoon in May, when he found himself at the top of Tuvim-Wiersze Street overlooking the yard of Shmulke's Hotel, where he observed a project underway.

Having duly noted the complaints from his Staatspolizei guests as to the dearth of toilet facilities, the commandant had issued orders for the immediate restoration of the privy behind the tavern. This was the same pungent structure in which Menke and Tsippe had been so unwarrantably interned overnight. A bull-necked staff sergeant (the same one, in fact, who had been the agent of their confinement) and a sleepy-eyed under officer were directing a pair of cadaverous Jews in the task. Their first order of business, after slapdash repairs had been made to the structure's exterior, was to tip the outhouse backward like a teapot lid until it rested horizontally upon the ground. That way the great mound of surplus excrement in the pit beneath it could be removed. A section of the board fence about the yard had been knocked down to make way for a farm wagon wheeled in to receive the volumes of waste dredged from the hole. Exposed to the sunlight, especially harsh for that season, the twin peaks of turd released a fetor so foul that the sergeant, having ordered the Jews to proceed in their work, quit the scene with his corporal gagging into a handkerchief.

"Don't stop," called the sergeant in parting, "till that pit is as empty as your *Judensau* heads."

It had been easy enough to resist temptation amidst all the quotidian awfulness. Of his lifelong addiction to rascality, Menke conceded, nothing remained but an occasional twinge, like the itching of an amputated limb. When the spring thaw had roused the dormant crickets in the rotting eaves of his house, the Menke of another day might have collected them in a sack; he might have dumped them in the window of a soldiers' billet, where they'd have skirled throughout the night like a chorus of bicycle bells. But such pranks would have borne the unmistakable stamp of the Herr Oberst's privileged Jew, and the Herr Oberst could no longer be counted on to protect him. Menke's nuisance would now be judged an act of sabotage. But, as with the partisans in the forest who blew up bridges and trains, wasn't sabotage what a *chutzpadik* Yid ought to be about?

"And aren't I," asked Menke, contradicting the objections of his dry throat and jangling nerves, "that dauntless Jew?"

A barbed wire barrier stood between Menke and Shmulke's tavern, but if you lay on your back in the gutter and deeply inhaled, you could just manage to slither crabwise under the ghetto boundary. Once beyond it Menke had only to shamble down a brief incline and scoot round into an alley on the near side of the wooden fence, where he could spy on the two laborers through a knothole. He recognized them: Leo Fajnhauz and Jossif Czacki, former partners in a small textile concern, both since relegated to warehouse porters and now shit shovelers. Their shirts were tied about their faces against the stench, laying bare torsos displaying hollow cavities where their stomachs should have been.

They persisted in their digging throughout that torrid afternoon, flinging their shovelfuls of dung into the bed of the wagon, while Menke watched vigilantly from the alley behind the yard. Toward dusk, they had emptied the pit to a depth beyond which their shovels could reach unless they lowered themselves into the hole itself. At that point the men looked about for the superintending sergeant, then turned to each other and shrugged.

"A grave for the Amalekites this should be," said Jossif, too loud for caution's sake.

And Leo, more diffidently, "Let's hope it isn't ours."

They shared a sigh and said in unison, "*Shoyn genug.*" Enough!

Then they set about heaving the privy back into its upright position over the cesspit and vacated the yard, only to return shortly thereafter leading Zundl the ragman's spavined plug horse Shoshana. They hitched Shoshana to the *schmutz* wagon and prodded her with a stick until they'd coaxed her into hauling the load, with a discernible limp, back out of the yard. (The horse would later be found lying dead in the Boulevard, swarmed over by flies and women slicing slabs of its scanty flesh to bear away to their cobwebbed skillets.)

Menke waited until the pair were well on their way toward wherever they were told to dump their freight, then stole into the deserted yard. He took up a long branch fallen from the dying beech tree that overhung the yard and entered the outhouse, where he thrust the branch into one of the openings in the newly sanded wooden seat. Having plumbed the depth of the excrement that remained in the pit, he extracted the branch and found it coated with perhaps a yardstick's worth of damp muck. Satisfied, he went round to the back of the facility and stretched on tiptoe to gain a handhold at the edge of the slanted roof; then he gave the structure a mighty tug. It tilted slowly backward, gathering momentum as Menke leapt out of the way, allowing the outhouse to topple with a shuddering thud into the dust. Menke held his breath until he was certain no one had been alerted by the sound; then, with much grunting and internal swearing, he dragged the prostrate structure several feet away from the shithole. He grasped the edge of the metal roof once more and heaved upward, taxing his stringy physique to the limit. Walking his hands up the rough-hewn boards, he gave the privy a shove with his shoulder until it rocked forward and was stationary again, restored to its original standing position.

Hastily he gathered up a bundle of the dry twigs and brittle branches scattered about the yard and lay them in a latticelike arrangement across the width of the open pit. Over them Menke sprinkled an armload of dead leaves so that they formed a kind of brushy doormat in front of the facility. Then he retreated behind the fence and knelt at his knothole again.

He hadn't long to wait. The staff sergeant, whom his under-officer addressed as Feldwebel Pfluger, returned as the sun was setting to inspect the day's labor. The early evening was beginning to cool a little, dissipating the nauseating odors that had vitiated the afternoon; a half-moon like a silver sail was just visible in the shell-pink sky. Seeing that the structure was vertical again and the yard absent of wagon and Jews, the sergeant must have assumed that the assigned task had been adequately accomplished; because he declared to his nodding subordinate that he intended to be the first to "inaugurate"—that was his word—the rehabilitated outhouse. Unbuckling the equipment belt that compassed his respectable girth, he stepped forward onto the carpet of leaves, which directly collapsed beneath him, dropping him into a waist-deep trough of warm shit.

"*Schiesse!*" he cried somewhat redundantly; "*Der mist!*"

His enraged clamor brought a party of officers charging from the rear of the tavern; though rather than help the portly sergeant, ineffectually aided by the corporal as he tried to scramble out of the mire, they stood about the pit convulsed with laughter.

Hidden behind the fence, Menke laughed along with them. He continued his sputtering laughter even after Sergeant Pfluger, having clawed his way out of the hole with his trousers and the skirts of his tunic caked in feces, changed his tone from anger to accusation. "This is the work of the Jews!" he declared, tears streaming from his piggy eyes. Then, by degrees, all merriment ceased except Menke's, who bit down hard on his fist to keep from revealing himself in his jollity.

But Menke too stopped laughing when, not long after the incident, the two former textile merchants were rounded up and summarily shot. The hapless Sergeant Pfluger was publicly dressed down and demoted for his negligence in what had come to be called an act of insurrection. A few of the officers got a kick out of seeing the lard-assed sergeant's abasement, but a lingering rancor had set in among the rank and file, many of whom had been partial to the bluffly paternal if blundering Pfluger. Neither were they placated by the pro forma execution of the shit shovelers: The outhouse fiasco, they recognized, had all the earmarks of a prank perpetrated by who else but the Jew to whom the commandant had shown such favor in the past. They knew him by name, Minky Klepfisch, the notorious jackass so often trailed by his faithful milk-and-water freak. The Obersturmführer may not yet be past objecting to any unauthorized assaults on his person, but an enterprising young ensign suggested what might be an even more pernicious way of getting even with the Hanswurst swine.

The reprisal was swift; it was a relatively simple matter to abduct her. The Bialovskys, who still suspected the girl of having supernatural powers, could hardly believe it had been so easy. One of the twin nephews, looking out a window where Tsippe-Itsl was hanging laundry on a line, thought that her bleached features were scarcely altered by the sheet thrown over her head. He nevertheless watched with an unhinged jaw as, in a quick but not especially stealthy operation, she was captured by a small band of common soldiers and spirited away.

She was taken to the town hall and sometime theater, now a barracks, where she was indecorously unloaded onto the floor, and there left to wriggle out of her sheet like (here the Freiburg-educated ensign again) "a metamorphosing larva." What emerged was no butterfly but a frightened, peaky creature whom the soldiers promptly relieved of her coarse cotton shift and drab underdrawers. Then they stood frozen, marveling at her ivory pallor and the disquieting grace of her small-boned anatomy. None dared approach her alien nakedness.

"Not with a ten-meter Schwanz would I touch that thing," announced a squeamish senior corporal, who seemed to be speaking for them all. Rising to the challenge, however, a strapping young private soldier stepped forth to show his mettle. Unbuttoning his trousers, he released a hypertrophied member with which he commenced to set what some might have regarded as a new standard for ingenuity in an act of defilement. Afterward, the others were emboldened and in a spirit of competition followed his lead.

"*Omne animal post coitum triste*," sighed Gershom after the trollop had left him (with her five hundred crowns), and waited for the sadness to overwhelm him. The stunning events of the evening were finally no more than an anomalous interlude. He was still all alone, lying in a disheveled bed in an empty (but for the leavings of his feast) hotel room in the middle of a continent whose soil was still sodden from the blood of its victims. That said, he was also at peace. It couldn't last of course. Despair would descend on him again like a poison fog despite any effort he might make to outrun it; soon enough, it would lay him low. For the time being, however, Gershom leaned back against the headboard and recalled how he had wanted to shut his eyes from a surfeit of ecstasy—but he couldn't help gazing transfixed at the rampant female as she rode him. Even at the height of his rapture, he couldn't lose the suspicion that she might turn at any moment into a serpent or hag, though he could see beyond the charade of her face paint that she was really just a girl.

In his languid thoughts, the libidinous cosmic drama that was the theme of his beloved *Zohar* replayed itself: how copulation on earth sympathetically reenacted the union of the Lord with his Shekhinah, his bride, and was thus a holy act. But there had seemed nothing particularly holy in their tempestuous animal thrusting and grinding. However, when—no longer passive— Gershom had wrapped his arms around his partner's full-bosomed torso, he wondered if her pronounced shoulder blades might be rudimentary wings.

He rose slowly from the bed and slouched over to the pier glass that hung between the tall windows, trickling rain like strings of glass beads. "*Hashmal*," he murmured. It was a word that in the mystical lexicon had several meanings, one of which was a kind of fun house mirror in which the observer is granted something like a God's-eye view of himself. What Gershom saw in the glass was a pigeon-breasted, broad-hipped, knobbly-kneed figure in drawstring undershorts and gartered socks. His ears were like bat's wings, his nose a dorsal fin—a laughable entity; in short, a clown. He thought again of the sainted Ari's exhortation to gather the scattered sparks of divinity and return them to their source. He thought of Franz Rosenzweig's dictum that those who forsake action for ecstasy have abandoned the hallowed tradition. He thought of Walter's conjecture that "only a fool's help is real help." And so, quick before the ludicrous vision of himself could turn back into the serious scholar, Gershom assigned the fool in the mirror a fool's errand.

He hired another car, this time a Tatra V8 shaped like a vented hard hat, from a company unaffiliated with the reconstruction and restoration committees. No camp survivor, his driver was not even a Jew, but the employee of a jackleg fleet hastily organized to grab a little business before the Soviets cracked down on private enterprise. A stolid, turtle-faced man in a seedy serge imitation of a chauffeur's livery, Mr. Hladik was willing to drive Gershom to Ultima Thule and back if the price was right. (The right price being the better part of the professor's wallet.) After Gershom and his driver had studied the map and pinpointed the destination—a village near the Polish-Byelorussian border some thirty versts (the distances were measured in versts now) of Grodno—there was little cause for more conversation between them. Gershom had no desire to know what Mr. Hladik had done during the war, and Mr. Hladik had no curiosity concerning Dr. Scholem's itinerary. The plan was to drive north for a day and a half to an inconsiderable rustic outpost for undisclosed reasons. Then, after a flying visit, they would carry on to Grodno, and from there Gershom would travel via a prearranged series of rail connections to Paris, arriving—if all went well—with a day to spare before his scheduled flight to Palestine.

The trip was largely uneventful but for the number of wrong turnings due to Mr. Hladik's inconsistent sense of direction and Gershom's poor map-reading skills; there was the usual bother at crossing borders that could shift like a snake's spine from week to week. Along the way Gershom had much time to reflect, which he failed to take advantage of, nor did he read— reading in moving vehicles anyway made him nauseous. He merely looked out dispassionately onto the mauve hills of Lower Silesia, the surviving medieval spires of Klodzko and Katowice, the monotonous liver-brown industrial landscapes of steelworks, foundries, and mines—the same smoldering satanic mills, in fact, that had helped fuel civilization's attempted self-destruction. Gershom had repeatedly, during his European sojourn, tried to stretch his apprehension to encompass the breadth and depth of the savagery, but for all its touted brilliance Dr. Scholem's brain had reached the limit of its elasticity. It had since snapped back into an unprecedented smallness, almost a coziness from which Gershom could witness the passing scenery without anger, pity, or remorse. His evening in the Hotel Europa had already receded into incomprehension, and he moved forward now only by virtue of the strength of a vague resolve.

The former shtetl of Zyldzce on that pied afternoon in autumn was almost unrecognizable from Gershom's previous visit. Where before it had had a nearly deserted, hole-in-corner atmosphere, today it appeared relatively thriving, though still bucolic in mood despite all of its provincial activity. The businesses around the market square all looked to be going concerns: A barber signaled the turn of a waiting patron seated among others on a bench outside his shop; an apothecary conferred in his doorway with a woman holding the hand of a child with a balloon tied to his finger; a butcher in a blood-stained apron embraced a flayed pink carcass in order to hoist it onto a hook in a window in front of which customers had gathered. A towheaded lad lounged atop a wagonload of fresh produce parked in front of a grocer's storefront; a peasant wife bearing bushel baskets on either shoulder—one full of mushrooms, the other wild berries—kicked a sashaying partridge hen from underfoot. Horses in their traces eyed with passing interest the dogs and untethered goats ferreting about the market for refuse. There were no beggars in sight. Gershom observed that the houses themselves, some painted now in bright pastels, seemed less crouched and cowering, more freestanding and independent of their neighbors. It was as if, having rid itself of a stiff-necked, otherworldly element, the sanitized village had reclaimed its native vitality. Who needed the Jews?

Gershom left Mr. Hladik sipping slivovitz in a snug tavern with a barn owl nailed over the transom for luck, and assured him he wouldn't be long. There was a bracing breeze circulating between the houses, sweeping through the puzzle of streets that Gershom remembered as leading toward the river. He made his way past a reopened brickyard, felt the current of warmth from its kilns, and had the oddly inappropriate sense of a homecoming. A laddered alley led him down the slope to the embankment, where some washerwomen were anchoring the laundry they'd laid out to dry with heavy stones. He crossed the reinforced footbridge beside an electrically powered millhouse to the old Jewish cemetery on the opposite bank of the Bug. The graveyard itself, enshrouded in nettles and scrub, had practically vanished from sight, as had the path that wound into the encroaching woods. Undiscouraged, Gershom proceeded into the trees and traversed the tufty meadow whose ground lacked its previous buoyancy, giving no indication of any prior desecration. After a stretch of virtual bushwhacking through dusty bindweed, gorse, and fern, he arrived at the fish-shaped granite outcrop with its yawning mouth.

The crude trellis-like door had disappeared, nor was there any votive offering at the foot of the rock face. From a pocket of his suit jacket Gershom withdrew a small flashlight and stooped to shine it into the cavern's entrance ahead of him. He ducked beneath the low overhang, straightened, and swept the torch beam about the craggy walls of that cold, sunless space, looking for signs that its former tenant might still be in residence. Not only was the cave barren of its onetime occupant, but there was no evidence that the book peddler had ever been there at all. Gone was his distinctive fetor and the straw-filled bed frame, his icon of a dressmaker's dummy. Of the stacks of weatherworn Yiddish novels not a single volume remained. Instead, along with a mildewed mattress, the once spartan refuge was strewn with empty Warka beer bottles and a couple of circular condom tins. Turning up his coat collar against the chill, Gershom registered the grotto's violation with as little disappointment as he had the absence of its departed resident. Had he really expected anything else? His mission was in any event purely symbolic; it needed no witness to receive the gesture.

He removed the well-thumbed grimoire from an inside pocket and asked the blessing of his dead friend Walter. Then he aimed the flashlight into what he'd previously assumed was a niche no larger than a chapel apse in the rear wall of the cave. "Darkness visible," thought Gershom, because the light illumined no immediate terminus of the cavern's confines. He took a few steps forward into the lengthening passage, advancing hesitantly until the peddler's former abode was well behind him. Was this the direction in which the peddler had taken his leave? Had the wizened old huckster opted for an interior journey, choosing a retreat into the bowels of the earth over re-emerging into what was still called (if somewhat sardonically) the land of the living? Would that poor bedraggled party have understood Gershom's ritual offering anyway? Gershom was hard-pressed enough to explain it to himself. Nevertheless he continued inching his way with resonant footfalls into the gloom, waiting for fear to overtake him. It didn't, but after proceeding for perhaps the length of a drafty shopping arcade, he decided he'd gone far enough, having reached a few steps shy of what he thought might be a point of no return.

He held the book out in front of him just in case some nameless entity might come out of the murk to retrieve it. ("*Adank*, Dr. Scholem," a grateful Prophet Elijah might greet him, adding with a doff of his fedora, "It's been missing, this volume, from a library in heaven.") Absent that, Gershom simply tossed the book away from him with a purposeful flick of his wrist. He tried to follow its trajectory with the beam of the flashlight but lost it in the stygian dark; nor did he hear it fall to the floor of the cave. Rather, it was as if he'd flung that magical primer known through the ages as the *Sefer Raziel* into some version of a bottomless lateral abyss.

What's the difference between a Jewish optimist and a Jewish pessimist?

The pessimist says, "Things can't get any worse."

The optimist says, "Of course they can!"

Thanks to the importation of more Jews from the outlying districts, the population of the ghetto had become insupportable. Some looked forward in their misery to the threatened resettlement, even if it meant journeying to places from which they might never return. It would at least be a reprieve from the slow death of their current straits. Just when they thought there were no further means of demoralizing them, however, the occupiers introduced yet another element: In the interest of impounding as many Jews in one place as could be gathered before deporting them en masse, they evacuated a group of *meshugayim*, of lunatics, from an institution in nearby Kotsk, transporting them by freight wagon to the end of a disused train spur outside of Zyldzce. In former times such unfortunates had been looked after; beggars and madmen were the objects of what charity the Jews, penurious themselves, could afford. But now that all were reduced to the condition of beggars, their houses packed to the rafters with the sick and desolate, the lunatics were left to fend for themselves.

Most were quite passive; wearing only castoff jumpers and soiled hospital gowns, they fetched up in courtyards and doorways where they quietly starved. Others, periodically agitated, were made even more ungovernable by hunger and exposure, creating havoc wherever they appeared—and they appeared in the oddest places: the sidecar of a Nazi Zündapp motorcycle, say, or hunkered like trolls under the footbridge in the river silt. For the soldiers they were merely another source of entertainment, whom they enjoyed goading into even more frenzied behavior: Say boo! and watch them run barefoot and gibbering through knee-deep mud after another spring downpour. One of them might assault some decrepit citizen whom they suspected of being in possession of a carrot or a lump of cheese; another might attack a person for no apparent reason at all—their actions were seldom informed by rationale. Occasionally a long-suppressed predator deprived of medication, in a burlesque of the Germans' own abuses, would pounce upon some incautious maiden. These hysterics inspired almost as much fear among the Zyldzcers as the mamzrim themselves, demonstrating as they did a mental collapse that many were already on the verge of succumbing to. Some did succumb, as if lunacy were as contagious as cholera.

Tsippe-Itsl had been delivered naked and coughing up blood on the doorstep of Menke's little house in Toyvl Street. Its lodgers half expected that, dying, the girl's ordinarily translucent flesh might simply conclude the business of dissolving into invisibility. So they were shocked to see how her unclad body had acquired a dappled pigmentation—a medley of greens, yellows, and angry reds—that it had never revealed in good health. At first afraid to touch her, the Bialovskys, whether out of compassion or guilt, had overcome their repugnance to try and give her some comfort. It was the loutish twins who had carried her to her bed and tucked her in, covering her almost tenderly with the ratty wool blanket as if afraid that its weight might increase her torment. (Later they managed to collar Dr. Zdrojewicz, the only licensed physician still practicing in Zyldzce, but the old man, unsound himself, took one look at Tsippe, shook his head, and departed.) Mama Bialovsky rose from her own torpor to stroke the girl's brow. Without leeches to bleed her with or the spleen of a she-goat for a poultice to draw out the pain, she tried her best to feed the girl the boiled offscourings that approximated a vegetable broth, which Tsippe refused. Forbidden to climb into bed with her, little Yanki, rather than throw one of his raging tantrums, seemed to deflate like a discarded hand puppet and whimper himself to sleep.

Unable to bring himself to approach the sick bed, Menke fled the house. The mixture of emotions that roiled in his breast were so new to him that he was unable to separate one from the other, or even to give them a name. They throttled and hectored him, those clashing sensations, as he strayed through the ghetto streets looking for he knew not what, until it came to him: He was seeking the gifts that Tsippe had received in her dream. But all the bicycles were now property of the Reich, and as for the rarity of a lady's support garment, Menke had no idea where to look for such an item exclusive of its wearer. (For all he knew brassieres were also forfeit to the Nazis.) Nevertheless, he would persist in scouring the quarter, stealing in his mind across boundaries, climbing mountains and wandering deserts in his quest. But after dark he was forced to obey the curfew like everyone else.

As he slumped back into the house, however, Menke happened to observe an open suitcase, one of those his guests had schlepped along with them in their displacement; and in it, amid clothes in a disarray that a vital Tsippe would never have allowed, was one of Froy Dobke Bialovsky's unoccupied staniks. It was a great beige, bullet-cupped, cantilevered affair, perhaps overlarge now for the woman's shrunken bosom, or simply obsolete in the absence of her vanity. Menke scooped it up and bore it like a trophy to the bed, where he draped it over the blanket in the area beneath which lay Tsippe-Itsl's rattling breast.

"What are you doing?" gasped Mama Dobke, reaching over him to snatch the superfluous garment from off the blanket. "You make a *khoyzek!*" A mockery.

Somewhere between shame and anger, Menke made to take back the garment, but paused when Tsippe's previously unfocused coral-pink eyes suddenly widened and fixed on her nominal husband. *"Mayn mann,"* she was heard to say (and even then Menke winced at the endearment); "Mayn mann," barely audible, "would you cry if a pear tree turned into a bird and flew away?"

He attributed her words to delirium, though they were in fact no more confounding than her typical everyday utterances. They made no sense, of course, but clutching at straws, Menke tried to read in them some glimmer of his vindication. For he'd rightly assumed that he was to blame; his ill-conceived prank had precipitated the act of retributive justice that led to the ruination of the girl. The *Soldaten*, in whose eyes he still retained a degree of exemption, had elected to inflict a proxy punishment on him via the person of an innocent Tsippe-Itsl.

Though she was in and out of consciousness, Menke never again left her bedside. He mopped her brow, dampened her lips; waited patiently for those moments when her eyelids fluttered like an ebbing moth's wings and she babbled more of the inanities that were her cradlesong to herself: "I saw one time a kitchen demon sneeze and the ribbons of flypaper sprayed out from his nose," exhaling a sound like a rustling of dry leaves then laboring to refill her lungs, "I heard him speak from out of his armpit . . ." "I think I was by *ha Shem* created," she panted, not without a hint of pride, "at twilight on the eve of the first Sabbath . . ." And once she squeezed Menke's fingers until they were numb, and said with a nostalgic resignation, "Mayn mann, I almost forgot you already."

When she took her last shallow breath some days later—by then all had lost track of time—Froy Bialovsky's husband, the spidery Reb Itche, who was never known to make a wry remark, observed, "In her case you couldn't tell whether the girl gave up the ghost or the ghost gave up the girl." The words were not spoken disrespectfully, yet Menke glared at the man with a detestation beyond any he'd thought himself capable of. He ultimately extended his loathing to include the entire party of his houseguests, as well as their host, himself, who was finally at fault for everything.

The work detail assigned to removing corpses carted Tsippe-Itsl away in a two-wheeled wagon containing other bodies. The twins had carried her, still bundled in her blanket, out to the wagon without Menke's assistance, following which she was taken to the mass burial site on the opposite side of the river. Since they were not allowed to leave their precinct without authorization, the Jews could no longer properly bury their dead. No matter, death was too commonplace to warrant special rites anymore; and as for the customs of mourning that were also prohibited, weren't the Zyldzcers, in their immobility, involved in a kind of perpetual sitting shivah?

Without the girl to provide for them, the family Bialovsky fell into a morose desuetude. (They hadn't far to fall.) They were barely sustained by the thin rations distributed on irregular days from the soup kitchen in the Lipkunskis' log house. The layabout nephews—Menke had studiously avoided distinguishing one thickheaded twin from the other—were finally driven to some course of action, but by the time they tried to locate the floating black market, it had been effectively shut down. Their scrounging expeditions were not much more successful, returning as they did with little more than gnawed turnips and yellow-brown lettuce leaves. (One of them caught a rat in a trap, which even their famished elders could only ogle in revulsion.) The once bouncing toddler Yanki, fed a mashed concoction of skunk cabbage and bog moss, spat it up and crawled about the floor looking for the more succulent potato bugs. Menke, who all his life had dined on whatever fare came to hand, and that on the fly, suffered less from hunger than from a malignant conscience.

Remorse, however, had not previously figured in Menke's repertoire, nor—despite his near pariah status among his neighbors—had loneliness. Not much given to introspection, it seemed to him now that his whole life had been spent in an effort to elude the truth. What truth? That the world was not, as the proverb had it, a wedding, and the time when wedding jesters were called for had come and gone. I'm all bluff, Menke concluded, and that bluff devoted in large part to pointlessly grabbing the attention of the rabbi's daughter. So where was she? Unable in his mournfulness to evoke a clear picture of Blume's comely Ponim, Menke worried that, if they crossed paths now, it would be as strangers. Just as every Jew—faces sere and distorted from tribulation—was a stranger to every other; and Menke, having glimpsed the stubble-headed skin-and-bones configuration in his mother's looking glass, was a stranger to himself.

Reluctant to abandon his watcher's posture in the chair beside the empty bed, Menke thought he sometimes heard the soughing of Tsippe's breath, though it was only the ragged sighs escaping his own diaphragm. What was he if he was no longer a *letz*, a clown? No one in particular, he supposed—or perhaps less than no one, merely the thing the Jews had become as viewed through the eyes of their despisers. Which had its advantages; since the non-persons the Hitlerites perceived them as might reside in a place below the surface of human emotions, where you were immune to pain and fear. For the nonperson it was only a small step to being nothing at all, a transition of little consequence in God's grand scheme. Tsippe-Itsl, for instance, had had only a brief distance to travel from her bed to her death. So why did she now seem so terribly far away?

A daft thought entered Menke's head: He might present himself at the home of Blume Vaynipl and appeal to the girl to intercede for him with her father; she should ask if he would mentor her friend in assisting him in the creation of his golem. Rejecting the idea for its obvious imbecility, Menke decided instead to apprentice himself to the stagnant disposition of his lodgers. He studied them: Froy Dobke Bialovsky slumped in a kitchen chair, her thick legs (embroidered in varicose veins) spread wide under an unlaundered housedress, while her husband Reb Itche knelt before her with his knobby head in her lap, allowing her to pick the mites from his few remaining hairs. The half sisters (what were their names?), diminished to matchsticks, embracing each other in their tearful incapacitation, while the querulous twins were reduced to swaying at their prayers like chastened cheder boys. The child with its unwiped bum sitting unattended on the floor, listlessly eyeing his mama's occupied lap. From them Menke learned the art of waiting.

He was well advanced in his mastery of that lackluster art when, on a night in late May, there came a knock at the door. It was a soft night, a breeze through the open window slightly alleviating the stuffiness of a house whose interior was redolent with the funk of perishable souls. No one made a move to answer the knock; it could not bode well—though it wasn't the insistent knock of ill tidings. That one would have been delivered with a rifle butt.

"It's your house," growled one of the nephews to Menke, who was once again lying supine atop the unlit stove. (The Bialovsky husband and wife had taken over the bed since Tsippe's demise.) "Since when did you remember it's my house?" muttered Menke, who nevertheless slid from the stove and padded with a thumping heart to the door. Opening it a crack, he spied a shrouded figure standing on the single stone step. There were no working streetlamps in the ghetto, but the wrought platinum moon above the tin rooftops sufficed to illumine a face that for Menke had always seemed to radiate its own light.

"Blume!" he gasped, thunderstruck to find her there, and aware of how late it was, threw open the door and entreated her, "It's after curfew; quick, come inside."

But the girl didn't budge from the step.

"Blume, it's a dangerous hour!" he cautioned.

Still she didn't move, but said something under her breath that Menke couldn't quite catch. She's here, he assumed, to heap more calumny on my head. Do your worst, he thought, then cupped an ear the better to hear her. "I want . . ." Having found her voice, she threw back her scarf somewhat dramatically as if to shake out the mane of her once luxuriant hair—though nothing of it had survived since the fumigation but a velveteen nap. "I want, before we die, to know a bisl love."

Menke was confused. His first thought was to reassure her that no one was going to die, before he remembered their grim reality. "Blume," he reasoned, looking sharply to right and left, "your papa loves you, and your cousins and friends and half the boys in Zyldzce . . ." *I love you,* though the sentiment had lately become sadly abstract.

The girl continued to hold him with her resolute gaze, until some flicker of her meaning began slowly to penetrate his murky brain. His mouth fell open at the utter impossibility of what she seemed to be requesting; a shudder passed through him like the beginnings of some internal mutiny. In what world, other than one turned upside-down, could he ever be appointed an instrument of Blume's desire?

Lest the light from inside expose them to a passing sentry, Menke quickly shut the door behind him. A throng of discordant thoughts crowded his head, all assuring him how utterly unprepared he was for this moment. Not that you could call him inexperienced. Hadn't he once, flush with the kopeks he'd earned in his travels, purchased a woman? (The memory of whose flab and fur still visited him with an unwelcome clarity.) It had been a squalid affair, endured less out of lust than from the wish to undergo an essential rite of passage. Afterward, the shame lingered, alongside the shame from the sin of Onan to which Menke was no stranger; the ethics of the ancestors had a lasting authority. Besides, what means had a young man of satisfying his impure appetites? The Jewish girls were virtuous, the Polish girls contemptuous, and Niobke der Tush, who lived in a shed at the edge of town, was a nursery of diseases. So Menke had suffered

his needfulness in silence and told himself he remained chaste for
Blume's sake. He would marry no one but her, in a ceremony that
could take place only in his imaginings. Because, in the end, he
could aspire to no higher station than that of Blume's fool.

While he stood still, rooted to the doorstep, the girl took his
hand—had she ever before taken his hand?—and led him into the
street. "Blume, this is craziness," he hissed, the words sounding
to his own ears less admonition than question. It was of course
beyond reckless to venture abroad at night, perilous even if you
felt you had entered into an unspoken covenant with the rabbi's
daughter, one that somehow ought to take precedence over the
danger. They had turned a corner, hugging the stuccoed wall of
a former tea shop, before Menke found his tongue again: "Blume,
where are we going?"

She paused to look at him, her fine features more pronounced
than ever as if in compensation for the scarcity of her hair.
"Zanzibar?" she shrugged. "Cloud Cuckoo Land?" How, given the
circumstances, could she find the temerity to tease him?

He had yet to shake off the weight of his long-standing
dejection—let alone the alarm of her unannounced visit—to
sufficiently rise to the moment. Moreover, Menke's own particular
strain of faintheartedness owed more to his anxiety over the role
he'd been charged with than the Gadarene foolhardiness of their
foray. True, the electrifying fact of being abroad in the night with
Blume went some distance toward mitigating their jeopardy. But
since the arrival of the Gestapo contingent, the occupiers had
increased their vigilance, the ghetto boundaries were less porous,
and death's dominion had been established ever more conclusively.
Of course, the topography of the shtetl had been imprinted on
their brains from birth; surely, Menke told himself, he could rely

on the girl's instincts, if not his own, to lead them undetected through its tortured alleys and lanes—but to what purpose?

He nevertheless acquiesced, following her from shadow to shadow, and as the darkness was mercifully vacant of soldiers, smugglers, and bedlamites, their luck held; though Menke wondered if some agency beyond *mazel* might be at work to keep them from being observed. They reached the ghetto barrier at Cinnamon Street, where, in another fortuitous instance, they found the razor wire partially tamped down—perhaps by smugglers (though was there anything left to smuggle?) or even the soldiers themselves, who were known to drive their bucket cars over the unspooled barriers on patrols. Without hesitation Blume had begun to pick her way over the wire, and Menke, only just become aware that she had yet to let go of his sweaty hand, had no recourse but to do the same.

Like every street on the eastern side of Zyldzce, Cinnamon sloped toward the river, and it was down its gentle gradient that Blume had begun to make a dash with Menke in tow. Breathlessly sprinting behind her, he would have liked to make some sly remark of the type he was notable for, but what fortitude he could lay claim to had been spent in advancing this far. Besides, he was still braced for the barked order to Halt! and the subsequent fusillade.

They scrambled across the rickety footbridge and started down the path that led beyond the graveyard into the woods, never once stopping to discuss where they might be headed. The track had been broadened and worn down of late by the frequent passage of wagon wheels, but the snatches of moonlight that flittered in the overarching branches barely lit their way. They were moving forward only on faith now—or rather on Menke's faith in Blume, which he hoped she was deserving of. Then the ovoid moon had disengaged itself, like a soap bubble released from a pipe, from the tangle of black boughs above them; it shone unobstructed now over a glade where the earth was freshly turned above recessed ground. Here, having recognized with a shared gravity the use of the site, the couple paused.

"Blume," whispered Menke, "why aren't we scared?"

He asked because he realized that, curiously, he wasn't: He felt all of a sudden as if they had wandered into the eye of the nightmare. All around them nocturnal hazards abounded; German squadrons prowled the forests, as did the marauding Armia Krajowa, the Polish Resistance, who loved the Jews no more than did the Nazis. Yet, though all logic and common sense disputed it, Menke entertained the possibility that they had entered an inviolable region wherein they could not be touched. He clung to this idea even as he understood how misguided was the conviction, whose source originated from nothing else but his proximity to the girl. But Menke would take his courage wherever he found it.

In answer to his question, however, Blume drew the babushka back over her shorn head and tightened the knot beneath her chin. "Who isn't scared?" she said, her voice still mellifluous despite its tremor, which caused Menke's stomach to turn over like a barrel churn.

It was then he noticed for the first time that she was wearing the dark lace-collared frock she reserved for the High Holidays. It hung on her gaunt body as limply as on a rack, while the delicate cast of her face was stretched taut over its bones.

"Blume," said Menke, making an effort to overcome the fevered palpitations of his heart, "you are as beautiful as a cat in sour cream."

This made her smile. It was a smile one might see through a blindfold when facing a firing squad.

They proceeded together along the footpath back into the trees on the other side of the clearing. At this stage the path was so flocked with weeds as to be nearly imperceptible, but Menke recalled how they'd trekked along it in their childhood, back when Blume was merely an angel-faced sprat and he an unruly cheder *bocher*; and while he didn't feel it his place to propose a destination, he began to think it likely that their steps were tending toward an old secret haunt. It had never, in fact, been a very well-kept secret; other youngsters had also discovered the grotto and explored its reaches as far as they dared. Some of the yeshiva boys declared it to be the Cave of Machpelah, which led all the way to the Holy Jerusalem, though none had to anyone's knowledge ever attempted the journey. The place had anyway been long since supplanted in their memories by more immediately pressing concerns.

Then the low-lying escarpment reared in front of them, with its limestone overhang shaped like the head of a wide-mouthed fish. "The Leviathan" was what the truant yeshiva scholars had somewhat predictably dubbed the piscine outcrop. The mouth of the fish, which formed the cavern's burrow-like entrance, was concealed by a mesh of intertwined twigs and creepers that served as a makeshift door. Neither Menke nor Blume spoke, both having acquired the habit of silence in keeping with the impetuousness of their expedition. Each stole a sheepish sidelong glance at the other, but it was Blume who took the initiative, lifting the flimsy portal out of the way. Directly a lemony light streamed from the opening and the two companions knelt to peer into the cave. What they saw, in place of the gaping emptiness of former days, was an oil lamp atop a pickle barrel illuminating a habitat of sorts. With no occupant in evidence, the cave's interior begged inspection.

This time Menke took the lead, trusting that Blume would follow, which she did, careless of disarranging the dress she'd donned for this singular occasion. They stooped through the tight fissure then straightened to take in their surroundings—the soggy pallet of rushes and the cracked porcelain ewer and basin beside it, the odd property of a dressmaker's dummy decked in a tallis and lady's undergarment, the crunching of God knew what under their feet. There was a chill and a dense, unsavory odor, and the improbable installation of several stacks of books leaning precariously against the chamber's knuckled wall. They were—as their spines attested—neither scriptural nor secular classics, but a miscellany of mostly schlock Yiddish novels. Still, you wouldn't have judged them trivial by the measure of Blume's enthusiasm as she swooped over them.

"Look, Menke!" she exclaimed, taking a volume from the top of a pile. Schooled by her father in the Hebrew canon, she had never in her private reading made much distinction between the sacrosanct and the profane. "Here's Yankev Dinezon's *Der Shvartzer yungermantshik*," she exulted, swapping the book in her hand for another, "and Avrom Reisen's *Damn the Nose, As Long As There Is a Dowry*—ach, don't you love that title!" She continued to comb the stacks, fondling individual books like spoils from a treasure chest. "Opatoshu's *Romance of a Horse Thief*, do you know it?" she mused, wholly absorbed by such an embarrassment of riches, "and—*gottenyu*—my favorite Isaac Meyer Dik . . ."

Watching her gleeful distraction, Menke wondered if Blume had maybe forgotten the reason behind their heedless escapade. The thought brought with it, surprisingly, an element of relief. They were, the two of them, like children again, who had trespassed together into some spellbound hermitage. It was a thrilling notion, made abruptly more persuasive by the materialization out of the blackness of what looked for all the world like an authentic ogre. "Welcome, *yingelakh*," he croaked hospitably, a bent figure in a long, patched coat with a gnawed whisk broom of a beard and a humped back. "It's good that they should find pleasure, the young people, in mayn excellent *biblyotek*."

It took a hair-raising instant for the intruders to unfreeze. Then, both shaken to the core, they exchanged a look that included an implicit agreement. Backing up an unsteady few steps, they turned about and attempted to scramble as one person through the grotto's constricted egress. For a moment they were wedged shoulder to shoulder in the tight passage before they managed to extricate themselves and tumble back out into the night.

They ran, retracing their steps, kicking through ferns and anemones and snatching at each other's fingers as they raced along the forest path. Somewhere in their headlong flight, one or the other, then both, began to chuckle. How ridiculous for them to have been so frightened by such a harmless old kucker with a face like a hairy excrescence, when the whole world was governed by archfiends. What a colossal joke! As they plunged farther into the woods, their laughter swelled, becoming fitful, a giddiness amplified by the sheer release of being able to laugh again. Having emerged from the trees back into the plowed clearing, each tried in vain to shush the other only to succumb to an even more full-throated burst of hilarity. So light-headed had Blume become, not to say out of breath, that she collapsed onto the mossy turf at the edge of the glade, and as she still held onto his hand, Menke was drawn to his knees on the cushioned ground alongside her.

But for their waning gaiety and the ringing stridulation of the cicadas, it was a quiet night, the hemlock-fragrant glade imparting nothing of what lay beneath. The moon, pale as a cataractous eye, still shed enough light to reveal to Menke that Blume's merriment had suddenly ceased and her face become tenacious again. She was leaning back on her elbows, a lissome girl in a holiday frock buttoned to the neck, its skirt fanning about her. Her headscarf lay in the grass behind her, the bone-deep beauty of her face at provocative odds with the bristles of her cropped head, while her eyes, still moist from laughing, directed their unyieldingly expectant gaze at the crouching young man.

Menke retained his insipid grin. "Mayn *bashert*," he wanted to declare as he knelt beside her, "my destined one." But instead he offered timidly, "Blume, so much room you take up in my head I should charge you rent," and when that elicited only a ghost of the smile he had previously roused, he tried again. "So Heshie asks Menachem the pickle man," he yammered, "'What kind pickles you got?' 'I got sour,' says Menachem, 'half-sour, gherkins, dill; lime pickles I got . . .'"

Blume put a finger to his lips. "Shah," she said. Then, with thoughtful deliberation (and visibly trembling fingers), she began to unbutton the smocked bodice of her dress. Menke watched her with eyes on stems, his heart stampeding as she opened the dress, pulled down the shoulders of her cambric chemise, and exposed her swan-white breasts to the moon. He tried but failed to swallow the lump in his throat, and gripped by a paralyzing awe, continued to kneel there adoring her this side of idolatry. But wasn't idolatry—an untimely thought chose that moment to insinuate itself—wasn't such worship a violation of the Second Commandment? Menke let go a guttural groan. "Feh on your

Commandments!" he heard himself exclaim. Tonight in this place where desire—the fervent aching to stroke, lick, nuzzle, and kiss—was stronger even than fear, he would love the girl as she wished to be loved and in the process become the man she deserved.

But before he could summon the nerve to take her in his arms and gather her warmth to himself, an amber beam, overruling the moonlight, enveloped them both in its brightness. The beam's focus sharpened to a concentrated circle of light, flitting like a will-o'-the-wisp over Blume's bare breasts. She sat up at once, hastening to cover herself with her arms, as a rude voice intoned, "Was haben wir hier?"

I n Jerusalem Gershom took to his bed, or rather the sofa with its deep, crocheted cushions in his study. There, as in every other room of his house, he was surrounded by books. The walnut shelves stretched from floor to ceiling so that, entering the house, you had the impression that the very red-tiled roof was upheld by walls, tiers, and pillars of books. You had the sense that its resident dwelled not so much in a quince-hedged cottage of timber and stone as in an edifice made of words. Gershom had amassed his own library with the same voracity with which he'd helped to gather the far-flung volumes stored at the Offenbach Depot. He'd made his home a similar repository, a comprehensive archive of Judaica spanning the range of texts from sacred to civil, antique to modern, many with brown and brittle pages faded from epochs of intense scrutiny, some with pages yet unread and uncut. Only now, as he browsed their tooled and banded spines from his prostration, he felt as if the books had turned their backs on him, and all the staggering knowledge he'd acquired from them had somehow been recalled by the works themselves.

He had scarcely left that sofa for the greater part of a year. The purple bougainvillea outside the barred casement window bloomed, withered, and blossomed again; goldcrests and warblers sang in the date palm, took flight, and returned; but Gershom was seldom moved to look out the window. There was even some snow in Jerusalem that winter, the climate of the old city on its promontory incompatible with the more temperate new town of Tel Aviv down on the coast—only an hour and what could seem light years away. Gershom's ruddy-cheeked Fanya, playing her part as the faithful hausfrau, was tolerant for a time. She fielded the many phone calls, discouraged visitors, and diplomatically declined invitations to formal dinners and prestigious conferences. For a while she even spoon-fed the convalescent his vegetable bouillon; she massaged his flat feet and read him the badgering letters from Hannah Arendt, the blandishing letters from Teddy Adorno, the dogmatic and casuistical ones from Martin Buber and Leo Strauss, while Gershom clapped his hands over his ears. Then she lost patience.

"Gershom," she told him, "you didn't hear the Irgun blew up the King David Hotel? You didn't feel the ground quake?" And later: "Gershom, Weizmann talked the British government into terminating the Mandate; he nudged the UN General Assembly into making a partition resolution for Palestine." "Gershom, Ben-Gurion has declared Israel a state! The Arabs are killing Jews, the Jews are killing Arabs—it's a bloodletting! Get off your *Hinterteil* and reenter already history."

"Fanya," replied Gershom sourly, adjusting the damp cloth over his eyes, "I came to the Yishuv to escape history."

"Nu," she said, "from history you can hide? Where the Jews go, so does history."

She was not without her dram of wisdom, Fanya.

When she still failed to rouse him from his malaise, she reminded him that no one was paying him a salary to lie doggo;

she advised him of the extent of his neglect, not just of his work but of her. "Not that you'd notice but I'm still a sensual being," she stated—Fanya in her shapeless housedress and carpet slippers, her dowager's double chin and thinning hair the color of rust. This got Gershom's attention enough that he raised the cloth over one eye. Fanya assured him that, while *he* might be done with physical intimacy, she was not. He unblinkered the other eye. Then she breezily confessed to a dalliance while he was away with Gershom's university colleague Hugo Bergmann.

Gershom sat bolt upright. "Fanya, what are you saying!"

Bergmann was a man Gershom had always respected not only for his philosophical acumen but for his quondam membership in the Prague circle that had included Franz Kafka. Whenever in proximity to Bergmann, Gershom found himself sniffing about his person, as if some tincture of Kafka's genius might have clung to the man's tobacco-scented tweeds. But Bergmann's affair with Gershom's first wife Escha had been the final indignity of their already failing marriage. It's true that his transition back to bachelorhood and his marriage soon after to Fanya had been virtually seamless, his friendship with Bergmann only slightly bruised in the process. But to be cuckolded twice by the same man: "This is unconscionable!" Gershom was struggling to get to his feet, the knit shawl sliding from about his shoulders.

Outraged, he was on the verge of telling his wife—eye for an eye—about the floozy in his hotel room in Prague, though he himself was still unconvinced of her materiality. Then he saw that Fanya was grinning, her broad face with its calf's eyes having recovered something of its youthful sauciness when she smiled.

"You're a wicked woman," accused Gershom, having realized that she'd lied to him. He would have given her an earful had he not so much admired the canny way she had jolted him out of his overextended *weltschmerz*. "I think I'll demand satisfaction from Bergmann all the same," he muttered. Fanya told him don't be an ass.

Later that same day he waited in futility at a taxi stand near his house; then, forbearance spent, he flagged down a paneled delivery van and offered the reluctant driver an inordinate sum to take him from the deceptively peaceful enclave of Rehavia up to Mount Scopus. When the man still wavered, Gershom reached through the window, stuffed the money into his vest pocket, and climbed purposefully into the backseat. The jug-eared driver removed the cash from his pocket, examined it, and slid it under his cap. Then he shifted the car into gear and abruptly accelerated.

He chose a bewilderingly circuitous route to the university, as if trying to lose imaginary pursuers. He wound between the crowded concrete tenements of the *haredi* quarter of Mea Shearim with its posters warning heathens and blasphemers to keep out. Bug-eyed and white-knuckled, the driver zigzagged among the fortified Arab houses and shanties of Wadi Al-Joz, dodging a fried cheese vendor, weaving between an immovable donkey and a man in a burnoose and bandolier. Then, as there was no way to avoid it, he began the ascent up the rocky corridor through Sheik Jarrah. This stretch had become a virtual no-man's-land since the outset of the war, subject now to frequent Arab attacks and land mines; but for Gershom, having just come out of a long retirement, the contours of the outside world had yet to reassume their former definition, and he remained remarkably oblivious to the danger.

Sweating rivulets, the driver navigated the switchbacks and managed to steer his vehicle, with its silent passenger and rattling scrap metal cargo, up the slope to the university without incident.

The campus sat on the ridge that had once been the vantage from which the Jews, prohibited from entering Jerusalem during Roman and Byzantine rule, were allowed to look down in bereavement upon their capital of times past. Now the faint thundering of the guns from below signaled that the Jews were attempting, after millennia, to take back the city again. Zion, it seemed (though sometimes regretfully to Gershom), was more than an idea; it was a palpable aspiration that would manifest itself by occupying geographical space rather than simply enduring in time. Palestine, or should he say "Israel"—the word resounded even louder in Gershom's mind than the distant crackling of artillery—was in a life-and-death struggle for its survival. But why couldn't the inevitable have been postponed just a little longer? The Jews had yet to rally sufficient strength to imagine the unimaginable that had only recently befallen them. Who could ask them so soon to imagine themselves as warriors?

On the hilltop campus the driver received Gershom's gratitude without response, his tires squealing as he sped away. Gershom promptly commenced nosing about the empty lecture halls, stalking past offices in which a few die-hard colleagues were sheltering in place due to the siege mentality that had gripped the school. He crossed a deserted quadrangle and entered the austere Modernist citadel of the library, long his personal sanctum. Toward the rear of the building, in back of the stacks, was a common room whose congenial wainscoted warmth was in contrast to the building's functional architecture. There, Gershom was not surprised to find, standing and seated, a party of elite university notables engaged in cheerless conversation. Bergmann was present, the smoke from his briar pipe wreathing the green-shaded library lamps on the end tables. A tall man with a walrus mustache, he loomed above the leather wingback chair in which a frumpish Martin Buber, yarmulke perched like a listing cupola atop his bald pate, sat brooding into his frosty beard. Adjacent them in an identical armchair sat their sartorial chancellor Judah Magnes, a deep frown distressing his otherwise urbane features. On the chancellor's right hand, resting his bony backside against a ticking radiator, his head bowed prayerfully, was Gershom's fellow archivist (also a Prague Circle alumnus) Felix Weltsch.

Along the way Gershom had prepared a wordy apology for his long absence, which was needless of course; all were aware of the crippling depression that had left him flattened these many months. Moreover, consumed as they were with lamenting the future of Zionism, they greeted him without bothering to inquire after his health, but rather as if he'd only stepped out briefly to relieve himself. "Scholem, at last!" said Magnes, casually waving the eyeglasses in his hand. Apparently he'd been expected. So, instead of an apology, Gershom offered the kind of droll observation that would come to characterize much of his speech in the ensuing years.

"Looks like we're still five short of a minyan," he quipped, which elicited only despondent grumbling.

These were the wise and indispensable men, whose philosophies had done much to shape the original vision of the Yishuv. Drop a bomb on the Jewish National Library and deprive Western civilization of some of its best minds. But they were also dreamers, and here in the face of the tumultuous present they appeared to Gershom, taking the atmosphere's temperature, like passengers stranded on the Raft of the Medusa. They were all, including himself, members of Brit Shalom, the Covenant of Peace movement, which had for decades called for a binational state shared equally by Arabs and Jews. It was an unrealistic cloud-castle fantasy from the first, that was being blown to pieces even as they spoke.

"We are," Bergmann had once grandiloquently submitted in the salons of the German Colony, "the last flicker of the humanist nationalist flame," and no one protested when he repeated the sentiment fatalistically in the past tense today.

"Neither to dominate nor be dominated," sighed Magnes, uttering the movement's guiding principle in a melancholy register; and Buber, sighing: "Look at us now, like yeast seeking dough."

Having settled himself cross-legged on the cushioned window seat, Gershom felt called upon to add his voice to the general requiem but somehow couldn't bring himself to contribute to the prevailing mood. After all, there was a war on and the puncturing of a utopian dream seemed suddenly the least of the collateral damage about to occur. Perhaps his lengthy bout of inertia had rendered him more clear-eyed after all. He knew as well as the others that the political career of Zionism would create a circumstance full of undying doubt, despair, and compromise precisely because it was taking place on earth and not the moon; he understood that now a stiff dose of realpolitik was inescapable. But when the heavy-lidded, waxen-faced Weltsch noted that Dr. Scholem was being conspicuously quiet, Gershom replied once again gnomically, "Me? I am the no-man from no-man's land."

The company's lamentations continued (exclusive of Gershom's counsel) throughout the days they spent—despite all their frantic communications—literally besieged, cut off by the fighting from traveling between the university and Jerusalem proper. Their collective jeremiad continued during their evacuation by armed motorcade from Mount Scopus and amidst the subsequent reports of murderous battles and their ambiguous conclusions; they persisted in their hand-wringing, these men of parts, through all the years of the university's exile from the hilltop campus to the less panoramic site near the nascent government complex at Givat Ram. They carried on grieving even as the militias of the Jewish Underground roared to the surface and were consolidated among the agile Israel Defense Forces, and the entire population—not excluding certain *éminences grises* who served in the emergency humanitarian agencies—was conscripted to the cause. Massacres were perpetrated on both sides, each with its own respective narrative of victimhood; unsatisfactory armistices were negotiated, flags were raised, bodies buried, the first Knesset established—and all the while Gershom kept his colleagues off-balance with a cagey irreverence regarding the fate of the new nation.

Attempts to engage him in serious discourse were often met with evasive rejoinders. Asked by Chancellor Magnes, poking his head into Gershom's library carrel, "Have you seen the *tokhes-lekker* Ben-Gurion picked for his finance minister?" Gershom replied without looking up from his work, "I keep mainly to the back of the house, so I don't see much."

Felix Weltsch, after a failed attempt at initiating an exchange about the embryonic nation's destiny, confided in his friend his recent diagnosis of an inoperable malignancy. "Cancer, shmancer," Gershom assured him, giving his back a friendly slap, "so long as you got your health." And when, soon after, the poor man began prematurely to plan his funeral, Gershom teased him, "Weltsch, you're such a *nudnik*, your hearse will have to follow the other cars."

Once Buber let a fart in Gershom's presence, and feigning panic-stricken alarm, Gershom inquired, "Do I smell Zyklon B?"

Ask after his well-being and the redoubtable scholar of Jewish mysticism might tell you, "It's not a question of staying healthy but finding a sickness you like."

In the classroom he frequently made jokes at his students' expense: "You're not completely useless, Mr. Yavnai," addressing an incurably feckless youth, "you can always be employed as a bad example." And to another student's boneheaded gloss concerning Rashi's incomplete commentary on Job: "Marvelous!" declared Gershom. "With such a *kop* you might have been a member of the Sanhedrin in the time of Akiva."

"Why," questioned an equally obtuse classmate, "why for such ignorance the exorbitant praise?"

Explained Gershom, "The Sanhedrin hadn't read Rashi either."

Ask him, "Professor, may I please close the window? It's cold outside," and he'd answer, "If you close the window, will it be warm outside?"

On an afternoon when he'd invited a select group of scholars to his home for tea and Fanya's homemade rugelakh, one young man, stupefied by his library, wondered, "Dr. Scholem, have you read all these books?"

"What," exclaimed his teacher, mimicking shock, "am I supposed to *read* this rubbish too?"

His soaring lectures might transpose a colorless classroom into a breathtakingly supernal realm, but they could also lead one through dark dialectical forests of thorns to places where you followed only at your own fraught risk.

"The absolute word is meaningless," Gershom was known to proclaim, his forefinger lifted (suggested one sharp-tongued student) like the flaming sword upheld by the angel at the gate of Paradise, "but it is also pregnant with meaning."

"At the core of the mystical experience," he asserted, "all religious authority is destroyed in the name of authority."

And, with his hands on his desk and his myopic eyes dilated with a fierce energy: "Holiness is a rustling of madness in the blood."

Though it surely couldn't have been attributed to the unresolvable paradoxes at the heart of his pedagogy (or to his bad jokes), one still had to wonder why one or two of his most gifted and devoted students, disciples really, took their own lives. But despite the somewhat Mephistophelian character at the center of what was becoming the cult of Scholem, all attested that there was a spirit of playfulness behind even Gershom's unkindest gibes.

S cratching at his head lice until his scalp began to bleed, Menke asked himself why he and Blume had not stayed hidden in the grotto. They might have evaded the ogre and groped their way into the cavern's darker recesses; they could have threaded its subterranean passages until they were disgorged into the garden of God's pet Jews. But what, he wondered, prying a loose tooth from his spongy gums—what if the cave had turned out to be a blind alley? Then he might have told the mamzrim, "I know where the Jews hid their treasure." They would have followed him, stooping single file into the grotto where Menke would have corralled them along with the ogre's repossessed books. He would have rolled a boulder in front of the entrance, dusted off his hands, and received universal plaudits from the people he'd delivered from evil. Blume would have cleaved to the hero with a fervid embrace, but Blume—it was discovered—had swallowed a bottle of Lysol and died in agony. A good Jewish daughter, though, she had waited for her father to precede her into kingdom come.

It happened that two members of the Judenrat, the honorable Rabbi Berel Moszczenik himself, head of the Old New Synagogue, and his brother-in-law Israel Erlich, both of them recent widowers, had escaped the ghetto. They had managed to make it as far as a nearby crofter's farm before they were tracked down and shot in the hen coop where they'd gone to ground. (The patrol also shot the farmer and his family for good measure.) Their delinquency had sullied the entire council with guilt by association; and so the surviving members were forced at gunpoint to assemble in the wagonyard behind the market, where they would face their just punishment. The rest of the ghetto's population, ambulatory or not, was called by order of the occupiers to witness the event.

It was a morning when mourning doves trilled, poppies and clover sprouted about the fence posts surrounding the yard, and mild breezes diffused the ordinarily horseshit-laden air. The freshness of the day was enough to make the gathered Jews wonder, at least those still capable of wondering, how the cruelty of the winter they'd just endured could extend into this pristine season. Menke Klepfisch, whose own punishment was that the barbarians had declined to murder him, was present among the crowd. He was there but not there, after the fashion of those who had seen things beyond which there was nothing more to behold. He saw but could not see Blume among the onlookers, held tottering by a pair of big-boned Balabustas, and was confident that she no longer saw him. He hoped she was equally blind to her fragile father leaning on the handle of the shovel he'd been issued along with the other members of the council. Once prominent shtetl dignitaries, the remnant of the Judenrat were reduced to a scarecrow brigade, already with one foot in the grave they'd been assigned to dig. It was a shallow grave whose measurements the Oberfeldwebel, a stalwart sergeant major in his cockaded field cap, had meticulously specified: "Fifteen meters in length," he bellowed, striding officiously back and forth, "three in width, one in depth . . ."

As the men began to dig in the packed earth, it soon became apparent that Rabbi Vaynipl, weighing little more than the long-handled implement he wielded, lacked the strength to proceed in the task. No one paid him much heed as he slumped to the ground, where he was left to sit wheezing and ignored so long as the others, with only slightly more stamina, continued their toil. Some did collapse but were soon reinvigorated by the menace of the malevolently snarling Alsatian dogs; the dogs tugged at leashes held by men in black uniforms wearing visored caps with death's-head insignias. These were members of a small elite *staffel* of the Allgemeine SS, arrived in Zyldzce to further enforce, in collaboration with the Gestapo echelon already in residence, the region's racial policy. Officially, they had authority over the occupying Wehrmacht officers, but were content to bide their time while the original invaders carried on with their own brand of brutishness.

Soldiers and attendant Polish citizens heaped scorn on the laborers throughout the insufferable period it took them to complete the trench. Then the Obersturmführer von Graf und Trach, appearing less raffish in his comportment since the coming of the death's-head unit, expressed his rather lukewarm satisfaction: Arching a brow, he allowed the monocle to drop from his eye to the end of its ribbon, which was apparently the signal for the sergeant major to instruct his subordinates to oblige the faltering Judenrat members to fall to their knees. So depleted were they that all complied almost thankfully; they knelt without protest at the lip of the excavation, all but the already seated old rabbi, whose drooping head suggested he might no longer be conscious. A nod from the commandant, and the sergeant major unholstered his service revolver, then strode behind the row of genuflecting offenders, pausing briefly to shoot each one in the back of the head. (When his own weapon had emptied of cartridges, he was instantly handed another by an enlisted man.) With every sonorous discharge blood and bone sprayed in a fleeting crimson plume from the scalp of each Jew as he tumbled in his turn into the pit.

Amid the keening that arose among the assembled who had not swooned outright, some voices could be heard murmuring Kaddish. It was then that the waning Rabbi Vaynipl was roused from his crumpled posture by the sergeant major's boot in his spine. He was raised from the ground by the collar of his tattered caftan, then handed his shovel and told to spread the dirt from the unearthed mound over the bodies lying in the trench. This was the moment, thought Menke, for the old rabbi to summon the occult powers that had lain dormant in his feeble breast all these months, and transform the shovel's handle into a serpent. The serpent's sting would change the sergeant major straightaway into a pillar of manure, which would in turn frighten off the rest of the awestruck Hitlerites. But instead the old man endeavored with his whistling exhalations to sprinkle a few shovelfuls of soil into the trough. His performance was so slow and painstaking, however, that the observing SS overseers could not withhold their impatience. *"Beeil dich!"* they shouted, *"Mach schnell!"* Again the commandant signaled the sergeant major, who, rather than waste another bullet, simply shoved the spent Rabbi Vaynipl head foremost into the pit. A hasty selection of sapless Yids were mustered to take up the abandoned shovels and finish filling in the open grave.

The moaning of the assembled had subsided, many struggling to keep from collapsing from the exhaustion of having stood for so long. The dogs had been muzzled and the late morning was eerily silent but for the birdsong and the *chuff* of the shovel blades biting into the mound of dirt, the pebbly sound of earth falling over the corpses in the long trench. Like everyone, Menke ached from standing, a pain intensified by the lingering lacerations bestowed by the soldiers who'd forced him to watch what they'd done to Blume—whose body, Menke now saw clearly, had gone limp in the arms of the women attempting to hold her up. As a consequence, she was spared the sight of the monstrosity that caused the Jews, Poles, and even the occupiers to grow still; it seemed there were yet things that could stop even a cauterized heart. For they were riveted, one and all, by the sight of an old man's leathery fist boring its way from beneath the surface of the earth, its fingers furling and unfurling in the air like tentacles.

Menke squeezed shut his eyes, though not before he'd had a glimpse of the rabbi's great clay creature towering above the heads of the ghetto dwellers. It would step forth at any moment and drag Rabbi Vaynipl root and branch out of the ground, then turn around to decimate the enemy. But the golem stood motionless, as impotent and defenseless as any other worn-out Yehudi. So it was left to Menke to back away from the throng and pluck from the base of a fence post an acacia sprout hung with a cluster of tiny pink buds. Then he knelt, if only in his mind, at the edge of the grave and tickled the palm of the upraised hand with the feathery root until the gnarled fingers closed around it. The commandant shouted for the Jews to continue spreading earth into the trench, covering over the grisly hand, but the sprout remained visible, its buds unfolding into blossoms, its slender stalk shooting up to become, all at once, a lofty flowering acacia tree. Without a second thought the Jews hoisted one another into its branches, where they remained embowered among its spreading limbs beyond the reach of their foes.

IF THE BEETLE-BROWED BLACKSMITH PERETZ the Hammer had looked up as he was being escorted into Lazrov the grain merchant's house—which the Geheime Staatspolizei and their SS cronies had taken over for their headquarters—he might have caught sight of Menke Klepfisch perched like a gargoyle on the roof. He would have seen the ragged *yungatsch* hugging his shins, resting his chin on the knees that poked through his torn cotton breeches. Reb Peretz was on his way to an interrogation that would result in his vicious maiming, as would the interrogations of Nathan Bressler, Ossip Epstein, and Yetta Kaleko. The crimes they were charged with were random and immaterial but gave the Gestapo interrogators an opportunity to make use of their diabolical playthings—the spiked oxtail, the strappado, "the goat," an electrical contraption with a crank that the interrogators were still trying to get the hang of. It was in any case a way of passing the time until the transport that would carry away the Jews was brought to the rail spur outside the wretched little town.

But the branch line had been blown up by some faction of the Resistance and the train was delayed indefinitely. The not-so-secret police and their SS auxiliary, there to expedite the wholesale removal of the Zyldzce ghetto, were becoming gallingly impatient. Nor was the morale of the occupying Wehrmacht regiment much better. The common soldiers had grown increasingly disgruntled by their backwater posting; the more they'd been compelled to terrorize the Jews, the more, it seemed, they abhorred the Jews for having been forced to inflict terror upon them. That said, the greater portion of their brutality was perhaps bred less from spite than boredom—which made of murder, unchecked by their senior officers, a recreational pastime. They felt anyway justified in pruning a population whose density further fouled an already contaminated atmosphere.

They killed the rachitic Luba Ratner, with her scrap of a daughter Hodl clinging to her skirts, for having accidentally made eye contact with their *Kamerads*; they killed the widow Sorl for scowling and Menassah the distiller whose fetal form lay across their path, though he might have been already dead. When at loose ends, the Soldaten took potshots at the errant berserkers from the Kotsk asylum, though more in fun than with lethal intent. Aim at their feet and they would leap, whoop, and perform lopsided dances, and none performed more animatedly, in a mud puddle or on a low-slung roof, than the mangy halfwit who had once secured the favor of the Obersturmführer himself. (Some, however, remarking on his basilisk stare, judged the undesirable a bad omen, and rather than shoot at him, merely spat and muttered a "Kaynehoreh" against the evil eye, a habit they'd picked up from the Yids.)

"He's gone and joined the meshugayim," repined Mama Bialovsky, surprised to find herself so distraught over Menke's defection from plain sense; while her mumpish nephews took some smug credit for having driven him out of his own home, if not his mind.

In truth, Menke had more or less forgotten he had a home, or anyway the overrun hovel a father he no longer even remembered had once thrown together with salvaged materials. The past was eclipsed by a present that bore little resemblance to anyplace he'd ever known. The aggregation of off-kilter houses and raveled streets was similar to the town he'd grown up in, but in this one the *sheydim* and *mazzikim*, along with flesh-devouring ghouls, were thicker on the ground than mortal men. In theory, though, if you simply ignored them, they would come to doubt their own existence; and denying the reality of these demonic arbiters had its subsidiary benefits as well, in that you found yourself denying by extension your own debased being.

This gave a person the advantage of being free to poke about the streets at his leisure, sleeping in the open, competing with dogs and children for scraps, conducting his own shadowy reconnaissance of the ghetto in extremis. He could spy on imps and ghosts, and listen unnoticed to neighbors exchanging their *loshen horeh*, their dolorous hearsay about the transports coming to take them God knew where. But surely, some argued, there could be no place worse than their own stinking ghetto—while others whispered of death factories where the chimneys flared from furnaces stoked with the bodies of Jews. Though even by the extraordinary standards of their current suffering, such things could not be imagined. Such things were the stuff of dark fairy tales. Moreover, the yehudim of Zyldzce had by and large lost the faculty of being curious about their fate, and were mostly too disheartened to care.

Meanwhile, beyond the shtetl, Operation Barbarossa had concluded in a disastrous rout of the Wehrmacht at Stalingrad, Allied bombers were reducing Cologne and the Ruhr to embers, and the Germans were in full retreat from North Africa—not that such news would have mattered much to Zyldzce's survivors, even had it reached their ears; since when had they belonged to the world beyond the ghetto? But the news increased the urgency among their overlords to have done with the filthy business of eradicating the Jews in their charge once and for all. After that they might get on with the more consequential endeavor of prosecuting a war whose victory for Deutschland was still predetermined. And so, the latecomer Gestapo subunit, weary of the playthings with which they could only mishandle one Jew at a time, were delighted when definitive orders came down from the Reichszentrale für die jüdische Auswanderung, the branch of the Generalgouvernement in Berlin responsible for all matters concerning the Yids: Finally they had been authorized to administer a blanket retribution with regard to the Jews under their jurisdiction. The Gestapo and their recently arrived SS complement, between whom there was only the finest of distinctions, invited the commanding officer of the occupying force and his lieutenants to attend a critical meeting at their headquarters to discuss the immediate implementation of a valedictory *Aktion*.

In the absence of the roving Einsatzgruppen squads with their mobile gas vans, Zyldzce's military command would have to rely on other more fundamental means of liquidating the ghetto. It was toward that end that the sober-faced council in their decorated black and gray uniforms were seated around the long table in what had been the merchant Lazrov's dining room. Throughout their congress the mood in the room was unusually grave, conscious as they were of personifying in a body the iron will of the Fatherland. Having unanimously agreed upon their method and the logistics involved, they were just wrapping up their deliberations when an intruder, a supremely unkempt specimen of the very people they were preparing to depopulate, appeared in the doorway. Conversation dwindled to an incredulous silence as heads turned toward the unwelcome visitor.

"I tried to see things from your point of view," pronounced Menke, his voice almost stentorian in its pitch, "but I couldn't get my head that far up my tushie."

The Obersturmführer von Graf und Trach, whose back

was to the door, swiveled about in his chair. "Minky," he asked speculatively, "is that you? You're looking a bit out at the elbows."

"I don't think of you so much as vultures," replied Menke, still clamorous, "but as something a vulture would eat."

Several men had risen to their feet, one of them—a high-ranking SS officer in tight-fitting tunic and trousers flared at the hip—drawing his weapon. "What is this creature?" he snarled.

Without bothering to stand himself, the commandant waved an informally defensive hand. "Gentlemen," he said with his air of imperturbable bonhomie, "allow me to introduce Minky Shnauze Mouth. Herr Minky has kindly condescended to entertain us during these tiresome months with his humorous badinage." The acknowledgement did nothing to dissolve the tension in the room.

But it was not with the purpose of diverting the mamzrim that Menke had breached the razor wire cordon behind Shmulke's tavern; then, finding the tavern empty, proceeded to the firehouse command post (also empty) and on to the joint headquarters of the Schutzstaffel and secret police in the grain merchant's house. Neither was it with the intent of martyring himself that he had gate-crashed that nether space, though even Menke must have been aware of inviting his martyrdom. It's doubtful, however, that the unsightly lad himself could have explained the irrepressible impulse that had brought him there. All he knew was that he'd awoken in the fodder bin in back of Meir Kaplan's goat shed with the conviction that the barbs and jests, which he'd thought himself entirely bereft of, had somehow replenished themselves in his sleep. Removing himself from the bin, he picked the clinging bits of straw and fly larvae from his jumper, stretched his stiff bones in the dewy mandarin dawn, and felt blessed. Vintage wisecracks tickled his brain like a sprinkling of manna; they prickled his scalp as when blind Samson's docked hair began to grow again. And so, before the moment passed and left him once more disarmed, Menke set off in search of a suitable venue in which to exercise his God-given talent.

"You are so ugly," he loudly announced, "I think your portrait will hang itself." He said this to no one in particular, though the officer with the unholstered Mauser, a crescent scar across his high cheek, seemed to take the remark personally. He aimed the gun directly at the intruder's grimy brow. But in the instant before he pulled the trigger, the Obersturmführer, with uncharacteristic alacrity, had leapt to his feet and deflected the pistol's muzzle with his swagger stick. The pistol discharged into the ceiling, plaster sprinkling onto the long table through a mist of lavender smoke; then the reverberant room became quiet again.

"Herr Oberst," roared the thwarted officer, the scar on his cheek angrily enkindled, "this is insupportable!"

"But amusing, Hauptmann Müller, no?" replied the commandant coolly.

The disposition of the room, however, seemed inclined in one accord toward no.

It should be noted that the Obersturmführer was not greatly esteemed among the presiding Schutzstaffel, reports of his practically absentee administration of the town and its environs having preceded their arrival. Aware of their censure, the commandant had made a concerted effort to redeem his reputation through an unimpeachable deportment. But there were times when he bridled under their judgment and was of a mind to defy their meddlesome authority. This was apparently one of those occasions.

"Gentlemen," he submitted, taking advantage of the gathering's still suspended animation, "don't you think that, in light of what his people would call—what is it they call it?—his chutzpah, the Jew at least deserves an opportunity to choose his own death? Minky," addressing the uninvited guest with his standard flightiness (though one might have detected a subtle quaver in his voice), "how would you like to die?"

There was a moment's heated confusion during which the assembled seemed unable to determine who was the greater offender, the jüdisch fool for his outrage or the commandant for his interposition. It was a moment too when the madcap Menke, encouraged by the stir his trespass had created, believed he might stall the pitiless forward progress of the almighty German Reich for the time it took him to make up his mind. Stagily stroking his chin, he wondered just how long he could sustain the hiatus— maybe until the Messiah was finally informed via ram's horn that his people were about to be blotted out? But along with what he took for the return of his wits, Menke had also recovered his sense of timing and knew that not another second should be lost.

In answer to the Herr Oberst's question—the man was after all deserving of an answer, for hadn't he (for what it was worth) saved Menke's life along with handing him the line?—Menke thoughtfully replied, "How about from old age?"

Then it was as if his response, while wholly unappreciated, had nevertheless broken a spell, releasing the company to pursue without further delay the vitally important matter at hand. Soldiers having entered the house, the Oberleutnant at their head saluted and declared that all was in readiness for the commencement of the Aktion; his men-at-arms only awaited the decisive order. That order was peremptorily given by the Schutzstaffel's Oberführer, a chinless, comfortably paunched, brightly complacent personage seated at the head of the table. (The commandant, reseated at the foot, appeared to have no voice at all in the immediate proceedings.) Punctuating the order with an affirming nod, the Oberführer transferred a sheaf of documents to the adjutant sitting next to him, who began stamping individual pages as if hammering coffin nails. The Oberleutnant and his cohort, efficiency incarnate, turned smartly and exited the premises.

The Wehrmacht officers and their SS minders, along with the Gestapo agents in their signature leather coats, also rose to vacate the room—though the Hauptmann Müller, the intruder's frustrated executioner, paused to notify the Obersturmführer that the business between them was yet unresolved. The Herr Oberst, for his part, made a ribald gesture toward the man's departing back, then rose and chucked Menke under the chin on his own way out the door.

"Funny fellow," he was heard somewhat wearily to say.

Outside in the streets, a noise emanating not from a shofar but a voice crackling over a bullhorn called on the Jews to leave their homes. "TAKE ONLY WHAT POSSESSIONS YOU CAN CARRY AND PROCEED WITH ALL DUE HASTE TO YOUR SYNAGOGUE."

The wire barrier had been withdrawn from the ghetto's periphery, enabling the German troops to pour in without allowing the Jews to leave. They were rousted from their crammed houses (*"Juden, sich beeilen! Schnell!"*), which were exhaustively searched, so that those found hiding in wardrobes and cellars, tangled among spider webs in attics, were soon ferreted out; they were pried from the packing crates and crawl spaces into which they'd contorted themselves and their children, and driven into the streets at bayonet point. But most emerged from their abject straits without resistance. This was due to the long lassitude that had left them docile, and because they realized that the imperative to leave their blighted habitations spelled the end of waiting for whatever they'd been waiting for.

The soldiers had been made to understand that the transit of the Jews from their various ratholes to the familiar sanctuary of the Old New Synagogue should be conducted, as much as possible, as an organized and well-regulated event. But such a large-scale undertaking could hardly be kept under wraps, and once the town's Polish citizenry got wind of it, whole families turned out like gawkers at a parade to watch the herding of their neighbors through the narrow streets. Such unruliness as there was came mostly from these jeering spectators, many of whom doubtless saw themselves as assisting the Germans in their clearance of the ghetto. Some had brought stock prods, others musical instruments—accordions, flutes—to accompany the grim cavalcade in its progress. To humor the occupiers, they struck up the anthem "Die Hitlerleute" and enjoined the Jews to sing along, while the soldiers, rather than discourage the strident chorale, rousingly supplied the lyrics. A few of the Polish youths were on horseback, the better to chase down any Zhids who might take a notion to break and run. But that would not be necessary, not until they had reached the synagogue courtyard where their belongings were confiscated—thus giving the lie to the reassurance that they'd been shepherded into a holding area to await their deportation.

In the meantime the spectacle provided no end of amusement for the rubberneckers, what with the stirring sight of the exodus itself—the scores of staggering ghetto denizens, ashen but for their yellow stars, their ranks swelling as they were joined by others plodding into the Boulevard from its tributary lanes. Families struggled under ungainly bundles and squalling children straddling their shoulders and cradled in their arms; they endeavored to marshal the fuddled pace of their old folks, some of whom were pushed in clanking wheelchairs, some carried on improvised litters or folded like malt sacks over the shoulders of stumbling youths. Here and there an elder begged to be left behind, plunking himself down in the midst of all that movement at peril of being trampled, beginning to chant the final confession prayer. There was Peyse Khantske's waifish daughter Teybl-Eydl, tears streaming in league with the monthly flow—her first?—that coursed down her leg. There was Lulke Ben-Shemesh attempting without breaking stride, and despite his wife's disparaging shrieks, to circumcise his newborn son with a dull pocket knife—this so the boy, at the risk of his mutilation, might enter paradise in accord with the covenant of Abraham.

There was no shortage of bloody footprints trailing after the halting advance of that shapeless formation. The morning air hummed with their moaning mixed with the whine of idling motorcycles, which blunted somewhat the barking of the dogs baring filed yellow teeth. At the margin of the crowd a bustling SS man with a turned-around cap was mounting his camera on a tripod to capture the entire breadth of the hellscape in vivid Agfacolor. So much was there to observe that it should have been enough (*dayenu*) just to watch the drama unfolding from the sidelines; but while they were cautioned by cursory warnings not to interfere in the operation, some of the Poles were moved to step beyond their role as onlookers and participate in the traveling scene.

Someone kicked the crutch out from under the arm of Lemel Hutzpit the joiner, who'd lost his handmade wooden leg; another

held a match to Bezalel Plok's venerable beard, tying his hands
behind him so he couldn't beat out the blaze. Several hooligans
tore the shift off Leah Lichtig and, enflamed by the sight of her
naked body, paltry though it was, dragged her from her mother's
side. Some of the harshest treatment was reserved for the
coachman Elyahu Schkopp, who years earlier had hidden a Polish
officer from his Soviet pursuers. His gentile acquaintances had
bargained with the Germans for his freedom, but when informed
of the reprieve, the wiry old Elyahu merely spat and joined his
fellow Jews. For his heroism he was pelted to a gory pulp with
jagged stones. So long as these minor disturbances did not impede
the ultimate performance of their duty, however, the soldiers were
inclined to look the other way.

As did their superiors, who congratulated themselves on
the relative orderliness with which the affair had so far been
carried out. Once the Jews had reached the flagstone courtyard
of the shulhoyf compound, they were divested of their suitcases
and duffels, which they were told they would no longer need,
and thereby disabused of any expectation of being relocated.
Most, upon realizing the deception, were simply too ground
down by fatigue and travail to comprehend, though one or
two made panicked efforts to escape. They were cut down by
submachine-gun fire before they'd even had a chance to fall
into the hands of their cudgel-waving neighbors. (There was
nonetheless the rare exception, such as the seamstress Hinde
Margalit, who succeeded in slipping from view and fleeing
all the way to the Bug, where she drowned her little son and
herself.) Deprived of their material goods and any pretense of
hope, and forbidden to rest, the Jews of Zyldzce were harried
through its portals into the great brick pile of the Old New

Synagogue. Once inside, their nostrils recoiled at the scent of kerosene, hundreds of liters of which the cavernous interior had been liberally doused in.

Their destruction would never be chronicled, since no one among them survived to describe it: There was no one to tell how the covered kiosk of the rosewood bima was turned into a pavilion of serrated flame. Red-crested blue flames ranged the hall, engulfing the benches and assailing the altar, devouring the ark of the Torah and spiraling upward around the fluted columns to overtake the mesh screen of the women's gallery. Dragon tongues of flame lapped the wall panels, causing the fanciful painted animals and zodiac symbols to bubble and peel from the boards. Flames mounted to the height of the vaulted octagonal rotunda, torching the ceiling, rupturing rafters that toppled in fulminations of sparks. The moisture contained in the bricks steamed like fumaroles until the walls began to buckle and come apart; explosive surges of hot air blasted the leaded windows and blew open the carved oaken doors, but by then the Jews had all been burned alive.

The fire must have spread haphazardly, perhaps moving from east to west, because it was near the synagogue's western wall that the bulk of the charred corpses were piled. The bodies on the top of the heap were totally incinerated, while those beneath them had been crushed and asphyxiated, their clothes left largely intact. Many were fused together and intricately entwined, like overbaked braided loaves, so that the Poles engaged by the Germans to bury them had to use pitchforks to tear them apart, extracting here a leg, there a carbonized head. But before their remains were carted away for burial, they were given a thorough going-over by scavengers in search of valuables the dead may have sewn into their clothing. Occasionally, shooing vultures from the ruins, they found a gold tooth, a brooch, or a czarist five-ruble coin, which they were thereafter relieved of (along with a backhanded smack) by the occupying officers. That is, unless they had managed to hide their loot in a shoe.

Before all that happened, however, Menke Klepfisch found himself left to his own devices in the grain merchant's empty dining room. Priorities having prevailed, the distraction of the obtrusive Jew had been entirely forgotten in the succeeding flurry of activity. Then Menke, who'd yet to budge from his spot, was left all alone to study a patterned wall upon which a framed *mizrakh* paper-cut was hung. This was the ornamental plaque that families mounted on the eastern wall of their homes to remind them of the direction toward which they should aim their prayers. (The Nazis would surely have removed it had they known what it was.) But try as he might, Menke couldn't recall the prayer for a kiddush ha Shem, the sanctification of the Name, the one that was invoked prior to self-sacrifice. Still in possession, however, of a raft of impertinence he'd yet to impart, he addressed himself directly to God.

"That part of You that can't be mentioned," he said without bitterness, "I'm told it wouldn't be worth mentioning even if it could be."

Then he departed the house. The streets outside were strangely vacant of passersby, all having been baited and hounded toward the looming shul, from whose vicinity an indistinct caterwauling could be heard. Unobserved and apparently discarded, Menke thought he might simply walk away. He could travel clandestinely over (or under) land to Arabia or Birobidzhan or maybe *Yenne Velt*, the Other Side—and from there lead squadrons of hobgoblins on incursions back into the world to sow confusion among the enemy. But just then a small party of soldiers emerged from between the stunted houses, squiring at rifle point a pair of the transplanted meshugeners. The soldiers had evidently been making a sweep of the town in their hunt for stray Jews who may have slipped through the net, and had snared two rag-mantled refugees from the Kotsk asylum. Still contemplating his imminent vanishing, Menke missed the moment when he might have ducked back into a doorway, and was clouted over the head with a rifle stock by an unseen soldier.

He reeled, his vision stippled with sparkling lights; the blood purled from his brow and trickled onto his outstretched tongue where it tasted of copper. But despite the blow, he managed to remain more or less upright as he was prodded into line with his bedlamite brethren. Lumberingly they proceeded into a gravelly avenue on both sides of which stood bystanders hurling obscenities. It was at that point in their shambling march that Menke angled his swimming head toward the soldier who'd struck him, an overweight Obergefreiter, a lance corporal with an unshaven porcine face.

"If they gave to you an enema," he said, "they could bury you in a matchbox."

The corporal couldn't have heard the Jew's remark over the din, yet Menke thought he discerned, through the runnel of blood stinging his eye, that the soldier's baleful expression had altered, softened from threatening to deeply injured. Also, he was speaking, and though the words were not audible, Menke believed he could read the man's lips all the same.

"Itzig, what was the meaning of it, your life?"

Menke didn't need to consider. "I was Blume's clown," he

replied, as if any schmuck would know. But the fat corporal was no longer looking at him, if indeed he ever had.

In the synagogue courtyard Menke and the meshugeners were thrust by the bayonets at their backsides into the procession trudging toward the building's hallowed entryway where it was swallowed up. As he tottered forward, Menke's vision was still impaired by the blood seeping into his eyes from his throbbing head wound. Regardless, he could see, when he squinted up at the building's scalloped dome, the great piebald Ziz bird perched upon its pinnacle; and astride the bridled bird in a diaphanous apple-green gown sat Tsippe-Itsl holding the reins. Clearly she'd been waiting for her doomed husband to appear and climb on board the giant fowl behind her. But the bird must have had its own agenda, because—perhaps impatient with Menke's tardiness—it suddenly took flight, its extended wings obscuring the sun and casting a shadow over the town. The resulting darkness was like a thick vapor that, once inhaled, suffuses the body, replacing the blood with an icy black ichor that freezes the bowels.

Arrayed beside the synagogue's open portals was an exuberant phalanx of ranking officers and secret police. The Obersturmführer von Graf und Trach was among them, his chiseled face wearing its typically cavalier expression, his monocle held in place by a vulpine brow, but it was apparent that he was no longer calling the shots. He and his senior staff had been shouldered aside by the black trench coats and Totenkopf caps, who'd taken charge of the operation, relegating the commandant and his lieutenants to virtual spectators. It was now the Schutzstaffel's bantam Oberführer who wielded the swagger stick. He waved it like a conductor's baton, sportively whacking the backs of foot-slogging individuals at the tail end of the column to hasten them through the synagogue doors. All but a handful of stragglers had already passed into the building, from which there exuded a caustic cloud of fuel oil fumes; but there was one stumbling Yid near the rear of their number whom the Oberführer chose to halt, jabbing him in the chest with his rattan stick.

"If it isn't . . . ," sparing a glance at the Wehrmacht commandant, "what did you call him, Herr Oberst? Der Kaiser . . . ?"

"Von Judenspass," the commandant grudgingly volunteered.

"Kaiser von Judenspass!" crowed the Oberführer. "Herr Kaiser, got any good *witzen* for us now?"

Menke's heart was tolling in his chest like a runaway clapper, but his head, in spite of its pounding, remained remarkably clear. Witzen, he reflected. Jokes. Jokes and japes—hadn't they been his charms against death? He might once have tucked them like *kvitel* prayers into all the mezuzahs in Zyldzce. But the invaders, looking for riches, had prized the mezuzahs from their doorposts, and Menke ought by all rights to be fresh out of jokes. Though surely he must have saved at least one enduring bit of business befitting the occasion.

"After the Czar was assassinated," he began—the effort involved recalling the breath of a spirit already on its way to other futures. The strutting SS officer cupped an ear to hear him over the cries from the building's interior—the baying of the *Sh'ma*, penitential prayers reserved for the High Holidays. "After the Czar was assassinated," declaimed Menke, "a government official says to a rabbi, 'I bet you know who is responsible.' 'Gevalt!' replies the rabbi, 'I got no idea, but it will conclude, the government, the same as it always does: They will blame it on the Jews and the beekeepers.' 'Why the beekeepers?' asks the official . . ."

At that the Oberführer, sniffing dismissively, placed a top boot polished to a mirror sheen in the small of Menke's back and gave him a shove. Weak-kneed as he was, Menke went sprawling across the synagogue threshold to join the rest of his accursed race. Then the officer struck a match on the heel of his boot and touched it to a pair of wicker torches that his subalterns held at the ready. Marinated in kerosene, they flared instantly, and with the head-wagging assent of his Shutzstaffel complement, the Oberführer gave the signal for the men to fling the burning brands into the shul. No sooner were the broad doors slammed shut than their commander turned again to his officers and repeated the Jew's final words: "Why the beekeepers?"

His audience seemed puzzled, some of them stifling coughs from the smoke that had begun to curl from beneath the doors and out of fissures between the bricks. Savoring their perplexity a moment, the Oberführer briskly delivered the punch line: "Answers the rabbi, 'Why the Jews?'" He added, with a sly grin, "I heard that one already."

The lieutenants, trench coats, and death's-heads grimaced slightly, then burst into appreciative laughter.

In Kabbalah it is incumbent upon the perfect master, once he has attained the ultimate height of his powers, to dive from that empyrean apex back into the abyss of the fallen world. There he is obliged to rescue from the *kelipot*, the husks of depravity that hold them hostage, the captive sparks of holiness, and elevate them to sanctity again. Gershom Scholem, in his effort to rescue the lost books of the Jews, had believed that he was, analogously, retrieving the stuff of what makes humans human, which had been forfeited during the cataclysm. He was conscious, however, that one who was less than a bona fide saint might find himself incapable of redeeming the sparks and raising up the souls they contained; he might even lose his own soul in the attempt, and be condemned to wander desecrated landscapes for the remainder of his days. Those landscapes need not be confined to the contemporary world—of which Gershom had recently had his fill—but might also include those of other centuries. In Gershom's case, it was the seventeenth or, to be precise, the year 1648.

That was the year of the Cossack Uprising in Eastern Europe, when the Hetman Bogdan Chmelnitzki, battling for independence from the Kingdom of Poland, decided, while he was at it, to slaughter the Jews as well. He accused them, ironically, of having "enslaved" the Ukrainians. Coincidentally, 1648 was the jubilee year that the *Zohar* had cited for the pending resurrection of the dead in the Holy Land. It was a year designated as propitious for the appearance of signs and wonders, though instead of miracles it had brought forth disaster. Nevertheless, that an "acceptable messianic moment" might also include a time of disasters was an idea that had figured frequently in kabbalistic writings since the period of the expulsion from Spain. The sufferings of the martyrs, it was popularly believed, hastened the redemption, and some insisted that the coming of Messiah was imminent in that very year. So it was not an entirely unanticipated revelation that, in 1648, a charismatic young man from Smyrna had declared himself to be that redeemer.

"And behold there was a man," wrote Nathan of Gaza, apostle to the self-proclaimed *mashiach* Sabbatai Zvi, "his size was one square cubit, his beard a cubit long, and his *membrum virile* a cubit and a span."

Gershom's epic exploration of the phenomenon of Sabbatai Zvi and his times was fated to become his magnum opus. He had launched himself heart and soul into the project before the war, though often during its composition he'd succumbed to doubts, sometimes asking himself if the subject was really worth such a monumental effort. After all, wasn't Sabbatai, in essence, a stark raving psycho? Hadn't he, when offered the choice between martyrdom and conversion—and here was the punch line to the joke of his fantastical existence—willingly chosen Islam over his fidelity to the Jewish people he'd promised to redeem? When not in a paralytic funk or in the rabid throes of an epileptic fit, he subverted and even defiled Jewish ritual with his scandalous behavior.

He once erected a canopy and had himself wed to the scrolls of Torah, an act that amounted to bigamy since he was already married, like the prophet Hosea, to a whore. (This was the featherbrained orphan Sarah, who was said to have appeared at the ceremony in a coat of skins stitched together by Mother Eve six thousand years before.) He claimed he could fly but refused to demonstrate that transcendent ability, since none were yet worthy of witnessing such a sight. He proclaimed one of his brothers the king of Turkey, the other the emperor of Rome, called women to the ark and exhorted them to pronounce along with him the ineffable name of God. Childless, he wrapped a large live fish in an infant's swaddling and cradled it lovingly. He feasted on fast days and fasted during feasts, conflated three holidays into one, and declared Monday the real Sabbath. His own fasts lasted for days, after which he might eat, in violation of the laws of *kashrus*, a paschal lamb with its dripping fat still on the bone. He scourged his spindly body with thorns, rolled naked in the snow, immersed himself in frozen ponds with his followers, some of whom died of hypothermia. He declared himself King Messiah and resolved to retrieve the Ten Lost Tribes from beyond the River Sambatyon, then lead them into Jerusalem riding a lion with a seven-headed dragon in its jaws. Had he not partnered with the boy genius Nathan of Gaza, who defended his every apostasy as evidence of his visionary godliness, he would have been confined to a madhouse. As it was, he was embraced as the foreordained and long-awaited savior of Jewry throughout all of Europe and the Ottoman Near East.

Gershom had come back to the project after the long interruption of the war, and the one in Israel after that, with a dithering ambivalence. Would he ever manage to recover his initial fascination with the enigma of Sabbatai's contradictory nature and his transcontinental influence with a fresh eye? Hadn't he had enough of false messiahs in the preceding years? But little by little the old enthusiasm began to return, or rather a new obsession that, in the end, bore small resemblance to Gershom's original preoccupation took hold.

Of course it was Nathan, Sabbatai's vital right hand, who had stage-managed his master's entire career. No charlatan, though, Nathan was a true believer: He had delved deep into the fathomless mysteries of the Lurianic Kabbalah and seen through its prism a vindication of Sabbatai's *ma'arim zarim*, his "strange acts." If, for instance, the prophet smashed in the door of a synagogue with an axe, it was in order to release the wayward souls imprisoned in its woodwork. If he compared a delegation of dissenting rabbis to unclean beasts, it was because the truth compelled him to reveal their previous incarnations. If he puzzled his disciples by his frequent and ferocious masturbation, it was in order to rescue the spirits of so-called backsliding children from his ejaculations. If bathers in the ritual bath, which was thronged to capacity with his adherents, remarked on the erubescent rash about his loins, it was explained how, in a childhood dream, Sabbatai had perceived the light of the Shekhinah, and its flame had seared his private parts. And if he elected to convert to Islam over the alternative of a beheading at the hands of the sultan in Constantinople, it was due to the sacred commandment of the *mitzvah ha-ba'ah baaverah* or "redemption through sin." This was the concept by which the Chosen One, having ascended to the summit of righteousness, must then risk the sacramental descent into the abyss beyond the "gates of impurity." Only there could he spring the traps that held the sparks of beatitude and raise them to perfection again

"The *Zohar*," wrote Nathan, "foretells of a king who is essentially good within but comes, by contrast, clothed in evil garments. The violation of the Torah is now its true fulfillment." "The Shekhinah," he wrote, inventing an imaginary midrashic source, "is destined to don the garments of Ishmael." "Only he who is himself guilty may remove the guilt of others," he wrote, adding Sabbatai's own lawless shibboleth: "Praise God who permits the forbidden!"

Not all of Sabbatai's followers bought this line of argument, but so many had already come so far that it seemed impossible to turn back. Their unconditional sanctioning of their standard-bearer's wild enormities had exiled them forever from common orthodoxy. A multitude of the faithful, in order to be worthy of the realization of his prophecy, had ceased all business dealings, put on sackcloth and ashes, and devoted themselves to Sabbatai's extreme measures of charity, penitence, and prayer. Some had torn the roofs from their houses to await the angels that would carry them off to the Holy Land. Some had seen miracles: They spotted the prophet Elijah at every turn, doffing his many disguises to announce in all his glory the advent of Mashiach; they were convinced that Christian churches were everywhere beginning to sink into the ground, and that a ship had docked as far away as the coast of Scotland, whose sailors spoke Hebrew and whose silken sails were emblazoned with the Star of David. Some had witnessed Sabbatai himself in his ecstasies and been swept into a hysteria that in turn drove the prophet into an even more frenzied rapture, until the force of his radiant mania became fully manifest and overwhelmed them all. They'd seen the cynosure in the shape of the planet Saturn shining on his brow and been transported by his sweet-toned voice singing psalms. In short, their whole world had been turned toches over teakettle, and it was too late to forswear their anointed leader now.

Despite the interminable litany of Sabbatai's follies, Gershom was moved to his own brand of admiration for the mystical sociopath. The reports of his heresies gave the scholar a piquant thrill similar to the one he'd experienced as a rebellious youth, when he was expelled from secondary school for his subversive ideas; they revived his exhilaration over being kicked out of his father's house for those same radical views, to say nothing of his checkered military career. Moreover, the downward spiral of Sabbatai's personal history seemed to parallel to a striking degree the tragic descent of Gershom's otherworldly Zionist vision into a base political reality—a correspondence that had incidentally broken his heart. And yet, had not the demagogue's antinomian instinct, springing as it did from a bond with his zealot worshippers' fear of death (most specifically from being trampled under the hooves of *haidamak* steeds)—hadn't his maverick personality awakened a powerful resurgence of the mythic strain in an otherwise arid religion?

At the same time, Sabbatai's deviant exploits conjured in Gershom's mind a picture of that outrageous eccentric himself, performing in his princely robes his crazy dance on the razor's edge between faith and anarchy. It was finally a comical image in keeping with Walter's judgment that "only a fool's help is real help." Sabbatai was that holy fool whose blissed-out visage, as glimpsed in Walter's Argus-eyed insight, contained the faces (all six hundred thousand of them to be exact) of God. Just as Walter had shown how Kafka had snatched humor from the jaws of dread, so had Gershom extracted the antic figure of Sabbatai Zvi from all his sacrilege, and positioning him midway on the spectrum between demon and redeemer, imagined the notorious heresiarch as a type of fabulous clown. And the clown that Gershom had conceived made him laugh. He laughed idiotically in fact, cackling like the ninety-year-old Sarah whinnying over the absurdity of finding herself with child; like Joseph, helplessly tickled over his unpantsed flight from the ravening lust of Potiphar's wife. Just shy of declaring "Sabbatai, c'est moi," Gershom laughed until the tears ran down his cheeks.

Meanwhile his reputation for impiety with respect to the existing political landscape—and nearly everything else— continued to unsettle his university colleagues. His mordant retorts, veering as they did from the whimsical to the oblique to the downright irritating, were bruited about to the discomfort of all concerned. When, over lunch in the faculty dining hall, the historian (and soon to be Knesset deputy) Ben-Zion Dinur expressed his guilt over having unavoidably missed the funeral of poor Dr. Weltsch, Gershom condoled, "Well, Dinur, you were never a mourning person."

Once, he and Martin Buber, Gershom's favorite target for poking fun at, were seated in adjoining stalls in the gentlemen's lavatory. The lugubrious Buber was as usual lamenting aloud some especially garotte-like twist of fate unfairly dealt to the Children of Israel.

"As you know, Gershom," he repined, "in the Talmudic academy of Shammai, it was deemed better never to have been born."

"So true," replied Gershom from his cubicle. "But, Martin, who is so fortunate? Not one in fifty thousand." As a coda to their exchange Gershom passed a currency note under the partition, asking Buber if he had two fives for a ten.

"There's no toilet paper in my stall," he explained.

In the lecture halls, he maintained his protean presence. He was able, in his disquisitions, to reverse course all of a sudden from exalted to droll, a talent that often left his students utterly befuddled. An example: In a seminar, while citing the Maharal's anti-Lurianic thesis that there is no direct continuity between exile and redemption, Gershom was interrupted by a scholar from America with a Bukharan skullcap crowning his golliwog hair.

"Do you not believe the state of Israel is itself the herald of Messiah?" queried the young fanatic.

Gershom stroked his chin, his long face souring into solemnity. "According to the third-century tana Jochanan ben-Hyrkanos," he responded, raising a portentous forefinger, "three things come unawares: the Messiah, a found article, and a scorpion."

"What exactly is that supposed to mean, Professor?" asked the irked Mr. Michnik.

"Ah, there you have me," replied Dr. Scholem.

As the student remained stymied by the cryptic rejoinder, Gershom added beneficently, "It's not that you're stupid, Mr. Michnik; you're just unlucky when you try to think."

Once, when he was describing Rabbi Cordovero's hidden theurgic system, according to which Man's deeds (and misdeeds) gravely affect the divine powers, a young lady from Tel Aviv, fashionable if not terribly astute, dared to challenge the sage's assertion—and hence the entire mystical program: "It says in Talmud Hagigah, 'Refrain from searching after the things that are too hard for you and from seeking the things that are hidden from you.'"

Gershom considered: "Isn't it dangerous for you, Miss Klugman, to use up your entire store of knowledge in a single sentence?"

To a particularly disputatious haredi postgraduate with reptilian eyes and earlocks like dangling confetti, Gershom remarked with that touch of cruelty that had made him renowned throughout the institution as a holy terror, "They don't make them like you anymore, Reb Yedvab, but just to be on the safe side, they should neuter you anyway."

Strangely, the greater part of his students seemed to delight in his jabs and sometimes even competed in inviting their own victimhood.

To cool his brain after the day's labors, Gershom took long walks through the divided city in late afternoon. As if a walk in Jerusalem could do anything but roil the brain into a fever. For one thing, it was always a shock to the system to emerge from the rich bounty of Nathan of Gaza's *Derush haTanninim* or Moses Cordovero's *Palm Tree of Deborah* into the conflicting sights of the current century. Of course, in the streets of Jerusalem the centuries were always laid bare, the still living memories of past millennia arrayed like unfurled banners—they brushed your face and flapped about your head as you passed among them. The aftermath of recent battles was everywhere, every passage littered with a moraine of pale yellow stones—though the archeologists would have a field day distinguishing the detritus of the latest fray from that left by the Romans, the Caliphs, the Crusaders, the Mamluks, and the Ottomans. In the Old City, Gershom walked through a succession of conquered and recaptured Jerusalems. The Jews had seized it now, but for how long?

Since the Jordanian siege had been lifted, there was a military presence in every twisted thoroughfare; watchful sentinels of opposing nations faced one another from behind whorls of barbed wire and barricades of ash cans filled with cement. But above the snarled web of the streets, the cupolas, steeples, and minarets still vied for their portion of the sun. The alleys were still fragrant with the scent of skewered meats, honey-drenched pastries, and the resinous smoke from nargilahs as tall as totem poles. In the Arab shuk the mercantile incentive still trumped the appetite for war, its vaulted passage alive with a hubbub of voices hustling inlaid boxes, Persian carpets, and ceramic tiles, which the kaffiyeh-clad merchants offered at prices they promised were practically gifts. Prayer notes fluttered like locusts' wings from the crannies in the Western Wall, and the Valley of Hinnom, as viewed from the parapet below the Tower of David, still lay in its perpetual shadow. To the east the eggshell sails of the windmill at Yemin Moshe were still turning; and if he looked to the far horizon, Gershom could just make out, luminous in the emerald light that is the prelude to the Jerusalem sunset, the spilled mercury of the Dead Sea.

But by then Gershom had had enough of the golden city's pageantry; it was time he got back to his eucalyptus-girded sanctuary in the Abarbanel Road. It was Tuesday evening and Fanya would be serving his favorite Bavarian pot roast; tomorrow was the baba ghanoush he'd developed a taste for since making Aliyah. After dinner, a hasty kiss upon Fanya's deep-creased brow then back to his study. He exited the Muslim Quarter of the Old City via the Damascus Gate, past the antiquarian bookstore nestled beneath its arch that he had often plumbed for treasures. He was pleased to see it was still open for business but would save the browsing for another day. He scarcely glanced at the newsstand in the plaza boasting the journals of a dozen nations, but took some note (as he trod over it) of the grainy photo on a loose page of *Haaretz*. It featured the nonchalant countenance of a newly appointed Shin Bet commander, who—a cigarette listing from

the corner of his lips—bore a marked resemblance to a chauffeur
Gershom had once hired during his European travels. He hurried
past the crater-faced coffee vendor with the ornate brass urn on his
back, the pear-shaped Bedouin women seated cross-legged behind
open sacks of almonds and dates, their outlined eyes all that
was visible through their veils. He passed the humpbacked old
bookseller with his whiskered jaw in constant motion presiding
over a weathered wooden cart. The cart contained a disordered
heap of back-numbered Yiddish romances and the odd handbook
of spells and incantations once so popular among the uneducated
Ostjuden. How, wondered Gershom, could such a throwback of a
shelf-worn luftmensch survive in this unsentimental climate? The
man must have some angelic benefactor.

"'There are only miracles,'" Gershom said to himself, quoting
Kafka, and shrugged. But if any of those rude faces and sublunary
sensations lingered in his mind, they were soon, once he'd
returned to his desk, translated along with the rest of the world
back into words.

ACKNOWLEDGMENTS

Three books were constant references during the composition of this novel: *A Mortuary of Books* by Elisabeth Gallas, *Stolen Words* by Mark Glickman, and *From a Ruined Garden* by Jack Kugelmass and Jonathan Boyarin.

ABOUT THE AUTHOR

Steve Stern has won six Pushcart Prizes, an
O. Henry Award, a Pushcart Writers' Choice
Award, and a National Jewish Book Award.
For thirty years, Stern taught at Skidmore
College, the majority of those years as Writer
in Residence. He has also been the recipient of
a Guggenheim Fellowhip, a Fulbright lecturer at
Bar-Ilan University in Tel Aviv, the Moss Chair
of Creative Writing at the University of Memphis,
and Lecturer in Jewish Studies for the Prague
Summer Seminars. He splits his time between
Brooklyn and Ballston Spa, New York.